Praise for
The Margot Affair

"Betrayal and desire fuel the story of Margot, the secret daughter of a twenty-year affair between a French politician and a famous actress. . . . It's impossible not to love Margot's delicate mixture of maturity and naïveté. . . . This is a startling, affecting first book by an author who is confident in her craft, who knows that a loving portrait includes flaws."

—*The New York Times*

"Lemoine captures with painful accuracy the clumsy ignorance of adolescence, unable to understand people, relationships and the delicate truces keeping marriages in balance. . . . This is what it means to come of age, and it is a messy business."

—LAUREN ELKIN, *Financial Times*

"Gorgeous . . . perfectly captures the heightened emotion and confusion of being a young woman with a bruised heart and limited experience . . . It asks the ultimate question about this most complicated of relationships: What will a mother do for her child?"

—SARAH LYALL, *The New York Times*

"Drumming with tension, *The Margot Affair* grapples with the complexity of familial love."

—*Marie Claire*

"[A] perfect mix of literary and entertaining . . . This is one of those books that you didn't know you needed until you read the first few pages and you go: oh, I'm home."

—*LitHub*

"Unusual and accomplished . . . Here [Lemoine] lifts the window slats not just on the covert behavior of consenting adults, but on many facets of bourgeois Parisian life."

—*The Economist*

"Deftly crafted, thoughtfully observed, this absorbing coming-of-age novel explores the tense and complex relationship between Anouk and Margot, the notions of family and motherhood, deceit and betrayal."

—*Daily Mail* (UK)

"One juicy book . . . It's a commentary about the tolls of secrets and power—and will make you feel like you're sitting in a Parisian café the whole time."

—*The Skimm*

"An engrossing, impressive debut novel that skillfully charts a young Frenchwoman's coming-of-age."

—*Kirkus Reviews*

"Sumptuous . . . The eclectic cast and rich Parisian backdrop deepen this dramatic exploration of family and the trials of early adulthood."

—*Publishers Weekly*

"A stunning debut, simmering with tension and sensuality . . . This jewel of a novel examines the in-between spaces in life. . . . A mesmerizing story by an important new voice."
—CRYSTAL HANA KIM, author of *If You Leave Me*

"A deeply immersive novel about the ways in which your family may fail you . . . Written in graceful prose carrying clairvoyant insights, its wisdom stayed with me."
—LING MA, author of *Severance*

"Sanaë Lemoine is fearless and almost unbearably tender in her exploration of all the ways we both exalt and wound one another."
—STACEY D'ERASMO, author of *Wonderland*

"Poised, coolly beguiling, and deeply compelling, Lemoine's debut casts a powerful spell."
—HERMIONE HOBY, author of *Neon in Daylight*

"With exquisite precision and insight, *The Margot Affair* builds to an unexpected heat."
—IDRA NOVEY, author of *Those Who Knew*

"A diary and a page-turner and a masterful debut, all at once."
—VICTOR LAVALLE, author of *The Changeling*

"Subtle, beautiful, serious."
—KAREN RUSSELL, author of *Swamplandia!*

THE
Margot Affair

A Novel

SANAË LEMOINE

HOGARTH

London   New York

The Margot Affair is a work of fiction. Names, characters, places, and incidents are the products of the author's imagination or are used fictitiously. Any resemblance to actual events, locales, or persons, living or dead, is entirely coincidental.

2021 Hogarth Trade Paperback Edition

Copyright © 2020 by Sanaë Lemoine
Book club guide copyright © 2021 by Penguin Random House LLC

All rights reserved.

Published in the United States by Hogarth, an imprint of Random House, a division of Penguin Random House LLC, New York.

HOGARTH is a trademark of the Random House Group Limited, and the H colophon is a trademark of Penguin Random House LLC.

RANDOM HOUSE BOOK CLUB & Design is a registered trademark of Penguin Random House LLC.

Originally published in hardcover in the United States by Hogarth, an imprint of Random House, a division of Penguin Random House LLC, in 2020.

LIBRARY OF CONGRESS CATALOGING-IN-PUBLICATION DATA
Names: Lemoine, Sanaë, author.
Title: The Margot Affair: a novel / Sanaë Lemoine.
Description: London; New York: Hogarth, [2020]
Identifiers: LCCN 2019036653 (print) | LCCN 2019036654 (ebook) |
ISBN 9781984854452 (paperback) | ISBN 9781984854445 (ebook)
Classification: LCC PS3612.E465 M37 2020 (print) |
LCC PS3612.E465 (ebook) | DDC 813/.6—dc23
LC record available at https://lccn.loc.gov/2019036653
LC ebook record available at https://lccn.loc.gov/2019036654

Printed in the United States of America on acid-free paper

randomhousebooks.com
randomhousebookclub.com

2 4 6 8 9 7 5 3 1

Book design by Dana Leigh Blanchette

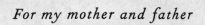
For my mother and father

I

1

Onstage my mother was her truest self. I would see the transformation within moments, a slow-building intimacy between herself and the audience. Mid-scene she would remove her shirt with the ease of a man, as if taking off a pair of socks. Then she would hold her red curls with both hands and lift them high enough to expose the length of her neck, jut out her elbows and accentuate the slope of her shoulders. She could be whomever she wanted. In her one-woman shows she would address the audience as though they were old friends. I could feel her effect on them as they tilted forward, eyes wide, their pores opening in her presence. She carried this effortless familiarity out into the world. With strangers, she was joyful and gracious. She dazzled. In other words, she was a true actress.

She had been acting since her teenage years, but it was a lead role in the nineties, when I was barely five years old, that propelled her career and led to her solo acts. The play in question was *Mère*, a short, forceful production that ran eighty minutes without an intermission. It had a small cast: a man, his

wife whom she played, their three young children, and the
man's father. It ended in a long scene where the mother kills
her children in a bathtub. The potential for such a violent act
wasn't at first visible in the mother—although there was a
hovering sense of unease, interspersed with moments of levity
and tenderness. At that age, no one told me my mother was
playing a woman who murders her children, but I knew off-
stage she would often choose to stay in character.

At home, she was a stranger to me. I wanted her to return to
where she'd come from, as if she could be reabsorbed into herself. She was turned inside out, her interior laid flat along her
skin for everyone to see. I preferred her right side out, a mother
in the conventional sense.

I wanted to be proud of my mother, and yet most of the
time I would find myself annoyed. What others admired in her
seemed exaggerated and theatrical to me.

Well, it *is* theater, Mathilde said, when I complained.

But I want to be moved by her. I want to stand on my feet
and clap with all of you.

What high school girl is moved by her mother?

A good one.

We love that you're not good, Théo said.

Théo and Mathilde were my mother's closest friends.
Mathilde was a renowned designer in the theater world, spe-
cializing in embroidery. She tailored my clothes and made me
dresses for special events. She had worked on the costumes for
Mère. Théo, her husband, was a dancer. My mother had trained
as a dancer in her youth and felt an instant kinship with Théo.

With me, my mother cultivated distance in a more deliberate way. I had memories of standing outside her room, knock-

ing on the door. *Maman,* I'd say, thinking she hadn't heard me. One day I transitioned to Anouk, hoping she might better respond to her name. Over time it became harder to say *Maman;* the soft consonants would belie the estrangement I so often felt around her. Anouk, on the other hand, ended with a sharp edge, and when I yelled her name, it was like throwing her over a cliff.

Her bedroom was smaller than mine, with a flimsy wooden door and a gap the size of my toe between the floor and paneling. I remember her voice on the other side, practicing the same line over and over again. *I should have pulled you from that dark place and covered you with kisses.* I would wait for her to open the door.

When we were alone, she'd look at me with a serious expression and say: We have to cut the cord. Too much affection is the greatest handicap. At those times, the difference between us would seem enormous, as if we were from two foreign countries, each speaking our own dialect. A mother is not a friend, she would like to emphasize, as if to justify our divergent views. It was true, we never whispered secrets to each other on the métro or hooked arms in the street. Those who didn't know us well thought we were alike—that I, too, would become an actor one day. They thought it was the kind of profession you acquired from your parent the way one writer engenders another writer. But I had half her physical grace, my voice had never carried the same musicality or appeal, and I didn't attract the stares of men on the street the way she did. She had little interest in turning me into a version of herself. She hadn't taught me to act or dance. She took excellent care of her skin and teeth, but she'd never nagged me to take on her habits. In private, I'd peruse her dresses in the closet, touching the soft fabrics and silks, so unlike the synthetic items I wore. Most of all, I resented her for leaving me with the task of being the careful one, having to monitor everything I said. Over time I'd refined a look of blankness that would be misinterpreted as shyness or indifference.

And yet, even when she repelled me, I loved her with abandon. I would wake to her sounds every morning: the wooden floorboards creaking beneath her feet and water gushing from the faucet when she filled the kettle. I knew she had made sacrifices for me. I knew motherhood clashed with her self-realization. Some days I recognized a younger self folded into her majestic, long body. A vulnerability flared on her surface and made me wonder whether we'd be friends if we were the same age.

I wondered this because we were very close. We lived as roommates. It's just the two of us together in this apartment, she would say, speaking with false affection, the old complaint seeping through. She called herself a single mother, as though she'd raised me on her own, but this wasn't entirely the truth: I had a father who visited.

Friends of hers would come by and stay overnight, most of them actors she worked with. Clothes drenched in stale smoke, they filled our home with loud opinions and ideas on how I should be parented. We had a cat for two years, a long animal with thick orange hair that we inherited from a friend who had moved to another country. The cat never assimilated, resisted being held, and came to me only when I cried, rubbing her torso against my legs when she sensed my distress. One summer she escaped through the open window of our kitchen and never returned.

By the time I was in high school, we had lived in three apartments, each one smaller than the last as we moved closer to the center of Paris and finally to the Left Bank. Anouk's friends didn't understand why she wanted to live in an expensive neighborhood steps away from the Jardin du Luxembourg. They wondered how she could afford the apartment on her own. They blamed her bourgeois parents. You're crawling back to your roots, they teased. But I knew it was something else. She loved Father, and this was a neighborhood he approved of. It was here, one afternoon in late June, not far from our street, that his other life crashed into ours, forever disturbing its arrangement.

I had just finished my French oral exams. I'd been wearing the same outfit all through the spring, black jeans faded gray from many washes and a blue tank top. I liked how the white lace of my bra showed under the thin straps of my top. At fifty-seven, Anouk was magnificent. Narrow hips and a lean stomach, a slight depression at her belly button, angular shoulders. Everything about her was long aside from her feet, the one ugly part of her body, red bunions and tiny toenails that she kept painted to distract from the feet themselves. They were the same size as mine. Even when she wore jeans in the middle of the summer, they slipped up her dry thighs with no resistance. I'd always known my mother was beautiful because of the comments friends and strangers alike made, but it was only in those previous months that I'd begun to understand how her beauty was rare. Most peoples' faces eventually dissolved into other parts, whereas hers had become more defined over time, the bones shifting to their right place in middle age.

We sat side by side at a small round table on the sidewalk of a café, facing those sand-colored buildings with their shallow wrought-iron balconies. We could see the gates of the park at the end of the street, their golden spikes, and the overflowing greenery behind. It was late afternoon, the hottest hour of the day, and the pale façades of the buildings reflected onto the pavement, trapping heat into a furnace beneath our feet. Anouk bathed in the sun, sleeveless, a straw hat on her head. I told her to cover her shoulders; they were turning pink.

She was an energetic talker, and I rarely had to prod her along in conversation. She was telling me about a play she was codirecting with a friend, who had less experience than she did. She knew the ins and outs of putting together a show, from writing the script to setting up the décor. Although she wasn't all that organized in her private life, she was a skilled director onstage. These actors, however, were novices. Anouk swung her neck to the side, cracking it gently. I shuddered at the sound of her body—the machinery made visible for a moment. She explained how it was important for her to know their lines. She'd garner more respect if she could correct them, finish their sentences.

How old are the actors? I asked.

Not much older than you, she said. They've just finished school. As soon as it's time to break for lunch they disappear for an *hour*. Imagine, a whole hour to eat a sandwich. Not one of them stays to rehearse. They lack your discipline.

I smiled at the compliment.

A few families walked by us on their way to the park. The street was otherwise quiet. I unwrapped the speculoos cookie that came with my coffee, and then thought better of eating it, not wanting to gain weight before the summer. Anouk hadn't finished her citron pressé. The lemon pulp settled on its surface in a thick layer. She drank it with no sugar.

Midsentence, Anouk paused. She had suddenly turned pale. What's wrong? I asked.

Her gaze was fixed on a woman across the street who walked back and forth along the opposite sidewalk. She held a phone to her ear. Nothing about her was familiar; I couldn't remember ever seeing her before. She was around my mother's age, dressed in a beige jacket and matching skirt, pale stockings and black heels, but didn't look like anyone Anouk would know. Her hair was short and elegantly coiffed, a dark brown color. She wore a delicate scarf with a floral pattern that moved in the air as she walked by. We could hear her melodious voice punctuated by small bursts of laughter, her heels clicking against the pavement.

Do you know her? I asked. Anouk shushed me and looked down at the table, as if bowing to hide her face. She then brusquely took a ten-euro bill from her wallet and threw it on the table. Did she want us to leave? She seemed to hesitate, staying put on the edge of her chair.

But you haven't even finished your drink! I said, gesturing at her citron pressé, where condensation marked the table around the glass.

Anouk's face usually expressed her emotional state in all its movements, her eyebrows sharpening like arrows, her mouth widening into oval shapes, her voice rising in volume. She derived energy from charging into a fire. She rarely stepped aside. And yet now she was immobile, her lips drawn shut, as though this action alone might contain her emotions. But what were they? Why had her body shut down so violently? She glanced up at the woman and seemed to flinch. My own skin prickled in response and I, too, recoiled from her.

Let's go, she said, standing up. She looked at the woman one last time and swept up her bag. As I got up, I saw the woman turn the corner and vanish from sight.

We took a shortcut through the park. We walked quickly and in silence, circling the fountain and the few tourists who sat on its edge. My sandals and feet were soon covered in a thin layer of dust from the gravel. We paused only once we'd arrived at Place Edmond Rostand to wait for the light. I tried to recall the woman's face. But all I could remember was her outfit, the jacket and square heels as she waved her hand in the air, and the electric effect she'd had on Anouk. Were it not for this, I would have found her banal, forgettable even, but now that I thought about it, she'd acted like an important person, taking up the width of the sidewalk with her phone conversation. A woman lifted from another world.

At home, Anouk told me that the woman we'd seen walking down the street by the café was Madame Lapierre, Father's wife.

I'd known about Madame Lapierre for as long as I could remember, though I'd never seen her in the flesh. I hadn't even seen an image of her. I knew she had two sons who were older than me, and I supposed I could call them my half brothers. I stayed away from the newspaper articles about Father. While his political career flourished, I pretended to have little interest in current events beyond the culture section. Anouk read the paper front to back when I wasn't watching.

I immediately knew it was her, Anouk said, pacing around the living room in circles. Her voice grew thin, saying how she'd always thought their paths would coincide once we moved to this neighborhood; in some ways it was bound to happen and she had steeled herself for the possibility of an encounter, but wasn't it strange how she'd instantly detected her presence, like a radar sensing a disturbance in the field? She knew my father's favorite park was the Jardin du Luxembourg. It made sense that he shared the same tastes as his wife, who exhibited her Roger Vivier shoes for all to see.

She was wearing the same shoes that Catherine Deneuve wore in *Belle de Jour*.

I winced when I remembered that Anouk had just bought a pair of similar heels for a fraction of the price.

Do you think she recognized us? I asked.

She'd have no idea who we are.

I looked away. In that moment, I saw it clearly, as if I'd been jerked from a stupor. Unlike Madame Lapierre and her sons, who enjoyed a public life with him and could claim him, we were nobodies, invisibles. I felt a layer scraped from me, a part of me gone. The exposure was sudden, and I shivered even though it was warm in the apartment. There were no public images to connect us to Father. If Madame Lapierre walked by me in the street, she wouldn't know who I was. I imagined her brushing past, wrapped in silk.

I had such a distinct image of him then in our home, seated on the leather couch with Anouk, standing by the sink drying dishes, turning the page of a newspaper at the dining room table. Just thinking about him triggered an intense familiarity. I was his only daughter and the youngest of his children. He was my father. But Madame Lapierre had shaken that image of him, like seeing a stranger in your home take possession of your belongings. We were, I realized, on the wrong side of Father's double life. I glanced over at Anouk, who had at last stopped pacing.

Is she what you expected? I asked.

I didn't have any expectations, she answered sharply and then disappeared into her room.

I stood in the kitchen alone, listening to our neighbors as they prepared dinner. So Father's other life had penetrated ours, in the same way that the sounds of families in the building swept through our apartment. But ours had been reconfigured, the elements settling into different corners, and I felt disoriented as I walked to my bedroom and shut the door.

I spent hours on the Internet searching for images. I zoomed into Madame Lapierre's face to see if she had more wrinkles than Anouk, to see if her arms were wide and unformed beneath the jacket. I looked for defects, a reason to find her less beautiful, and I studied the photos as if they contained some kind of truth, evidence of why he stayed with her. Until then I had resisted the temptation to stalk them. Anouk believed if I didn't look them up, it would be easier to live with the secret. But now that she had walked into our lives, I looked at dozens of photos of her, making up for lost time, and felt an unfamiliar greed overwhelm me. There was so much to discover.

Madame Lapierre had been pretty, with round cheeks and long, straight hair, dark eyebrows over almond-shaped eyes, a beauty mark at the corner of her lips that I hadn't seen from a distance. Her style had become more severe over the years, jackets with shoulder pads, narrow skirts that stopped at her knees. She came from a prestigious literary family, the daughter of a writer who belonged to the Académie française, whose members were known as *les immortels*. Alain Robert was an old man with a tanned, wrinkled face and brilliant blue eyes, who appeared on posters in métro stations because he was always writing a new book on the dismal state of French literature and politics. It made sense that she would go on to marry a promising young politician who would become the minister of culture—my father.

When I was younger, I'd had a strange thought. If Anouk died, would Madame Lapierre adopt me? Would she and Father take me in? I projected my own idealized version of a mother onto this woman: maternal, warm, gentle. Anouk had raised me to think of her with disdain and avoid her name around the house, but in private I felt an inexplicable draw. I imagined how she would care for me. Hold my hand, take my temperature when I was sick, accompany me to school in the mornings. I imagined a look of concern on her face, *the poor girl has lost her mother*, it said.

But if I died, what would happen to Anouk?

The more I learned about Madame Lapierre in the press, the more I felt my intuition had been correct—she was a discreet woman who didn't flaunt where she came from. Yes, she wore expensive outfits, but she wasn't the kind to give lengthy interviews that revealed sensational details about her life. When she spoke about her sons, it was with simple affection. She described the apartment that she and Father had lived in since before the boys were born, and the summers spent with her maternal grandparents in Dordogne. One photo showed her embracing the boys, her smile conveying contented bliss.

That night I had the first of a series of recurring dreams. Anouk and I were in a swimming pool. There was no bottom, and she needed to get out of the pool. I have to get out of here, she kept telling me, but she couldn't pull herself out with the sheer strength of her arms. I offered her my shoulders. She stepped on them, one foot after the other, and pulled herself out of the pool. I drowned.

2

I remember those last weeks of August with surreal precision. The food we ate, the music we listened to, the heat of the pavement seeping through my sandals, the stillness of a city asleep. Everyone we knew had left for the summer.

Paris was more polluted in the heat, the air on the streets dusty and stagnant, making our eyes prickle. I walked around squinting, having always forgotten my sunglasses. Inside our apartment, the fan circulated warm air as we sponged ourselves dry with towels. Not a single breeze when we opened the windows. It made us irritable, being at the limit of our physical comfort. I couldn't understand how people in tropical countries were so patient with one another.

Our apartment had two floors. The second, where the bedrooms were, was like an attic, with slanted ceilings held by thick beams. A spacious bathroom with black and white tiles separated the two bedrooms. There was a bathtub with clawed feet and an old mirror hanging on the wall. I liked seeing the reflection of my face blurred in the scratched silver. In the

colder months when Anouk kept the heat on low, not wanting
to waste money, I fantasized that our home was a sanatorium in
the Alps and I the tuberculosis patient.

If I stood on her bed and looked through the window, I
could see our neighborhood stretching out between the park
and Place Monge. We called this our wasteland because the
métro stations were all a fifteen-minute walk away. We relied
on our feet, whereas Father drove to see us.

An American singer with ropes of long charcoal hair had
died very young the previous month, and her deep voice
poured from the radio, embracing us even if we didn't always
understand the meaning of her words.

With my best friend, Juliette, gone until September, I spent
the summer mostly alone, the weeks bleeding into one another.
We spoke on the phone and emailed passionate accounts of our
days in long, rococo sentences. She told me about her grandmother who was sick with cancer and her grandfather who escaped the house every morning to call his mistress from the
village *tabac* where he bought the paper. Though she'd never
met him, Juliette knew who my father was. But even so, I
couldn't bring myself to tell her about our sighting of Madame
Lapierre. Instead, I told her about the movies I'd gone to see
by myself, the afternoons spent by the fountain in the Jardin du
Luxembourg, eyeing a boy who was older, a university student
with curly hair. I had waited for him to notice me, but I was so
much younger than he was.

At the lycée, a social structure had been established years
ago, and only a few had the privilege of going out with whomever they wanted. That didn't include Juliette or me. It had
little to do with looks at this point, because even the girls who

bloomed overnight stayed in their place, remaining unpopular, as if they hadn't changed at all. I wondered if I was ugly. I knew I lacked Anouk's beauty, but I wondered to what extent I was forgettable, or if I had inherited some of her light.

I didn't wait around for the boy in the Jardin du Luxembourg, as I'd written to Juliette; in fact, I spent almost no time there that summer, despite how quiet it was, the city drained of people. I was afraid of seeing Madame Lapierre again, so I avoided going on the other side of the park in the sixth arrondissement. What if she glanced at me and something in my face revealed me? What if I saw her with Father?

I stayed at home reading, fanning myself with papers, saving photos of Madame Lapierre and her sons in a folder I'd called *the others*. I waited for Anouk to mention her again, but she behaved as if that afternoon had been consciously erased from her memory. It maddened me that she went about her days ignoring our encounter with Madame Lapierre.

On the morning of my seventeenth birthday, I woke up with a jolt. It had seemed more important than the others, a year closer to adulthood and only one more year of school left. I stretched out under the thin sheet. We had nothing planned and the day opened up to me, as blank and dull as every other summer day.

Anouk and I didn't celebrate birthdays with great enthusiasm. On her birthday, I would give her a small gift and say the words first thing in the morning, *Joyeux anniversaire,* to be over and done with it. Celebrations made me uncomfortable, perhaps because she hadn't taught me how to enjoy them.

I wandered through the apartment. I knew Anouk was awake. I'd seen her dirty cup in the sink, and the bathtub was wet from her morning shower. I could hear her repeating lines in her bedroom, but today was my birthday, and I wanted her attention. I knocked on her door and said her name loudly. She ignored me.

It invaded me all of a sudden, a dark, complicated feeling.

The door finally flew open and I drew back from it, startled. My mother's skin glowed. In that moment, I hated her for not teaching me to take better care of myself. She didn't share her creams with me, either.

You know I'm working, she said. Her voice had an edge, but she wasn't as angry as I'd expected. What do you want?

For you to stop being so loud, I said. I'm trying to read.

She paused, her hand curling around the door. Her posture relaxed and she smiled. It's your birthday, she said, as if just remembering. Happy birthday, my darling. I'll make you some hot chocolate.

In this heat I would have preferred a bowl of cold cereal, but this was the sole indulgence she liked to offer me on the day of my birth. She made it with whole milk and a dash of cream, and pieces of dark chocolate. She set it on the table in front of me. One year wiser, she said. She watched me eat. I dipped a piece of buttered toast into the chocolate. Pools of salty grease collected on its surface.

What do you want for your birthday? she asked.

I put down the piece of toast and wiped my fingers. I pretended to think about her question for a moment, but the answer was already at the tip of my tongue.

I want Madame Lapierre to know about us, and then I want him to leave her and live with us. I spoke calmly, hoping to sound flippant, as if I didn't care.

She rolled her eyes. You always ask for the impossible. Your father would never live with us.

But maybe if she knew about us, she would leave him, and he'd be forced to move in.

I'm sure she knows something.

You told me she has no idea who we are.

Not about us specifically, but she's an intelligent woman. I wouldn't take her for a fool. Anouk laughed nervously and ran her fingers through her hair. I studied her more closely.

You were hoping we'd run into her one day.

She knows, Anouk repeated, ignoring me.

How can you be so certain?

I was shaken by her conviction. I trusted her for the most part, but it seemed she was drawing this conclusion just from having seen Madame Lapierre that brief instant and had interpreted its meaning long before that day. Anouk eyed me from the kitchen counter.

Anyway, what makes you think *she'd* ever want to leave him?

I took a sip of chocolate, and the hot, viscous liquid caught in the back of my throat. The soaked bread had the texture of papier-mâché.

And what makes you think *I* want him living with us? she asked.

Anouk moved to the living room and sat on her armchair. I could see her from the corner of my eye. She rested her feet on the foot massager and turned it on. A gift from Father. It rumbled to life, sending gentle vibrations up her legs. She had it on the lowest setting.

I didn't mean it seriously, I said, noticing the defensiveness in my voice.

Let me tell you something. Your father and Madame Lapierre haven't been intimate in years. They sleep in separate bedrooms. It's a marriage of convenience. A platonic partnership.

How do you know?

What?

That he doesn't sleep with her?

Anouk laughed in her theatrical fashion and turned up the speed on the massager.

You're right, Margot, she said more gently. We don't know anything about them. We don't know what their relationship is like from the inside. You can't know what someone else's intimacy looks like. I know they eat together, do their laundry together.

Anouk closed her eyes. She wore a large shirt that covered her thighs, but as her feet lifted from the bump of the massager, I caught glimpses of dark snatches between her legs.

What you don't know, Anouk said, is that your father doesn't like change. He'd be incapable of assuming responsibility if we suddenly appeared in other areas of his life.

That's absurd, I said, my head snapping back. I pushed away my bowl of chocolate, having lost my appetite. I searched for the words to persuade my mother otherwise, but I couldn't find them.

Oh my God, don't stare at me with those big eyes. Are you going to cry? Look how he's spoiled you, crying at the smallest frustrations. Anouk spoke to me as if I wasn't hers. Heat rose to my cheeks and along my neck.

Why are you being so cruel? And on my birthday.

Don't be dramatic.

I just wish we could live with him.

You always want the last word. And now you probably want to live with her as well. Anouk avoided saying her name—Madame Lapierre or Claire—even though she knew it well. Sometimes she called her *la dame,* the lady.

She turned off the foot massager. One morning, you'll come downstairs and I won't be here. Then you can have him all to yourself. But don't expect him to move in. You'll eat breakfast alone and he'll visit you when he finds it convenient.

Nothing frightened me more than the possibility of my mother's disappearance, though I also felt a pulsing thrill as she spoke those words. If she abandoned me, I'd have a concrete reason to blame her, other than this confused feeling of unhappiness. I scoured my brain for insults.

Yes, I said, maybe I would go live with them. She's probably a better mother than you. You haven't been a good mother.

Is there such a thing as a *good mother?*

People at school used to tease me about being dirty.

Always caring about what others think.

You forgot to bathe me.

Children misremember and can't be trusted.

You didn't speak to me for months.

She turned away. I wasn't sure if this one was true, but I had a vague recollection of her silence weighing on me, when I was six or seven, as if my presence offended her in some deep way.

What do you want? she asked, as if finally absorbing my words. How did I raise a daughter who complains, who is never satisfied with what she has, who can't see her privilege?

Her eyes were wide and shiny. She walked over to me. I nursed you, she said. I gave you milk from here. She jabbed at her chest. Her small breasts hung beneath the material of her shirt. I pictured the inverted nipple on her left breast and wondered if it had been difficult to feed me from there, if her nipple had always been inside out.

I was quiet. I felt ashamed, of course, but I didn't want to admit being wrong. I didn't know how to apologize. I had only wanted to tell her that I missed my father and wanted more of him.

We stared at each other for a while. Then she came over to me and sat at the table. She touched my hand, sending a bolt of terror and warmth up my arm.

When Anouk sent me to summer camps and people didn't know anything about my life, I pretended I had a father who lived with us. Over a bowl of hot chocolate, as we all dipped bread into the liquid until the crust fell apart, I invented a different life for my new friends. My father was a professor who left papers scattered in the apartment. He was a businessman who traveled the world. He was on unemployment, a lazy man who couldn't even provide for his family.

Don't you want to grow old together? I asked.

She shook her head. There you go again with your fairy-tale life. No one is ever happy in private.

You're wrong, I said. Look at you. You always seem happy.

That is your interpretation. Her eyes sparkled and she let go of my hand.

3

I last saw Father a week after my birthday. That day I had woken up before Anouk and stood in the doorway of her bedroom, watching her sleep. Her body faced away from me, covered in a white sheet. I knew the shape of her beautiful legs beneath the sheet, the delicate slope of her calves, although from where I stood, they rose like a fat vein on an arm, a formless tube. She rarely slept later than I did, but she had gone to bed past midnight the night before. I called out her name and she rolled toward the sound of my voice. She opened her eyes. She didn't seem to register who I was, and for a moment her face was blank.

She smiled at me. You are so grown up, she said. I noticed she had forgotten to remove her eye shadow before going to sleep, a green powder that made her eyelids seem porous.

At your age I was in boarding school, she reminded me. She made herself mustard and mayonnaise sandwiches and waited for her mother to write her letters, but they never came, and so instead she ate and gained weight. She ate her friend's portion of spaghetti because all the other girls were guarding their figures. They were nourished by the letters they received from their parents during mealtimes.

Her brother, who was two years older and had been her confidant throughout her childhood, had graduated the year before and was studying to be a doctor in Lyon. He was too busy to come home during her breaks and so she often returned to an empty house.

The summer before her last year at school, she had swallowed all the pills she could find in her mother's cabinet.

I made myself vomit right away, she told me, and then I fell asleep in broad daylight on the floor of my bedroom. When I woke up the next morning, life had gone on as it always had. My mother never found out. We had been growing apart for a while, but her negligence in that moment struck me especially hard. How couldn't she see my cry for help? Didn't she find it strange that I'd slept for twenty hours without interruption? Instead we ate toast and drank coffee like any proper family.

This was the first I'd heard of the pills. I studied Anouk's face for a clue.

Did you really want to kill yourself? I asked.

I thought I did.

Her answer surprised me. She took such good care of herself and seemed to relish her life. I tried to imagine her at my age, less joyful, not in control. It was hard to picture.

I should have gone to therapy, Anouk said, but instead I became an actor.

I felt a tender pain in my gut. My instinct was to shut out her voice. Was she telling me this to excuse the kind of mother she was to me? And what kind of lesson did she want to teach me?

Why was she like that with you? I asked.

My mother? Anouk paused and rubbed her temples. Let's see, maybe because she was self-involved, didn't care, or wasn't happy in her marriage.

I understood the subtext: You are more fortunate than I was.

Anouk pulled the pillow from behind her head and leaned it against the wall. Her hair curled around her neck. It shone a copper red, while mine was brown and flat. I saw her age in the purple veins running over her arms and the creases around her eyes and mouth. Her skin was looser but also softer than mine. My skin was tight and shiny across my face as the fan spat hot air onto us.

I'm going downstairs, I announced. I closed the door behind me and climbed down the stairs.

The previous night, a few of Anouk's friends had stayed over. They were asleep on our two couches. I dreaded cleaning up after them. They dampened our towels and ate our food. Sometimes they hid cigarette stubs behind the cushions on the couch. I had seen them refill a bottle of vodka with water, as if we couldn't tell when it froze overnight. Don't be a snob, Anouk always said. Many of them worked on a seasonal schedule and weren't lucky like us. Théo and Mathilde were different. They were like family; they cooked and helped us put away our things, and they preferred to sleep at home, even if it meant taking a taxi late into the night.

The morning light pushed through the closed blinds of the

living room, striping it with yellow ribbons. I made my way to the kitchen and stood by the sink, the window slightly ajar, a cool breeze sweeping across my face. I waited for everyone to wake up and leave. Father would be here in an hour.

Our apartment was empty by the time he arrived. Anouk was upstairs on the phone with her brother, a cardiologist who now lived in Strasbourg with his wife, while I waited in the kitchen. I heard his keys jingle in the lock and the sound of his footsteps in the entrance. He had arrived at last, and I was light-headed with anticipation. I pictured him taking off his shoes and placing his briefcase on a chair. I waited for him to walk through the entrance hallway and find me.

The moment I saw him, a wave of euphoria surged inside me and spread along my skin. I touched my neck, cooling the red splotches with my fingers. He came over to me with a smile. I stayed seated at the table as he kissed me on both cheeks. I pretended indifference, as though we did this every morning, but it was hard to hide the excitement I felt each time I saw him. As soon as he entered the apartment, I had to stop whatever I was doing. I became distracted by the sounds of him untying his shoelaces and putting away his coat or jacket and could no longer focus on the task at hand.

There was Father: stout around the chest but not particularly fat. He had a large nose with cavernous nostrils and a skin tinged gray from years of smoking, although he had stopped long before I was born. His nostrils were hairless despite being so impressively big. He was of average height, barely taller than Anouk. His teeth were square and evenly shaped, and his eyes a pale hazel bordering on yellow, just like mine. Mathilde once described him as classically attractive, a man who hadn't gone unnoticed by other women at the time of meeting Anouk in his thirties. I thought it was less a matter of looks and more about the way he presented himself, with precision and care. The opposite of slovenly. He wore an ironed cotton shirt tucked into dark blue trousers. I admired that he was always elegantly dressed and clean-shaven—even on weekends, in case he had to run into the office.

The kitchen was narrow. We had placed the long side of a rectangular table against the wall with two chairs side by side and another one at the head. Father and I sat on the same side, both staring at the white wall. I liked not having to look at his face when we spoke.

Happy birthday, he said, pulling out a gift from under the table. He had been holding it when he walked in, and I hadn't noticed. I thanked him. Father had called me on my birthday in the late evening, after dinner. I had checked my phone every hour, waiting for his call, worried he had forgotten because I knew how upset he would be, but also hoping he wouldn't call so I could indulge in my sadness, give shape to my anger, feel that dark twinge of satisfaction. Not a good father. I wondered if Anouk had reminded him of the date at the last minute. He called every year and sometimes we saw each other, but most often he was caught up at work.

I opened the gift. A book by a contemporary philosopher.

I heard a fascinating interview on the radio with this man, Father said, and I thought of you right away. He was talking about cultural difference. You're intelligent. I know you'll enjoy it.

I leafed through the book, pretending to read a sentence here and there. I could smell the soap on his skin. I hadn't seen him in weeks. His hair, brown and thin, fanned across his forehead as if he'd just taken off a sweater.

How was your birthday? he asked.

Oh, it was fine. I put the book down. Did you think of me?

Of course. Father furrowed his brow. Are you asking because I didn't spend the day with you?

I looked at his hands. They were on the table in front of him, where one would put a plate, the nails clipped short. His skin was smooth and pale, even though he had driven trucks, carried cases of wine, and tilled the vegetable patch with his mother throughout his adolescence. That was a long time ago. Since then, his hands touched paper, books, microphones, the leather handle of his briefcase.

No, I said, I'm not upset.

That's good.

I arranged the napkins on the table into a neat pile. Can I tell you something? I asked, looking away from him.

Of course, Margot.

My stomach constricted. I hadn't planned on telling him, but before I could change my mind, I opened my mouth.

I saw her the other day. Your wife, Claire.

The thought of saying those words had been exciting moments before, but now I was nervous, unsure of what I wanted from him.

Father tensed, his neck jerking slightly, before he regained his composure. Where was that? he asked.

Close to the Luxembourg. We were sitting at a café and we saw her on the street. I crossed my legs under the chair, skimming the cold tiles with my toes.

Your mother was with you?

She's the one who recognized her. I had no idea what she looked like.

Father glanced away from me. The silence bothered me, so I ventured forward. We left right away, I said.

He surprised me by taking my hands in his, and I was startled by the warm, fragile skin. It was like touching the hands of an old woman.

Was your mother upset?

Not really. But don't worry, I added, I don't think she saw us.

Even if she did, she wouldn't recognize you.

I paused and thought carefully about what to say next. The apartment was quiet. Anouk had finished her phone conversation and would appear at any moment.

Have you ever said something about us by accident? I asked.

Father shook his head. It doesn't work that way. I'm not ashamed of you. I don't feel like I'm hiding you and your mother.

You don't?

I searched his face to see if he was lying, but his expression wasn't easy to decipher. He was a practiced liar. Anouk had implied Madame Lapierre suspected her husband was unfaithful, and a small part of me couldn't help but believe she was right.

Would you ever tell her about us? I asked.

He ignored my question, and instead said it would be easier once I was no longer in school, once I was an adult.

Was it because as a woman I'd blend into the cohort of men and women who surrounded him, one more person at a business meeting, and perhaps one day I'd work alongside him on

a campaign? Whereas as a young girl I stood out? He seemed
to think this was almost over—not the secret of our family but
the weight of taking great measures to dissimulate.

I can't stop thinking about her, I said, interrupting him.
And when I saw her the other day, I realized I don't know anything about her.

What do you want to know?

Would she like me?

Yes, he answered, a little too quickly.

Would I like her?

Eventually. He smiled.

What would I like about her, then?

His demeanor relaxed, and he spoke gently. I was to understand that unlike Anouk, who was all on the outside, Madame
Lapierre had a hidden, inner resilience. Most people didn't see
it at first and thought she was shy. She had driven herself twice
to the hospital when she went into labor. She was an excellent
cook. I would love her food. She didn't have Anouk's strong-
headedness. She was more flexible.

His words echoed around me in the small space of the
kitchen. They were hard to absorb. Where had he been when
she went into labor? Was she kinder than Anouk? Why had he
chosen a woman so different from my mother? Would she
want anything to do with me? Although these questions
swirled in my head, I was unable to say them aloud. I tried to
match his description to the memory of the woman on the
street. I noticed the way he compared her to Anouk. It was
obvious he couldn't think of one without the other. I had
known he was a married man since I was a little girl, and yet I

felt betrayed, as if I'd just found out he was having an affair. What did her voice sound like up close? And did they sit on the couch watching television, their legs touching? I was less interested in their sons, who no longer lived at home. One of them was married and lived in Brussels, and the other was at university in London. As I listened in a daze, it occurred to me that my mother's intuition was misplaced, and what she believed to be a marriage of convenience without a trace of affection was in reality something much closer to what she herself had with him.

You love them both? I asked. The boldness of my question surprised me.

He swallowed with difficulty, as if I'd asked him to eat a pile of fish bones. I could see it pained him.

Above all, I love my children, he said.

We heard Anouk walk down the stairs, and we waited for her in silence. She entered the kitchen and raised her eyebrows. I don't think she'd heard a word of our conversation, but still I blushed deeply. She kissed Father and smoothed his hair. *Bonjour, ma chérie,* he said. He stood and busied himself with breakfast preparations.

Sliced bread in the toaster, the espresso maker simmering on the stove, butter softening on a plate. A vanilla yogurt for Anouk. She sat at the table without seeing the food. As usual, she was uninterested in eating at home. She rarely enjoyed cooking for others, and grocery shopping was a chore she avoided at all costs. But when we ate out at a restaurant, she was the first to order steak with foie gras, and never gave a thought to her weight or mine. She would devour what was placed in front of her with great appetite, often having dessert all to herself. I pushed the toasted bread in her direction and she picked at a piece, crumbling it between her fingers.

Father took great pleasure in his food. He smothered his piece of bread with butter, filling the air pockets and spreading it to the edges. He ate half a baguette quickly, taking big bites and chewing with his entire mouth. His parents had raised him on pasta, rice, and cheap cuts of meat. As a kid he ate day-old bread dipped in Nesquik, and I assumed this was why he preferred his bread stale and untoasted.

He was born in a small town in the north of France where the sky was grayer than a Paris winter. His parents had worked hard to offer their children a solid education in the nearest city. Later, he moved to Paris to study literature on a scholarship. He was the youngest in his graduating class to pass *l'agrégation*. He taught literature for years before transitioning to politics, with the blessing of his father-in-law.

I saw Father's outsiderness in small ways. He had never become a true Parisian, even after decades of living here. I saw it in his clothes. He was conscious of labels, but he preferred classic cuts, and had worn the same brand of socks and underwear since his twenties. He wanted to be la crème de la crème, and yet he justified his place, rather than asserting it the way a native does. He dropped names and chose restaurants that had been open for years and had the seal of approval from critics, never the newest spots. He compensated by teasing Parisians while also mocking the town he was from, as if he belonged to neither place. I thought this apartment, with Anouk and me, was where he felt most comfortable and complete.

Madame Lapierre came from an upper-class, highly educated family. For her entire life she had lived in the sixteenth arrondissement, close to Passy, and I struggled to picture Father in those spaces. I imagined him sitting on the edge of a leather couch, or always staring out of a window, wanting to be elsewhere.

I was relieved he wasn't from Paris. It made him different from the rest of us. He seemed more heroic coming from the middle of nowhere, though some critics claimed it made him narrow-minded and conservative. I didn't understand what that meant concretely. I worried about what would happen to him if it all disappeared, if he lost the privilege of being la crème de la crème, if he was no longer invited to the important parties or able to afford lunch at Brasserie Lipp. I saw how his eyes lit up in marvel when we spoke about the Jardin du Luxembourg, how his optimism bordered on the naive. I've been fortunate in my career, he'd say, and I know it can all disappear in the blink of an eye, but if it does, I can return to a simpler life.

He had first visited Paris with his sister, his parents, and two aunts. They drove in a car so small he had to sit in the trunk with his knees pressed against the back window. His sister was hidden in the skirts of an aunt who prayed each time a truck pummeled down the road. She thought anyone driving in the opposite direction would surely crash into them. Paris was an enormous city compared to the town he was from, with its mere five thousand inhabitants.

Anouk couldn't have come from a more different family. Raised in the affluent town of Le Vésinet, in the suburbs of Paris, she went to boarding school and spent her summers in Saint-Tropez, driving on a motorcycle with her friends, sometimes wearing nothing but shoes. When they retired, her parents moved to a beautiful house in Burgundy. We saw them once a year at most. Father had been very close to his parents.

On the surface, my parents seemed like opposites. She belonged, no matter the city or country she found herself in. Knowing how to properly put on makeup mattered more to her than learning how to drive. She didn't care how others perceived her, nor did she try to please everyone around her. He was less secure, and when he felt threatened, he shut down, becoming silent, his mouth drawn into a thin line. Anouk encouraged him to a more liberal stance in his private and political life. Most of her friends were socialists; she usually voted center-left.

I knew they still made love. Sometimes they disappeared for an hour or two in her bedroom. Once I had knocked on her door, wanting to ask a question, and she had taken a while to open it. When she finally did, she was wrapped in a towel, her cheeks flushed and her hair tied up, damp strands pushed behind her ears, a face removed of makeup.

On weekends like this, when we ate breakfast together, it almost felt as though we lived together. We had woken up in the same apartment, walked down the stairs, and participated in this daily ritual.

Have you thought about your plans for next year? Father asked. In high school I'd chosen the prestigious *scientifique* track, mostly for him, not because I enjoyed the curriculum. I hated math.

I'm not sure. I was thinking of applying to Sciences Po.

Sciences politiques. He sounded pleased. Are you following in my footsteps?

She just likes to pretend she's not my daughter, Anouk said, turning to him.

You say that only because I don't want to be an artist.

It's a very good school, Father said, and you don't have to study politics. How about sociology or law? You'll have to prepare your dossier and written exams in the winter.

She thinks you will finance it, Anouk said. Although there was a note of humor in her voice, I was upset by her comment.

I could get a scholarship.

Father finished his coffee and glanced around the kitchen with a look of satisfaction. Anouk rarely cooked with the expensive pots and pans he had purchased over the years. She still preferred to use a scratched-up pan from her student years.

And where would you live if you could choose anywhere in Paris? Father asked me.

The Right Bank.

I don't like how cramped the streets are around there. Don't you enjoy being close to the park?

I'd have more space if I lived in the eleventh or nineteenth.

Don't you feel like you have enough space right here? Anouk interrupted.

It's not bad, I said, knowing that Father helped pay for our rent.

When you were little, Margot, he said, you wanted to be an architect. You'd spend hours drawing houses.

I listened to him, remembering how for each house I imagined the three of us living in the space together.

You had an obsession with centers, he continued. You would draw us in different rooms of the house, depending on what our center was. It was the room that best reflected our personalities, not the geographic middle of the house, but the space that carried the soul of its inhabitant.

For you, it was the kitchen, I said, smiling at him. A large kitchen with only the best equipment.

Ah, yes, I should have been a chef.

What was my center? Anouk asked.

An empty room with floor-to-ceiling mirrors, I said, not missing a beat.

Are you calling me a narcissist?

You like to look at yourself when you rehearse.

What was your center, Margot? Father asked.

I don't remember.

What would it be today?

I can't see my center.

Try to see it.

I looked around the kitchen and then through the living room, which opened onto the balcony where Anouk and I tanned our legs in the warmer months as we waited for Father to come striding down the street. The balcony was a neutral space that allowed me to step away from my mother and father without ever leaving them. It gave me the impression of being at the end of the world, hovering between the street and my life with Anouk.

The balcony, I told him. It's between the apartment and the street.

A purgatory, Anouk said.

You can see through the glass doors into the apartment, he said. My daughter is a voyeur.

Thieves enter through balconies, Anouk continued, and murderers.

You feel the call of the void, he said, and it's exhilarating. You want to know what it would be like to fly.

Or what it feels like to die, Anouk replied.

We laughed at her morbid comment. I stacked our bowls and carried them to the counter, filled the sink with hot water, and left the dishes to soak. Particles of food floated to the surface. Father tied a white apron around his waist and rolled up his sleeves. Whenever he was here, he did the dishes. Anouk stayed in the kitchen with him. I excused myself and went to my room, taking the book Father had given me for my birthday. I put it on the shelf with the other books, lay down on my narrow bed, and spread my legs and arms until they fell over the sides. I hadn't intended on applying to Sciences Po; it was simply the first idea that came to mind when Father asked, knowing it would impress him.

When I emerged for a glass of water a few hours later, I passed by Anouk and Father in the living room. They sat on the couch, watching a travel show. The windows were wide open, and the television screen was bleached by the late-morning light, but they didn't seem to notice or mind. He held her feet on his lap and massaged her toes. She loved to have her feet touched.

The kitchen was spotless. Father had even dried and put away all our dishes. I stuck my head out the window. It was humid and the air smelled damp and bitter, like animals left outside in the rain. It would storm later. In the distance, the sky was dark with massive clouds.

I returned to my room and lay on the bed, staring at the ceiling. The rain started falling a half hour later. I turned on my computer and watched a show about young students who set themselves on fire as a form of protest. It troubled me most that the students didn't always die. Sometimes their hearts continued to beat despite the flames melting their skin. What kind of anger and despair did it take to set yourself ablaze? I wasn't able to imagine such an intense feeling of pain. Was it like being skinned, the way one peels an apple by pulling away its protection? How quickly those defenses could be stripped away, the skin removed, blood streaming along the muscles. This is how Anouk appeared to me sometimes, a tangle of organs, bright red and glaring at me.

Father left in the early afternoon. As he tied his shoelaces, I asked when we would see him again. I don't know yet, my darling, he said. I stared at the thin black hairs on his ankles. I knew he was a busy man. My anger bloomed and disappeared as quickly as snow melting on skin. I couldn't stay angry at him for too long. I waited in the entryway as he put on his jacket. He kissed me on the cheeks, his hand resting on my shoulder for a moment, and then picked up his briefcase and walked out.

That night, we went to dinner at Théo and Mathilde's place. They lived in the nineteenth, close to the Parc de Belleville. Anouk and I walked up the hill from the métro station and followed a street along the park. We were silent, both lost in our own thoughts, and it seemed to me that Anouk was preoccupied; it was unlike her to go for minutes without addressing me when we were out together. The streets were steep, and the dark foliage surrounding this section of the park gave it a shielded, hidden quality, so different from the grandeur of the Luxembourg, where the pointy iron gates could be seen from afar.

When we arrived at their building, Anouk had regained her energy. She typed in the code and pushed the door open with a forceful shove, barely holding it long enough for me to slip through behind her.

The front door was unlocked, and we let ourselves in without knocking. Anouk walked ahead of me, into the kitchen where Mathilde was preparing a vinaigrette. I watched my mother pick at the crust of a quiche still cooling in its pan. In other peoples' kitchens, she couldn't keep her fingers away from food when it was hot, fragrant, untouched. She was the first to break off the crisp edge of a cake. There was one window in the kitchen close to the stove. I stood by it, looking down at the tops of the recycling bins in the courtyard.

Mathilde asked me to taste the vinaigrette and see if it needed more salt or oil, but of course it was perfect; I could've sipped it from the cup. The secret ingredient was a teaspoon of mayonnaise. Théo was in the other room, setting the table.

We often came here for dinner on Sundays, even more frequently in the summer when our schedules were looser and I didn't have to study for exams, daylight brightening the sky until late into the night. I remembered being younger and watching the adults drink wine at the table over empty plates while I fell asleep on the couch, covered in Mathilde's hand-stitched blankets. I'd listen to Anouk talk about Father, seeking their advice, asking if they thought this or that was justified. I sensed that our family weighed on Mathilde and Théo, who loved us greatly and wanted to provide support, but were the only ones in our circle aware of his identity.

I felt that Mathilde enabled Anouk's choices. She was too fluid in how she handled my mother, perhaps afraid of offending her if she unleashed her true opinions. Although she didn't outwardly disapprove of Father, she was so reserved on the subject that I assumed she saw him as a poor choice. It's because she doesn't know him, I reasoned with myself. Théo was more of a listener than a prescriber, and he preferred to sit back and watch. Maybe it wasn't their place to judge, or maybe they had tried to change Anouk in the past and had failed. You have more agency than you like to believe, Mathilde once told Anouk, who answered that she enjoyed how different our family unit was from more traditional configurations. I did not for one minute believe her.

On any given day, ours could feel like an ordinary life. Like most families, we sometimes ate our meals in silence. We had been sick and torn up in each other's presence. I was often in a bad mood around Father, wanting more of him, but then I would disappear after we had finished eating, preferring to read or be alone. I had wanted to slap Anouk for chewing too loudly. The sound of her blowing dead skin from her feet as she pumiced over a bathtub drove me into a frenzy. When I say *we,* I meant the two of us.

And then there was the banality of waiting. Weeks going by, waiting for him, hating him for being gone, wondering if he loved us, missing him, believing he was better than everyone else because time with him was precious. That is how we lived, in a constant state of anticipation.

On mornings when Anouk slept in, I stood on our balcony and looked down at the street. The pavement was so far away that I could no longer see any cracks. I watched people trotting down our street without ever raising their heads. I imagined hundreds of men and women who shared their lives with two partners. There were so many of us, children of these double families who dreamed of the other side.

That night, like all the others since seeing Madame Lapierre, I awoke with the skin of my body chilled and wet, and a strong desire to tumble to the other side, to have the separate spheres of our lives collide. I lay paralyzed in bed with the desire to break free from this routine. I felt it pumping through me, wild and exciting.

4

I stood against a wall, a glass of warm champagne in my hand as I watched Anouk weave through the crowd to find her friends. The play hadn't been very good, and the actors took a while to emerge from the dressing rooms. I was impatient to go home.

Anouk wanted me to accompany her to these parties. She thought I might enjoy them, meet people who could expand my horizons. She wanted me to be comfortable among strangers and learn how to socialize. She worried that I had only one friend, Juliette, and she thought it was unhealthy to spend the rest of my time alone. Don't look so bored, she'd whisper angrily. I wasn't bored. I was tired, and sometimes I had to pinch my leg to stay awake. All I could think about was getting home, wrapping myself between the sheets of my bed, away from the drone of voices. People rarely spoke to me and I didn't encourage conversation, preferring to stay in a corner, out of sight. Older male actors sometimes flirted with me until they found out I was Anouk's daughter, and then they sped away. I sipped on the champagne, enjoying the prickle of bubbles bursting along my tongue. The actors appeared through the swinging doors and there was a general movement in their direction; they were soon surrounded by loud exclamations, whistles, clapping.

I became aware of a presence beside me, a man also standing against the wall, observing the actors from afar. I glanced at him. He was tall with light brown hair, almost golden, long enough to be tucked behind his ears. I guessed he was in his forties, though I wasn't a good judge of age. He wore jeans and a dark shirt with the sleeves rolled up his forearms.

He noticed me staring at him. You were smart, he said, nodding at my glass of champagne. You got something to drink before the crowds descended. The table where they served drinks was now hidden by a mass of people.

The play made them thirsty, I said.

I studied him. His face was handsome, with a slightly crooked nose and pale blue eyes. His hands were hidden deep in his jean pockets. Perhaps he'd spoken to me out of pity, because I looked lonely.

He asked why I was here.

I'm accompanying my mother, I said, pointing at Anouk. She's an actor.

A great one, too, he said. Anouk Louve.

So, he knew her. I waited for him to walk away or ask me for a favor.

Your mother was a rising star when I started my career as a journalist. He spoke as though this were no longer the case for her, and I felt a stab of hurt in my chest.

He introduced himself as David Perrin. I recognized his

name instantly. He wrote long profiles on artists, and I knew Anouk would have loved to have him write a piece about her. I thought about encouraging him, asking whether he'd seen her recent performances, saying she had changed over the years, her work was more mature, perhaps it had less of the physical dazzle from when she was a dancer, but it was still good, better even. I held back, feeling drained from the thought of having to envelop her with praise. I didn't want to talk about her.

David asked if I'd liked the play. I told him the truth, that I thought it was contrived and pretentious. I hadn't liked the ironic distance the actors cultivated onstage, speaking and moving in such an affected way, their faces expressionless throughout most of the dialogue. I wanted emotion, to feel connected to their lives and be moved. I wanted to be rooted to my seat at the end, holding on to those last moments, unable to leave the theater. Instead I'd stood up as soon as our row started to clear.

It's not authentic, I added, scouring my brain for something to impress him. I mentioned an exhibit on Dada at Beaubourg. It was trying to be Dada, a nonplay, I explained to David, but it had none of the energy, the political impetus, nor the invention of Dada.

He seemed amused by my comparison. I hadn't thought about it that way, he said, but I can see what you mean. You want the characters to wrestle with their emotions.

Are you writing a review? I finally asked, feeling stupid.

I wasn't going to, but maybe I will now. I'm intrigued by the parallel to Dada. I overheard one of the actors talk about automatic writing for this play, and anyway, I've been meaning to see the exhibit at Beaubourg.

It's a remarkable collection, I said, choosing my words with care, wanting to sound intelligent.

You speak like an art student.

I blushed. Do I? I'm still in high school.

He examined my face. I thought you were older, he said, after a pause. I became uncomfortably aware of the crowd around us. Perhaps Anouk would see us, not that it mattered.

It's my last year.

I didn't know Anouk Louve had a daughter your age.

She doesn't often talk about me.

There's such a solitary quality to her work. It never occurred to me that she might be a parent.

How old did you think I was?

In your twenties.

It must be my height. I was tall like my mother, and people often made this error.

A soft smile formed on his lips. Some of your mother's roles have been complete transformations, he said.

I was certain he was referring to *Mère,* about the woman who kills her children, the role that propelled Anouk's career, making her name known beyond the Parisian circles of experimental theater. I knew it had been a demanding role because she had to be onstage the entire time, aside from a few minutes when she changed her costume.

She takes her work seriously, I said. Sometimes she continues to inhabit a role even when she's at home. I can tell she's trapped in the character's mind.

What is that like?

I considered his question. It's like being with a stranger, I said. It's that same sensation of seeing, out of the corner of your eye, someone you don't know walking around your house.

It must be unsettling.

Well, I've grown used to it.

You admire her, he said. I can tell. He sounded sure of his statement.

I defer to her, but I don't want to be like her, I quickly added.

It's normal. You don't want to be like her because she's your mother.

His eyes creased at the corners as he smiled. I finished my champagne. When Anouk drank, the alcohol evaporated into her body, whereas each sip I took felt strangled and unnatural. I liked the shape of David's mouth. His lips were wide and tinged red for a man.

Can I tell you a secret? he asked. He leaned closer. Often, I'll meet the child of a famous actor and I'm struck by their ordinariness. They're not beautiful like their parent, they've been eclipsed, or they simply lack their sparkle. In some rare cases, however, they are just like their parent. They might not see it yet, but they have those same extraordinary qualities, a shine that sets them apart in a crowd. For example, Charlotte Gainsbourg, who isn't classically beautiful, and yet you can't tear your eyes away from her.

David stared at me intently. I felt the sudden urge to have him like me.

Are you saying I'm not classically beautiful? I asked, barely feeling the muscles around my mouth.

He smiled and tilted his head in a half shake.

You carry your mother's beauty, but in you it's less glaring and intimidating. Just like Charlotte.

The floor beneath me seemed to open up. I thought I felt Anouk close by, though when I looked for her, she was nowhere to be seen.

I see you're on a first-name basis with the Gainsbourgs, I said, my voice playful. I didn't mind that I was blushing.

David laughed. I was trying to give you a compliment, but instead I've embarrassed you.

You haven't embarrassed me. I brushed a strand of hair behind my ear.

Is your father an actor as well? he asked, scanning the crowd.

The back of my head knocked against the wall. He's not, I said.

I'd love to meet the man who married the famous Anouk Louve.

My parents never married.

David nodded slowly. I could see your mother not believing in marriage. Nowadays the norm is to *not* get married, isn't it?

I was glad he'd misread my words rather than drawing the more obvious conclusion, that my father was already married to someone else.

I wouldn't know what the norms are. I'm not looking for a husband.

David laughed. You're too young to be thinking about these things. You know, I remember early on, at the time of *Mère*, there was a lot of speculation about your mother's personal life. Rumors. But I don't remember hearing about you. She told everyone she was alone.

I wondered how much he knew, and which rumors he was referring to.

I may be misremembering, he said.

Father had stopped teaching that year. He had seen Anouk perform in *Mère* three times. Back then, he could appear in public without causing a stir.

So how come you know so much about my mother?

Everyone knew her at that time. She was a sensation. We were always surprised that she showed up to events alone. Your father must be a very private man.

I noticed how David was making casual assumptions and then pausing to see how I'd respond. The champagne had risen to my head. I was swayed by his questions. I wanted to show him something he didn't know, tear our world open by its seams. How satisfying to hold a piece of information that the other person wants. I smiled mysteriously.

I told him my father was surprisingly private for someone who'd made a career out of being a public figure.

The moment the words slipped from my mouth, a shock ran through me, and what had felt clever moments ago now seemed reckless. I held my breath, hoping to aspirate what I'd said back inside.

David's face tightened and he shifted on his feet before regaining his expression from a moment before. I sensed he was measuring my words with a new understanding. The conversations around us were loud—people were drunk and excited to gather after the play—but now their voices grew distant and a stillness enveloped us.

I saw Anouk locked in a conversation with an actor. She would come looking for me soon. I should go find her.

David took a card from his pocket and handed it to me. If you'd ever like to talk, he said. I hope our paths will cross again, Mademoiselle Louve.

I watched him walk away, a gentle warmth lapping my toes. It was like sitting close to a window and being caught unaware by a beam of light, noticing the shift of temperature as it travels over you, heating your skin for an instant.

5

I was longing to see Juliette after our summer apart. I waited for her outside the lycée on our first day back to school. We had a half day of classes to pick up our schedule and meet our class teacher. I saw her on the other side of the street, wearing a jean skirt and a black T-shirt. She waved at me. She wore sandals with a low heel, and they tapped loudly on the pavement as she quickened her pace.

We hugged for a long time, my face in her hair. From afar, it looked thick and wavy, but up close it was airy and light. It smelled like her shampoo, which hadn't changed since we'd met, a combination of linen, milk, and vanilla. I have so much to tell you, she said. Her nose and cheeks were tanned, and new freckles had sprouted on her forehead.

How did you tan in Brittany? I asked. The region where her parents lived was notorious for its gray and cold summers.

It rained almost every day, she said. But the sun is always there, even behind the clouds. It's insidious, plus I never wore sunscreen. She shrugged, seeming pleased with her complexion.

I missed you, I said. I wondered if she noticed the two kilos I'd lost.

Juliette and I had been friends ever since we both arrived at the lycée, when we were fifteen. We'd been the new girls. We hadn't known each other for a long time, in the grand scheme of things, just two years, but to us it felt like a lifetime. We had quickly established the rare closeness of childhood friends.

She lived alone in a small studio. Her parents had left Paris a year ago, when her father found a job running a dairy production in a rural part of Brittany, and she had asked to stay so she could continue attending our school. The town her parents were moving to had only a primary and middle school, and she'd have to travel almost an hour for a good high school, though I suspected it had more to do with Paris and our friendship than the academics.

I spent several nights a month at her place without the supervision of our parents. We cooked dinner, shared clothes, studied, took turns in the narrow shower stall, and spent so much time together that Anouk no longer asked when I'd be home on school nights if I told her I was going to Juliette's.

Anouk had promised Juliette's mother she'd keep an eye on us, but she'd never stepped a foot inside the studio. I sometimes wondered if Juliette was lonely and missed her parents and sister, though most days I envied her freedom. She had entered adulthood before me. I'd lost my virginity six months sooner than she had, but she'd had an orgasm during sex first. Most of all, I envied her relationship with her mother. *Maman*, she'd say, her voice soft and reaching to a higher pitch of affection, whereas mine grew defensive if Anouk ever called, because it wasn't to speak sweetly or ask about my well-being.

She called to say I had forgotten something essential, like turning off the lights or how to be a good daughter. I knew Juliette's mother judged Anouk for her style of parenting, and
when I saw her, she showered me with affection, the way one
feeds a starving child.

In some ways, Juliette appeared less dependent on her
mother than I was, and yet I assumed she was closer to hers.
Her mother stayed with her for three or four days at a time,
working remotely at the small kitchen table, her computer and
glasses the only equipment she needed. She slept in the same
bed as her daughter—there was nowhere else but the floor—
the same bed I slept in when I stayed with Juliette. Her mother
was discreet. She kept her suitcase upright in the corner of the
studio, her toiletry bag propped on its flat edge, her shoes
neatly aligned in the entrance. I had once seen her in a nightgown when I stopped by to give Juliette a homework assignment, and that moment—the shape of her mother's slight
frame beneath the thin material, an old thing she wore to
sleep—seemed unbearably intimate. I'd looked in her toiletry
bag and found only moisturizing cream, a toothbrush, and
toothpaste. She wore no perfume or makeup. Her most feminine gesture was when she tied her hair to keep it away from
her face.

She visited at least once a month and sent Juliette packages
of cookies, chocolate, tea, and shampoo, as if to save Juliette
from a trip to the Franprix on her way home from school. I
admired my friend's independence and maturity, how she kept
the studio clean and tidy, even wiping down the bathroom sink
after I brushed my teeth and periodically removing the white
calcareous streaks in the shower stall.

Juliette and I ran into the hallway to look at our class assignments pinned on the wall. I had dreaded this day all summer, going back to school, but it felt less awful with Juliette. Sciences didn't come to us naturally, and though we studied hard, we rarely came at the top of the class in math and physics-chemistry. Thankfully, we were in the same class. We had Madame Roullé in physics-chemistry again, who liked to return our tests in ascending order, from the worst grades to the best. Those who got lower than ten out of twenty had their tests thrown onto their desks. The others were handed theirs lovingly. It was almost impossible to get above fifteen in her class. She liked to tell us our work was a pile of *merde* and if we continued like this, we'd fail and have to repeat the school year. But there would be no time to absorb the humiliation. It wasn't worth the energy; we always had more tests to study for, and in the spring, we'd have mock exams on Saturdays to prepare for the Bac.

We were curious about our philosophy teacher, Monsieur H., who was new to the faculty. We'd heard he was young, in his early thirties, and had taught in America for a few years.

As it happened, philosophy was our first class the following day. Monsieur H. arrived five minutes late but didn't seem to mind his lateness or be in a great rush. He wrote his name on the board with confident strokes, as if we didn't know who he was from looking at our printed schedules, and only then did he turn around to greet us.

Welcome to your first philosophy class, he said. His voice was warm and his smile kind. He wore a dark blue suit with a white shirt and no tie, the top buttons undone. He was lanky in an adolescent way and looked younger than his age. I felt the girls in our class lurch at his presence. He sat on the edge of his desk, one leg straight and the other propped on a chair. He'll be eaten alive, Juliette whispered into my ear.

What do you think his first name is? I asked her. Monsieur H. looked at me. My cheeks flushed. I lowered my head and placed the tip of my pen against the blue lines of my notebook, ready to transcribe his words.

Put your pens down for now, he said. Today we are going to talk about the concept of space. What we know of space, and how it affects us. He paused and stood from the desk.

We will also consider boundaries. How we construct boundaries, and the different kinds of boundaries that exist, both physical and imagined. What kinds of problems arise when we talk about boundaries?

There was a silence in the class. Monsieur H. repeated the question. Someone raised their hand, a boy at the back of the class.

Depends on who's setting those boundaries, he said. And if those boundaries interfere with someone else.

That's exactly right, Monsieur H. said. First we need to define what constitutes *personal* space, and what it means to respect someone else's space. Because when are we most susceptible to creating boundaries?

When we are afraid, the student answered.

Yes, when we feel threatened, to protect ourselves, or perhaps when we want order, when we don't understand something, when we are faced with the unknown. One of the ways we try to make sense of the unknown is by categorizing it and setting rules, isn't it? We want to contain it, classify it, make it ours. But I'm getting ahead of myself. He stopped speaking and surveyed us. I'd like us to begin on a much smaller scale with an exercise. You'll have to stand up from your desks.

We looked at one another, unsure whether we should actually stand up in the classroom.

Come on, let's get our blood moving. Step away from your desks, Monsieur H. said. Make sure no part of your body is touching a chair or table or even your bag.

The chairs grated against the floor. We pushed them under our desks and stepped behind them.

Now close your eyes.

My eyelids struggled to stay shut against the brightness of the classroom. Everyone was silent. We waited for Monsieur H. to speak.

He told us to visualize a new space around us. Imagine the edges of this space, the boundaries, either hard obstructions or the more ephemeral kind like the line of a horizon, or simply the limits of your eyesight. Begin to define this space. It can be anything. A house, a room in this building, a cathedral. Pay attention to the details.

Specks of color floated behind my closed lids. At first, I couldn't see anything but a dark orange pressing through my eyelids. What is your center? Father had asked, pushing me to articulate where I belonged in our home.

Slowly an image began to take form. I imagined a horizon with clouds thickening in the sky. A town in the distance and a church surrounded by houses. Green fields stretched out in every direction. I was inside an old house. The floor was covered in a layer of brown dust.

Is anyone else in your space aside from you? Monsieur H. asked us.

I saw a man in the kitchen, standing over a sink. This kitchen was a place of family gatherings, old photos pinned to the walls documenting births and weddings, a television in the corner, and a long table covered with a plastic tablecloth. The man faced away from me; I couldn't see his face, but I knew he was young from the strong movement of his arms as they plunged into the sink. Footsteps creaked in the hallway, a long hallway lined with closed doors behind which there were bedrooms, wooden bed frames and closets, and then a bathroom at the very end, mold blooming around the bathtub and a medicine cabinet filled with expired aspirin.

I returned to the kitchen. I could barely feel the floor of the classroom beneath my feet. The man in the kitchen finished washing dishes. He placed the last plate on a dish rack and turned around. Water trickled down his forearms, plastering his hairs in dark streaks. He looked for a towel. It was Father, in the center of his home, much younger, his body leaner and his skin radiating with health. This was how I imagined his childhood house. No one had ever described it to me, nor had I seen photos of the house, but here with shut eyes I saw it clearly. The lace curtains on the windows, the flowers planted in the narrow strip of soil between his house and the road.

Monsieur H. interrupted the silence and told us to open our eyes and regain our seats. He asked us to take ten minutes to write about the exercise. Describe your process of visualizing a space, he said. What had we seen first? What kinds of boundaries did we define? What details did we notice? Were there areas where our mind expanded endlessly? He wrote these questions on the board.

Go on, he said. Pick up your pens and write.

Juliette and I sneaked glances at each other. Shouldn't we be studying Kant or Hobbes? As if reading our thoughts, Monsieur H. reassured us. For next week, you'll be assigned a text by Descartes, but for now I'd like to expand your minds before constraining them.

As we bowed down to our notebooks, he continued to write on the board. *Sensory versus Intellectual Perception. Awareness. Negative and Positive Space.*

After two hours of philosophy, there came one hour of English for me, German for Juliette, a lunch break, one hour of history-geography, and two hours of math. The classes followed one after the other with five-minute intervals between each one. The day ended at five. Juliette and I walked out onto the street together. We glanced over at Chez Albert, the café across from the lycée. It was informally reserved for the older students, and now that we were in our last year, we could go there. Through the windows I recognized familiar faces. The tables were almost all taken, people ordered coffees, no one was studying in earnest that first week. What would I study next year? I was incapable of projecting myself into the future. Would I leave home if I stayed in Paris? Would I actually apply to Sciences Po? The class with Monsieur H. made me want to do something else, maybe with words. I wished I was like Juliette. She'd always known she wanted to be a filmmaker. She wanted to create and went about her day absorbing it like a sponge.

Let's go to my place, Juliette said, interrupting my thoughts. I sighed in relief and followed her to the métro station. I could already see us walking up the several flights of lopsided stairs, arriving breathless at the top, the fresh scent of her laundry drying on a wooden rack, and the late-afternoon light dappling her bed. We would sit on her bed with bowls of pasta and talk for hours.

Were we shaped by the spaces in which we existed? At home, our apartment was all boundaries: each wall encasing us without the risk of being seen, a private space when Father was there. The boundaries had been there my entire life, and I'd always respected them. Outside it was more complicated. In the past three years we'd stopped going to restaurants together, both Father and Anouk were too recognizable. So, in that way, our realm of possibility had gotten smaller over time, the space in which we could move freely reduced to our apartment, the center of my world.

Juliette was parentless and alone in her studio for the most part, but out of choice. I noticed she didn't bother me about coming over. She accepted that we would always sleep at hers. And perhaps she sensed this, my craving to exist in other spaces, the immediate ease with which I adopted the left side of her bed, showered after her, ate the same breakfast she'd been eating her entire life. I liked being in her home—to be taken in as a friend, a daughter, to belong elsewhere. At Juliette's, it felt as though my lungs were filled with more air, and the heaviness in my limbs would evaporate until I grew light enough to hover right above the ground, able to breathe at last.

6

A few years before, in late autumn, Father had taken me to a remote beach town on the coast of Normandy. It was Anouk's idea that we spend a weekend together—father and daughter bonding time—given that she had rehearsals on Saturday and Sunday. I packed days in advance and waited by the door when it was time to go, throwing myself down the stairs upon hearing his car stop in front of our building.

We drove through the deserted town. It was damp and unseasonably warm. A few boats were still moored in the port. The beach curved along the coast and was separated from the town by a stone wall with stairs on either end. We came prepared for rain and wind, wearing waterproof jackets and boots. The tide was low, and from afar a white mist hovered over the sand. We never made it all the way to the edge of the water.

Father booked two nights at a luxurious hotel a half hour from the town, an old mansion renovated into a spa, with an *étoilé* chef at the restaurant. People came for the seaweed treatments and massages.

We were served lemon verbena tea in the lobby. The woman at the reception recognized him and greeted us warmly. So, you are his goddaughter, she said, satisfied to have remembered this personal detail. He's told me about you. I've reserved adjoining rooms with a king-size bed for Mademoiselle.

Father beamed at her. The muscles in my face ached from holding a smile. I followed the woman up the carpeted stairs, Father climbing behind.

I asked if he came here often. A long time ago, he said, he'd brought his mother to this hotel. She was sick and the seawater eased some of the pain in her legs. I hadn't met my grandmother. She died before I was old enough to ask about her. Anouk had told me about Father's childhood. His mother was a simple woman, kind and generous. She had known about Anouk and had treated her with respect and *délicatesse,* though she was worried the stress of juggling two families would be too much. It was not the straightforward life she had imagined for her eldest child.

In the afternoon we drove back to the town and parked by the beach. The wet sand spread out like packed dirt for hundreds of meters. In the distance I saw the ocean, a dark blue laced with white spray, fading into the sky. We walked along the stone wall.

Ever since he'd become appointed minister of culture a few months before, he'd stopped speaking about his work. In the past he liked to describe the literary festivals, authors I might have heard of, his frustration with colleagues who didn't answer emails on the weekend. But now when I asked how it was going, he was vague, often repeating the same words. *Ça va, ça va,* he'd say, *it's all fine.* His attempts to reassure me showed that he was more stressed than in the past; his work carried a different kind of weight. I pictured him in his office at the Palais-Royal and tried to imagine his daily activities.

Father had always appeared on the rise, working his way to greatness. Lately he sounded less confident, or maybe he wasn't allowed to speak as openly. I continued to listen to every word, probing him with a question whenever there was a lull in our conversations. I wanted him to know that I was interested, and he could speak to me. I loved it most when his voice quickened, signaling an excitement roiling just beneath the surface. He told me he liked explaining his work to me because I understood its complexities. He'd once said I was smarter than most people my age, and that he wished the interns he hired right out of university were as discerning as his own daughter. I remembered these praises whenever Father retreated into a shell of silence. And in turn, I swelled with pride when he confided in me, that same shine illuminating his eyes.

We were alone on the beach. The wind had picked up and I tucked my hands in my pockets. We walked in silence, but I sensed he was preparing to say something. He cleared his throat and spoke in a softer voice.

When you were born, your mother went to the *mairie* to declare you as her daughter. I didn't go with her. We decided it was better this way, not to have my name on your birth certificate.

I turned the words around in my head. Father was nervous to see my reaction, but this wasn't news to me. I had known his name wasn't on my birth certificate for years. I'd overheard Mathilde and Anouk discussing the certificate late at night when they thought I was asleep. Their voices had traveled up the stairs to my bedroom, where I kept the door ajar. Anouk regretted not forcing him to accompany her after my birth, and they had argued about it.

But you are my father, I eventually said.

Of course, *ma chérie*, but without my name on the certificate, you're not officially recognized as my child.

The words shouldn't have mattered as much—I'd gone about most of my life pretending there was no father—but they hit me with an unfamiliar force. I felt my ribs constrict. I glanced over at him. His head was bent, and he avoided looking at me.

I've decided to give you my name. Your mother and I will go to the *mairie* to amend the certificate.

I nodded.

I'm going to officially recognize you as my daughter.

I could tell he wanted me to express my enthusiasm, tell him this was a good thing, well done, *Papa*, with a pat on the back. I forced a smile along my lips.

And my assets will be equally divided between you and your brothers, should anything happen.

What about Anouk? I thought. Perhaps he assumed I'd take care of her.

The wind flapped his coat open, revealing a wool sweater. He always walked with his feet parted open and his hands folded behind his back. Why recognize me now if he hadn't at my birth? This was a question I often returned to later and that I regretted not asking in the moment. I must have been in shock. All I could manage was: Are you sick, is something wrong?

Oh no, he said, there's nothing to be concerned about. I'll live to be ninety years old. And your mother will live to a hundred. He breathed in deeply. I love this smell, he said, of the salt in the air, the humidity. I prefer this kind of weather, when the sky is covered.

It occurred to me that no one we knew would ever visit this beach in November.

For dinner, Father took us to a seafood restaurant on the outskirts of town. The chef was once a close friend and Father hoped he'd still be there. It had been almost a decade since they'd seen each other. It was dark and there were no lampposts to guide us, but Father remembered the way, and ten minutes later he pointed at a restaurant on the corner of two sleepy streets. It had wide, square windows and was the only source of light on the street. Inside, the décor was unassuming. White tablecloths and napkins, a few black-and-white framed photos hanging on the walls. The server seated us by one of the windows. Father asked if Pierre was there, and the server's expression immediately became amiable. The chef is in the kitchen, he said. I'll let him know you are here.

Father leaned toward me as he buttered a piece of bread. This restaurant doesn't care about its appearance, he said. You come for the food. He looked around with visible pleasure. It hasn't changed since it opened in the eighties. No one cares who you are. I glanced at the other customers, mostly retired couples. During the summer this room is packed, he added, but the service is always impeccable.

A tall man wearing a white chef's jacket walked over to our table. He grabbed Father's arm with familiarity. Father stood and kissed him on both cheeks. It's such a joy to see you again, said the chef. Monsieur Le Ministre! They stayed like that for a moment, soaking each other up.

The chef turned to me. You look like your father when he was younger. What a beautiful young woman you've become.

Bonsoir, Monsieur, I said. It's a pleasure to meet you.

And polite, the chef said, turning to Father. How old is she now?

I felt my heart jump to my throat. I was afraid Father had forgotten my age. Fourteen, he answered, not missing a beat.

You don't remember coming here, do you? the chef asked. His soft eyes narrowed slightly as he studied my face. You were four or five, but I can assure you that you ate an entire bowl of asparagus soup!

Father laughed. Pierre also made you a beautiful dish with avocado. He sliced it thin as paper and presented the slices fanned out on a plate. The moment you saw the avocado, Margot, you took your fork and smashed it.

How else was she going to eat it? the chef asked. She has good instincts, like her father.

She has much better instincts than I do, Father said.

The chef patted his arm and told him to sit down and enjoy the meal. He would take care of us tonight.

Until then, it hadn't occurred to me that someone from Father's circle knew about me. Had the chef met Anouk? He sounded comfortable with the arrangement, and at the time I assumed he, too, had a second family.

Father ate with great appetite. The salt-cured cod was layered with creamy mashed potatoes and presented in a small cocotte. The mussels bathed in a white wine and garlic sauce that we both finished with our spoons. My lips were sore from the salt. Father ordered a bottle of white wine and served me a glass. I'd had alcohol before, but never with an adult. Even before taking a sip, I felt drunk from the meal. For dessert, the chef brought out crêpes Suzette, a dessert Father always ordered at restaurants, and lit the crêpes on fire. Father lifted them with the rounded back of his spoon, allowing the liquor to slide onto the plate and under the crêpe. I could smell the burnt sugar and oranges. Look at those edges, he said, prodding with his spoon. It reminds me of lace.

I felt fine leaving the restaurant, but once in my room, I doubled over from an intense pain in my stomach. I ran to the bathroom and violently emptied myself into the toilet. I removed my shoes and undressed, dropping each article of clothing onto the floor, a negligence I wouldn't dare at home.

The mirror was the length of the wall, longer than my bedroom, and my reflection followed me as I walked from one end of the bathroom to the other. It was one of the first times I'd looked at myself in a mirror like this one, really paused to look, not like when I brushed my hair or washed my hands, a quick glance at my face. I knew my body was developed for my age, my hips already thicker than my waist. The features on my face were small and faded aside from freckles speckling my cheekbones. And there was my mouth. I had Anouk's lips. Wide and pale pink. When she wore lipstick, her mouth turned into a red wound, so bright it looked like someone had slashed her face. On an adult face it was striking. On my face it was grotesque. I imagined my mouth swallowing me whole. I knew it was jarring, a sensual and fleshy opening on my narrow, small head.

I took a long shower, lathering myself with the hotel soap and scrubbing my armpits and between my legs with a small towel.

The bed was monstrous in its width. Should I sleep horizontally? I opened the sheets and stepped inside. I slept on one side of the bed, almost at its edge. My entire life I'd slept in a single bed. Throughout the night I stretched a leg or arm to the center by accident, touching the cold sheets, and recoiled. I didn't mean to, I should have loved this bed, taken advantage of its grandness. I listened for neighbors above me, for Father sleeping in the room next to mine, separated by a thick wooden door, but the room was a vast silence.

Somehow, I managed to sleep in fits and starts, until I was awoken by the sun flooding the room. I'd forgotten to close the curtains. From the bed I had a view of green fields separated by dark hedges. I remembered the day before, when Father had called me his goddaughter. It was shocking to hear him lie, not because of the lie itself but because of how he said it, with flawless confidence, the way one speaks the truth. I had listened hard for the deception. His tone of voice had been the same at the hotel and with Pierre. Perhaps he believed I wasn't entirely his until he was named my father on the birth certificate. Perhaps he was divided in two. I rolled onto the other side of the bed, forgetting about the expanse, and my warm skin shuddered against the cold sheets.

When we left the hotel a few hours later, the woman at the reception stepped out from behind her desk and waved at us. It was raining and we hurried to the car. Father pulled out from the driveway, down a tree-lined path and onto the main road.

Did you have a nice weekend, *ma chérie*? he asked. I stared through the window and said yes.

We drove on the highway for an hour without speaking. I was still staring through the window when I felt the car swerve to the left and hit the small bumps that divide the lanes. I looked at Father as he held the steering wheel with both hands. We still had another hour and a half on the road, perhaps longer if there was traffic once we got to Porte de Saint-Cloud. He told me he needed to sleep for a few minutes on the side of the road. We pulled up at the next rest stop. Didn't you sleep last night? I asked. He had worked until very late, he explained, preparing for an important meeting the next day.

He turned off the motor and propped his elbow against the door. I only need fifteen minutes, he said. He leaned his forehead into his hand and closed his eyes. In a few minutes he was snoring. I watched him sleep. His eyelids were pale, almost white, and the skin on his forehead was red and irritated. His mouth drooped down into a frown. Asleep, he looked older. I wondered if I should also sleep, but I was restless and every time I shut my eyes, I continued to see his face. I looked ahead through the windshield and waited.

When he woke up, fifteen minutes later, as if he had an internal alarm, he rubbed his eyes and turned on the ignition. A moment later we were on the highway again.

When you were young, he said, I'd come to see you before you fell asleep. I knew you'd be in bed at around eight thirty. I'd have dinner with Claire and the boys, I'd do the dishes, and then I'd tell them I needed to go back to the office. But I'd come see you. I'd sit on the chair beside your bed. Sometimes you wouldn't fall asleep for an hour or two. You would hold my hand against your cheek, and when I tried to remove it, thinking you'd fallen asleep, you'd snap your eyes open. You'd glare at me in the dark, daring me to leave.

Father laughed and shook his head. Once you asked if I could cut off my hand and leave it there with you. You said: Wouldn't it be great if we could cut off your hand? You can go, just leave me your hand.

I kept my eyes ahead of me as he spoke.

I couldn't move, he said, or do much else. You had my right hand, and it was too dark to read. I had to sit there and wait for you to fall asleep. But I was never bored, and I never wanted to leave.

After that weekend, I wondered what it might mean for Father to embrace Anouk and me in a public manner. If he was claiming me as his legitimate daughter, wasn't there a risk that others might find out, like his wife and sons or his colleagues? I thought I'd known what our lives would look like for a long time, and now I was no longer sure. The chef at the restaurant had known about me, so I imagined that Father had confided in a close circle of friends and colleagues. Who else knew about us? I began to see myself as his secret rather than a nonexistence.

When I filled out the form at the beginning of every school year, writing *actor* for Anouk's profession and leaving the line blank for my father, I sensed something was wrong, but I couldn't always place my finger on this feeling of unease. I had been given one father and when he was there, he filled my world, even managed to eclipse Anouk. My love for him often felt overwhelming, complete. I remember being younger and seeing him walk through our door after a long stretch of absence. It was like a magician's trick. His presence shone brighter than my mother's, for she was always there, bludgeoning me with her performances. I had precise memories of him, quiet afternoons, lunches at a brasserie with a view on the Luxembourg, the weekend in Normandy—each one finite and engraved. And when we were apart, I replayed those scenes until they became my entire life, not just a day here and there.

I wouldn't have said it aloud, but I was also convinced of my untouchable status as his only daughter and the youngest. No matter if we were his second family, Anouk his lover, no matter I wasn't officially his kin. I'd come last and was freshest in his mind.

This was not the story of François Mitterrand, once president of France, and his hidden daughter, Mazarine. I knew better than to imagine the grandeur of a president. Mitterrand had split his holidays between both families, the women and children stood together at his funeral, whereas Father's worlds existed on parallel planes, never intersecting. I sometimes wondered if he had more to lose as someone less powerful, as a politician who was still building his career.

But perhaps what Mitterrand's daughter and I had in common, and what we shared with countless other daughters, was the vision of our father as an all-encompassing being. This man who would not get sick or ever abandon us. I knew deep down that he was a great man, a father who loved me.

I often returned to our conversation on the beach. I remembered him snoring in the car, depleted from a night of working while he was away with me for the weekend. I remembered being a child, his hand holding my cheek as I tried to stay awake for him. I felt his exhaustion pressing down on us, the burden of hiding me but also wanting to please me, protect me, when really I was asking for his entire world. I lived in a strange space, caught between the guilt of being his weakness and the desire to be everything.

Lately, though, I was losing him. The birth certificate never came in the mail, and I didn't have the courage to ask Anouk. Without a formal document, there was nothing concrete binding us. He could abandon me. I wasn't stupid. Even I understood the value of written agreements. If one day he was important like Mitterrand, what would I become to him? Something that needed to be kept suppressed. And it occurred to me that Anouk was just as complicit and perhaps wanted this, preferred it, not to be known.

7

I wrote to David one early morning before going to class. My desk was positioned against the window, and when I raised my head, I could see the rooftops of the buildings across the street. A pale light filled the sky. I knew it was time to get dressed when the grocery store next door lifted its metal shutters.

I told David, simply and in the plainest language I could, that my mother was involved with a married man, a politician, and that was why I'd been elusive when answering his questions. Very few people know about their relationship. I then closed my computer, put on some clothes, and went downstairs for breakfast.

Throughout the day I thought about David reading my email. I'd left it deliberately vague, and I wondered if he'd even know who I was referring to. He might have little interest in Anouk being with a politician, let alone a married one. A part of me always imagined that telling someone who shouldn't know would feel seismic, cathartic, a load lifted from my shoulders, and I was surprised that not much changed. The sky didn't fall on me, and I felt neither better nor worse.

I came home to a reply from David. He was glad to have met me, he said. It was a reminder of the serendipity of chance encounters. My email had confirmed the rumors about my parents. After seeing me, he had gone through old files from when he covered politics in the '90s and early 2000s, specifically the presidential election of 2002, when the National Front had made it to the final round. He'd found the speculations about my father, a promising young politician who had just slipped into their field of vision. He asked if I was referring to the current minister of culture.

We wrote to each other once or twice a day. It must be difficult for you, he said, being your parents' secret. We exchanged details about our lives. He described his days at the office, the Nespresso machine the editor in chief had brought from home and kept on his desk for an endless supply of coffee, the man who played the guitar on Tuesdays at his métro station, a story he was writing on Emmanuelle Devos, and her collaboration with the great director Arnaud Desplechin. I looked forward to reading his emails, and I put more care into crafting my replies, wanting to be familiar without sounding juvenile. I was keenly aware of the gap in our ages, and it took me longer than usual to articulate my thoughts. I read my emails twice before pressing send.

What if I no longer wanted to be their secret? What if I wanted a different life? I embedded these questions in the middle of descriptions of our home life. I wrote about Anouk's strangeness, aggrandizing her quirks. I made my childhood sound glamorous and neglected. I was afraid of boring him with stories about my mother. I told him so, saying I knew I was much younger than he was. Reading your emails erases any difference in age between us, David said. They say wisdom comes with experience, and you have plenty.

One night very late, when I should have been asleep, we exchanged a series of very short emails.

You know who my father is, I wrote, feeling emboldened by our new friendship or whatever it was. I found it easier to be frank in writing, hidden by my screen. What are you going to do with that information?

Do you want me to do something? he asked. I'll honor your privacy. You have my word.

But what if I wanted you to do something?

It took him twenty minutes to reply.

What are you thinking?

Could someone else find out?

It can happen. It's a risk you take when you lead a public life, and you have to be careful.

You would need evidence, a precipitating event, a photo.

Have you spoken to your mother about this?

I didn't reply. I was annoyed that he brought the conversation back to Anouk. I didn't want this decision to belong to her. I showered and prepared my outfit for the next day. It was almost midnight and I had to be awake at six, but I still glanced at my computer one last time before going to bed. He had written a longer message.

In your shoes I'd be having the same thoughts, he wrote, but I doubt I'd have the courage to tell my story. . . . If you choose to speak about your family, and I mean beyond a private conversation, you'll have to be comfortable with your life drastically changing. If it's something you want to do, I could help you.

I thanked him. I asked if it could hurt Father's career.

It depends. It would certainly have an effect, but the greater one would be on his families.

David offered to write a piece about us, but in that case, he would first have to interview Anouk and me. He'd contact my father for a comment. I wanted our story to be out in the open, I admitted, but I didn't want to be connected to the leak. I dreaded the interviews, the attention beforehand, and most of all, Anouk's involvement. Of course, I couldn't tell her about my correspondence with David. I knew she'd disapprove and forbid me from saying another word, because she thought Father was incapable of leaving his wife. I decided they were both cowards. I wanted to crack open our family and force him into the limelight. When I told Anouk life wasn't fair, she replied by saying life was never fair. It's not fair that we share him, that we are second to his family, that I've never told anyone other than Juliette about him. Soon it'll no longer matter. Next year, once I'm grown up, he won't think of me as his little girl anymore, and then what? You'll always be his daughter, she would say, but her words failed to reassure me. What if he thought I no longer needed his affection and presence? And with the elections the following year, we would see even less of him.

I continued to search for photos of Madame Lapierre. I saw her and Father at a gala, both wearing elegant evening attire. I stared at her face until she was grainy, the white of her teeth blending into her cheeks. I was glad to see her dress creasing at her hips in a vulgar manner.

David suggested passing along the story to an old friend of his, a freelance journalist who sometimes wrote tabloid pieces. For this, I gave him a photo of Father and me, taken by Anouk when I was fifteen. His arm was around my shoulders, and my long hair covered half of my face as I turned to face him. He was smiling, on the verge of laughter. I looked younger, but we were both recognizable. It was one of the few photos I knew Father had at home. I didn't know where he kept it, perhaps he'd lost it. We had given him a copy of it for Christmas the previous year.

The Sunday after my second week of class, Théo picked me up and took me to the swimming pool before the outdoor section closed for the year. Anouk was at rehearsals all weekend and Mathilde was putting the finishing touches on costumes for a Molière play. We swam a few laps to cool down before sitting on the grass. We had forgotten our towels, but we were too hot to care. The sun dried us within minutes.

I looked around at the late-summer bodies. Bronzed, some with sunburns along their thighs and shoulders, others stubbornly pale. Mathilde was fair-skinned and didn't like the sun. I'd never asked Théo how old he was. I guessed fifty, but he could have been anywhere between forty and sixty with his dancer's body. He was like Anouk in that way, but more ageless for being a man, or so she liked to say. Only the wrinkles and spots on his hands betrayed signs of aging. Mathilde, on the other hand, had turned forty-nine this year and was vocal about her age. She dyed her hair a beautiful crimson and wore no makeup. She had always been rounder than Anouk, her face full and smooth like the moon, and it made her appear younger.

Théo and Mathilde didn't have children. It was a topic they avoided in conversation, and the one time I'd asked Anouk about it, she had dismissed me. Had they wanted and tried? I was afraid to ask again, in case it brought up other difficult questions.

My fingers tapped on my knee. I thought about David and when the first article would appear. On Monday, he'd said. Tomorrow. It occurred to me that nothing might happen. The piece would go unnoticed and our lives would continue quietly, folded into the sleeve of a giant city.

Théo noticed my agitated state and asked if something was wrong.

I already have piles of homework to do.

I hated high school, he said. I wasn't the best student. I feel like my life only started when I left.

Thank you, I said, sighing.

It'll be over before you know it.

I nodded, glancing down at my tanned legs. Soon they'd lose their glow from the summer.

Are there any interesting boys in your class?

Théo's question made me smile. I thought about the boys in my class. Most of them looked and acted young, half of them wore glasses. They were either too consumed by school or lacked brain cells. Instead, my mind went to David.

I met someone at one of Anouk's after-parties, I said, instantly regretting I'd opened my mouth. But it won't go anywhere.

Théo studied my face. Why do you say that? Because he's an actor?

I laughed. I would never date an actor. He's much older.

How much older?

Double my age. I blushed deeply.

We sat in silence for a few minutes. I picked at strands of grass between my toes.

It'll pass, Théo said, touching my arm.

What will?

You wanting to distance yourself from your mother.

It's what she wants.

I know it looks that way sometimes. She's always been independent, but you are precious to her.

Our conversation was making me uncomfortable, and I thought of how to change the subject. Tell me how you met Mathilde, I asked. I knew this was a story Théo loved to tell, but I'd heard it only in bits and pieces.

His eyes lit up as he described seeing her for the first time. She'd been sitting in a café by the window around the corner from his apartment. He had walked by the café a hundred times but had never ventured inside because of its drab exterior. He pushed open the door and chose a table close to hers. The coffee he ordered was watery and the servers frowned when he didn't order a second one. He waited almost three hours before approaching her.

It's a miracle she didn't leave before you spoke to her, I said.

She was writing in a notepad, and every time she bent over to look into her bag I thought, This is it, she's getting her wallet to pay.

Maybe she was watching you, too.

She was completely absorbed by her work.

What was she wearing?

A long yellow dress with a belt, Théo said, without hesitating. He had a photographic memory. When I walked up to her table, I saw she wasn't writing; she was sketching. From where I stood, they looked like clusters of grapes. She was drawing a dress covered in pearls. I asked if I could sit at her table. We soon discovered that we both worked in theater. We even had friends in common, but somehow, we'd never met.

Did you know my mother at this point?

Mathilde did. She'd created the costumes for *Mère*. I met your mother through her.

What happened next?

I ordered two glasses of wine and a platter of cheese. The bread was stale, it was like a dry sponge, and the cheese was terrible, but we still ate everything, breaking the bread into small pieces, gulping it down with wine. At one point, during a lull in the conversation, I leaned over the table and kissed her on the lips.

You kissed her, I exclaimed. The audacity!

It was the wine. It took me another week to kiss her properly.

Théo and Mathilde had been like second parents to me, and it was both thrilling and strange to hear such an intimate account of their first meeting. They had taken care of me when I was younger, running baths and preparing dinner when Anouk worked late. After I turned twelve and Anouk decided I was old enough to be on my own, I saw them less, but they still dropped by from time to time to keep me company.

They were among the few to know about Father and to have spent time with him. I wondered if tomorrow they'd be accused of spilling the affair to the press.

Earth to Margot, Théo said, waving his hand across my face. The light caught in between his fingers. All I could hear were the shrieks from children as they threw themselves into the pool.

At home, I found Anouk on her mustard bedsheets, the ones she loved because they brought out a warm hue in her skin. She leaned over her feet with a black pumice stone. White particles of dust floated to the floor, collecting at the foot of her bed.

How was the pool? she asked, without raising her head.

Refreshing, but we forgot our towels.

It was probably crowded. I hate being surrounded by people in bathing suits.

Théo told me the story of how he met Mathilde.

Anouk paused, the stone hovering over her right heel. It's a nice story, isn't it? Though remember that no couple is perfect. She looked up at me. Her eyes traveled down my body. Sweat beaded above my lips. I felt the heaviness of my hair, knotted and pulling on my skull. Thank God you're not ugly, she said. It'll be easier for you to find a job one day.

Do you think I look like you? I asked, remembering David's words.

It's all a matter of perception, isn't it?

But concretely, if you take my face, my chest, my stomach, am I like you?

She returned to scraping dead skin from her heels.

Do we have the same traits? She frowned. Maybe. But is that enough? How would I know if you're *like* me? Resemblance runs deeper than how you and I *look*. For example, I keep thinking about this very fat woman. I sat next to her on the train last night. She was so large that her body spilled onto my seat and I had to draw in my elbows to give her more space. I kept waiting for her to stand, and when she did, she moved with incredible grace, as if her feet were made of feathers. There was nothing dense about her. She stood silently, without any effort. It was beautiful. She reminded me of a dancer.

Anouk stood from the bed and raised her arms, but her movements were false, as if she were parodying a ballerina about to perform at the Bolshoi.

At first glance, we were different, she said. And yet I felt close to this woman.

I turned and walked away from Anouk. Only a beautiful and thin person would think like that.

I paused at the doorway of my bedroom, staring at the black screen of my computer, feeling its pull, but did my best to ignore it.

For dinner Mathilde made a tomato tart with fennel salad. She had bought the tomatoes at the market and they spilled juice onto the cutting board as she sliced them open. She always made her own crust and shaped it like a true *pâtissier,* leveling off the edges until it was flush against the mold. Beneath the tomatoes, she added a layer of parsley pesto and grated cheese. I helped her pick fennel fronds for the salad.

Théo listened to the news in the living room while Anouk showered upstairs. I moved to the balcony with my math book. I could barely focus. The sky was hours away from sunset, but the moon was already there, half-formed and white. On the hottest night of the summer we had slept on the balcony. We were woken by cars puttering below, the sun licking our heads. My body ached from its heat. It was like waking up after drinking an entire bottle of wine.

I went indoors. Théo changed the station and the voice of the American singer who had died filled the apartment. Her voice was deep and as rough as sandpaper. I wanted to plunge into her throat and never leave. She had been a tiny person, always wearing platform shoes that gave her the appearance of a stork.

Anouk came down the stairs, her hair dripping onto her shoulders. She didn't like to use a towel, claiming it traumatized her curls. She sat on the couch with her legs crossed high up at her thighs. She could do that, make her legs look like two entwined serpents.

We had a late dinner. The sun was low in the sky. We each ate two pieces of tart, holding it with our fingers like pizza. Mathilde had added almonds and feta to the thin slices of fennel. They had marinated in the lemon dressing. She had a gift with cooking. I knew our neighbors were often jealous of the aromas spilling from our apartment, and Father always preferred her leftovers to anyone else's. Even Anouk was invigorated by the meal and mopped up her plate with bread.

Tomorrow our lives would change. The article would appear in print and on the Web in the morning. I had set off the machine and there it was, rumbling to life, unbeknownst to anyone else at this table. Somehow, I managed to eat, slowly taking bites, and after a while I felt a warmth spread across my abdomen, a wave of pleasure wash over me. My anxiety was so acute it was like being aroused. I drank more water to cool the heat in my neck.

The radio stayed on in the background and Théo swayed his head to the tune of the woman singing. Her song rippled with sadness and when it ended, the commentator praised her, saying her voice was mature.

I washed my face with water, but I went to bed without showering, my armpits sour and my hair smelling of chlorine. I tossed and turned, waiting for morning to come, for our lives to be divided in two stages, before and after. I felt certain that I'd done well, that my act was justified. The curtains were open and from my bed I saw the sky fade from a dark gray to a golden pink. The night was almost over. As I closed my eyes again, I imagined one day explaining myself to Father. I waited for you to choose me, I'd say.

8

I opened my eyes on Monday morning, a dull beating in my head. I had slept two or three hours at the most. Sounds from the street floated to my bedroom. It was late, time to get up and go to school. For a moment I forgot what had changed overnight, and then my mind woke up, firing a million thoughts.

The apartment was peaceful. I showered and untangled my hair. My clothes were on a chair, where I'd left them the night before, and I pulled them over my body, barely feeling the material. Downstairs, I heard a chair scrape against the kitchen floor.

Anouk sat at the kitchen table with a pot of coffee and the newspapers from the morning delivery spread out in front of her. She preferred to read on paper and was subscribed to two magazines and three newspapers. I suspected she did it to keep up with Father. But it was an unusual sight at this time in the morning—she rarely ate breakfast with me on weekdays, and most days I yelled goodbye from the front door, without having seen her emerge from her bedroom. She looked up at me as

I entered the kitchen and fixed me with a stare. Her pupils were large, her lashes painted in mascara. She wore a linen shirt tucked into her jeans and socks on her feet, as if ready to leave the apartment.

You're up early, I said. I served myself a bowl of coffee and sat next to her. Without a word, she held up the newspaper with the headline:

Lapierre has an affair with theater actor Anouk Louve! Minister of Culture, husband of Claire Lapierre, lives a double life!

I had prepared myself for seeing our names in print, and yet it was strange to see them there. A dizzying sense of panic came over me at first. It took almost no effort to appear surprised. I ran my fingers over the paper.

They know who we are, Anouk said, her voice expressionless. I had expected an outburst, but her demeanor was surprisingly calm.

What do you mean?

The press knows about your father.

She avoided my eyes. I knew it was bound to happen one day, but even so—I don't know why it feels like I'm reading my obituary. She paused and looked at me. Her hair was pulled away from her face into a tight bun. She pressed her finger against the image, a headshot I had chosen, knowing it was one of her favorite photographs. Hair tamed into glossy waves and combed behind her ears, her Modigliani neck accentuated by a dark background. The image was black and white, and her lips appeared less immense. She was angular and fierce, and most important, ageless.

Who would do this to us? she said.

I stayed silent.

She shook her head. Though isn't it strange that earlier this summer, we see his wife close to where we live, and now the public knows? It's something of a miracle that we'd never come across her before, given that we've lived in the same city our entire lives. I can't help but wonder if that meant something.

Anouk paced around the kitchen. She was animated as she spoke, her features aggrandized. Her mouth took up the bottom half of her face, and her penciled eyebrows jumped into her forehead. She held a cup in one hand, and the coffee sloshed up the sides, spilling onto the counter when she set it down.

Maybe the press has known for a while, but why did they decide to break the story today? She continued to speculate. They must have a reason for choosing this moment in time. Or if your father has anything to do with this. She shook her head. Impossible. He hates any attention on his personal life. He must be miserable. She sat down and stared at me from across the table, as if I held the answers to her questions.

Other people knew about us, I said, from his circle. I'd wanted to sound confident, but the words came out no louder than a whisper.

Not as many as you'd think.

I took a shaky sip of my coffee. It was hot and bitter. Anouk grasped my wrist. Her fingers were warm for once, but the sudden physical contact frightened me.

You should stay home today, she said.

We sat in front of the television, Anouk on the tip of her chair, her body rigid. We watched the news, a travel show, a report on markets in Spain. I waited for her to speak again but she was fixated on the screen. I wondered how David had passed along the story to another reporter, whether he'd been asked to reveal his source. I'd assumed he would tell the journalist in confidence, give him the photos, and that would be enough. The article made no mention of who had divulged the story, but I became increasingly nervous, chastising myself for not being more careful. What if he'd told someone about me and our email exchanges? What if he'd shown them?

Mathilde arrived an hour later and held Anouk in her arms for a long time. I couldn't remember ever seeing them embrace. She sat next to me and rubbed my shoulders.

What are you going to do now? she asked Anouk.

Nothing. She grimaced. I know he'll be furious. It's not what he wanted.

Why? I asked, interrupting her. You think he'll be angry?

You know your father.

Maybe it won't be that terrible, Mathilde said.

Oh, it will. I'm sure he's in denial.

But you must have spoken about it, I said. Didn't you have a plan for something like this?

The plan was to continue as we always have. Two separate lives for your father.

I kept my phone close by, the way I did on my birthdays, willing for him to call. As the day went on, the article was picked up by other news outlets. I received messages from acquaintances at school; girls who never spoke to me expressed a confused range of emotions. *You're in the news! Are you okay? I didn't know you had a famous father.* They usually gathered around in the courtyard designated for smoking. Diane, Camille, Laura. I wasn't popular enough to mingle with them. Juliette and I looked down on them for being vapid.

I went to my room and sent a message to Juliette. She didn't read the news, and I was afraid she might overhear the gossip. I explained why I wasn't in class today. My heart thundered as I typed the words: *The press knows about my father.*

She replied a half hour later, between math and biology class. *I'm so sorry, Margot. Meet me at my place tonight? I'll be home by 6:30.*

We spent the rest of the morning in the living room watching television. Mathilde prepared lunch, a salad with radishes and slices of cheese. She bought a fresh baguette and tidied the kitchen, setting the dishwasher to run and cleaning the stove. Anouk migrated to a corner of the couch, her legs drawn into her chest, as she furiously typed on her phone.

Who are you writing to? I asked.

It's none of your business, she replied.

I tried to silence the clanging in my chest. It grew louder and louder by the hour. I was restless. We hadn't heard anything from Father. I kept my phone with me in case he called. Where was he? I briefly considered Madame Lapierre, imagining a confrontation between them, Father telling her that he wasn't ashamed of us. I tried to disregard Anouk's comment about him being furious, which was not an outcome I'd anticipated, but if he was indeed upset, would he speak harshly about us? Would he diminish his involvement and say we were a mistake? I'd never seen him angry at me. I stood on our balcony and looked down at the sidewalk, wondering if the men and women who lingered outside our building were waiting for an interview.

It was dark when I decided to go see Juliette. I'm staying the night, I told Anouk.

Be careful of what you tell her.

Juliette doesn't care about public opinion. She doesn't even read the news, I said defensively.

You don't know her parents.

They're not in Paris. Why would they care?

You haven't known each other very long.

I hated the suspicious tone of Anouk's comment, as though Juliette couldn't be trusted. I slipped on my shoes and waved goodbye to Mathilde.

Juliette was waiting for me at the entrance of her building. She held the door open with her foot. Her studio was on the seventh floor and she had the strongest calves from all the stairs she had to climb. When we came home together, she liked to take my hand as if I were a suitcase that could be tugged along. By the time I got to her floor, I was always out of breath. I fell into her arms. I told her we hadn't heard from him all day.

I promise it wasn't me, she said as soon as I stepped into her apartment. I haven't told a soul, not even my mother.

We sat on her bed, our legs crossed, facing each other. I know it wasn't you, I said.

Who do you think it was? She scrutinized my face.

I shrugged. A lot of people found out over the years.

Are you relieved it's out in the open?

I feel lighter, I admitted, but I'm worried because Anouk is convinced that he's going to deny the article.

What do you mean?

Pretend he isn't having an affair, say I'm not his daughter.

He wouldn't do that.

But as soon as the words left her mouth, I sensed Juliette was wrong. How could she know his reaction? She had never met him. She repeated herself with conviction, perhaps because she'd seen the dread on my face, then quickly changed the subject to talking about the classes I'd missed.

We worked on our math homework, but within minutes my mind wandered, and I thought about Father. I leaned against a pillow, feeling drugged. Juliette knew better than to ask questions. She continued to solve the math proof while I watched her. We fell asleep early, an hour after eating. I woke up during the night to Juliette going to the bathroom. She closed the curtains with a paper clip before coming back to bed.

I lay there for what felt like years, my eyes closed, waiting for the alarm to ring. When it finally rang at six, we rolled out of bed and took turns showering. We ate bowls of muesli with chocolate powder to sweeten the milk. You can borrow anything you like, Juliette said, gesturing at her wardrobe. I took a pair of her jeans that I loved, even though they were too tight around the waist. We left our bowls to soak in the sink and went to school.

The week went by at a different rhythm, the days long and bloated, time defined only by the sun rising and setting. At school, a few people whispered and stared, but for the most part my classmates didn't seem to know or care enough, and the teachers would never indulge us with their attention, at least not publicly. Juliette and I sat side by side, going through the motions of being students. We listened to our teachers and took notes as we had been trained to do for years.

There were more articles in the days that followed. Anouk's career as an actor resurfaced, her iconic role in *Mère* discussed and dissected, and whether she had hinted at the affair in her one-woman shows. The critics found nothing in her art that implied an affair with Lapierre.

As Anouk had predicted, Father began by denying the affair, saying we had no relation to him. It took him a week to finally admit to the relationship. He communicated this in a written statement. I was crushed. I'd wanted him to recognize me, and there he was in the days following the reveal, pretending I wasn't his daughter, claiming he'd never been involved with Anouk Louve. New photos of Father with Madame Lapierre emerged. In them she wore a stiff jacket, the material creasing at her elbows. She had the marble look of a woman who would eat only government-rationed food if war broke out. I poured my energy into blaming her, as if Father's denial was her doing. The articles spiked for a few days and then petered out. Within two weeks, the public seemed to have lost interest. It was remarkable, how quickly the winds could change, once other news stories returned to their rightful place.

I waited for David to email me. We hadn't been in touch since the news story broke. He wrote the following week, asking how I was and if there was anything he could do to help. It was not the public response from my father that he'd expected.

My first impulse was to blame him. I knew he wasn't responsible for Father's denial, but his email was short and formal, and it lacked the warmth of his previous ones, as if he wanted to establish distance now that we'd gotten past the news story. What could he do to help? I responded in two lines, saying we were fine. It would greatly please my mother if you would interview her one day, I wrote. She loved your piece on Emmanuelle Devos.

I hadn't planned on asking him to interview Anouk. It was an idea that formed as I wrote the email, and later I found it foolish. If David and Anouk met, he might allude to knowing me, and she would immediately sense something was amiss because I'd failed to mention our encounter. She could be skilled at drawing connections between people, especially when she was suspicious. At the same time, it had been a year since the last magazine piece on Anouk. I knew she'd be flattered and would pounce on the opportunity, and when Father saw the piece, he'd be reminded of her talent as an actor. It was one more way to say: Here we are.

We have to take responsibility for who we are, Anouk said, sounding defeated. I don't think his wife is behind all of this. The denial feels like something your father would do. Anyway, the journalists aren't interested because he stayed with his wife. It's an ordinary ending.

I felt I'd played my only card. It should have transformed my life for the better, replaced those years of keeping his identity hidden with legitimacy. Instead it had cracked open our house and overturned our lives.

He could still leave her, I said.

He won't have the courage.

Are you sure?

Oh, that was never on the table. Anouk's eyes shone from the strain. I told you, didn't I?

When will we see him?

I don't know.

She combed her hair and showed me the grays that had sprouted all of a sudden. They've always been there, I told her. She wanted me to pluck them with tweezers. There was no point in arguing with her. I stood behind her and yanked them out, one at a time, placing them on the table for her to see. She stared at the small pile of hairs. I am like Marie-Antoinette, she said, whose hair had supposedly turned white overnight after she was captured. At least my mother hadn't lost her sense of drama. We should have grown closer in that moment, but I'd never felt lonelier. My skin hummed with a new agitation, and I withdrew from her.

She loved him. I had known she loved him, but I saw it even more in the last days of September, when she washed his handkerchiefs and ironed them carefully. She knew how important it was for him to wear clean, laundered clothes. I hadn't thought of my parents like this in a while. Perhaps they had stayed together all these years because they loved each other and not because of me, and perhaps if I'd never been born, Father would have left his wife for Anouk.

I was miserable. The lines around Anouk's mouth ran deeper; the skin under her eyes was purple. If I touched her there, I knew I'd feel the flutter of her heart. Her friends, aside from Mathilde and Théo, were angry. They, too, had been left in the dark all these years, always told that my father was an actor who'd left Anouk before I was born. They stopped coming by, and our apartment was very quiet for once. Anouk was a woman of principle—she would lie or take secrets to her grave if needed—and because of this her friends trusted her with their most embarrassing secrets. Perhaps this was why Father had chosen her to be his partner. Some of her friends, however, liked the attention of the press, good and bad news alike. They were natural gossipers. I doubted Father would suspect Anouk of leaking the affair, but he might still indirectly blame her.

Why haven't we heard from him yet? I eventually asked.

Anouk looked at me as if I couldn't possibly understand.

Because he's afraid. He's always wanted to please everyone, and he's failed in the most public way.

One evening I came home to find the apartment empty. Anouk had been here every night for two weeks and I had expected to find her at home. I walked through the rooms. There wasn't much visible evidence of Father, save for a few old articles of clothing, the handkerchiefs, and a block of Comté cheese in the fridge.

I stood in the middle of the living room, staring aimlessly at our furniture, seeing it with new eyes. The frayed edges of our couch, the secondhand coffee table, the cheap bookshelf with a faux *bois* covering. Father hadn't bought us beautiful objects, and I resented him for not giving us more. I knew Anouk made a point of being independent, but now that I looked around, I was embarrassed by what I saw.

Father stored his cello behind our winter coats, the only item of value his parents had bought him. He loved it dearly. The cello was dark and glossy with voluminous curves. The spike slid out from underneath. It was a heavy instrument. Outside, rain splattered onto our balcony. I imagined him at home with Madame Lapierre, sitting on a leather couch, holding her feet on his lap. They also listened to the rain, a pleasant pitter-patter to their ears.

I lifted the cello into the air and slammed it down. The bottom cracked and the spine caved in. For a moment, pleasure flooded my chest. Yes, this is it. I would call him, I would write to him, and find the harshest words to describe how we felt. Did he think he could pretend we didn't exist?

Soon, though, I started to feel terrible. I picked up the splinters of wood, knowing it would be impossible to repair the cello without telling Anouk.

I walked to my room in a stupor and lay down on the bed. I cried for a long time, holding my knees into my chest and biting the material of my jeans. I closed my eyes, wishing I could vanish just for a second. The violence of this thought always had a soothing effect on me. I stayed on the bed, the window open, until the rain stopped. A cold wind swept through my room.

Through the window I heard a couple argue on the street. The woman's shoes echoed on the pavement as she walked back and forth. I caught a few words of their conversation and let myself slip into their world. *You forgot to buy the milk. You are never on time. Of course I love you.*

Of course you were wanted, he'd said, when I cried in the car after our weekend in Normandy. I didn't want to go home to Anouk without him. I'd blamed him for not wanting a daughter after all, for not recognizing me at my birth. You were wanted, *ma chérie*, he told me a second time.

As I listened to the couple argue, a foolish hope warmed me, a relief so powerful it felt like alcohol flowing through my veins. This will pass.

9

The weeks sped by and September turned into October, the leaves changing from green to golden and rust, littering our neighborhood. The mornings were thick with fog. Our lives pressed on with the same uncertainties and hopes. We had exams almost every week, philosophy essays, long math *devoirs,* which Juliette and I labored over until midnight, often calling each other before going to sleep to compare our proofs. We slept from midnight to six, before starting all over again.

Unlike other mothers, Anouk rarely fretted over my grades or asked after my homework. She thought the schooling system was barbaric and stifled creativity. You are too serious, she would often tell me. Perhaps she was right, but it was all I knew, and I was protective of it. Either way, Father's approval mattered to me, and he would want to know I'd done well on the Bac.

One morning, Anouk told me she'd been approached by a journalist, David Perrin. The one who wrote a profile on Fabrice Luchini.

He must be famous, I said, keeping my voice neutral.

He wants to interview me. Imagine that. It must be because of the news of your father.

I sensed her conflict. She had turned down other interview requests since the revelation, preferring to remain private about her life with Father. We had both kept to ourselves, shutting down any friends who asked too many questions. What if he asked her personal questions about their relationship? She wasn't prepared to betray him after staying silent for two decades.

But she couldn't refuse a professional opportunity, an interview with David Perrin, and before she said it out loud, I knew she would accept.

I had planned on staying at Juliette's that evening. I was afraid of being in the same room as David and Anouk, in case she sensed a familiarity between us. But on the morning of the interview, just as I prepared to leave for school, Anouk insisted I come home right after. She wanted me to participate.

I don't like interviews, I reminded her.

We need to symbolize closeness, she said, the wholesomeness of a mother and daughter.

But I have mountains of homework to do, and Juliette is expecting me.

You're behaving like a spoiled child. I'm asking you for one favor. She turned her back on me. I could tell she was nervous to be alone with a journalist whom she admired. It was unlike her to ask for my help, but given the press attention on us those past few weeks, I understood this wasn't easy for her.

Anouk rattled on about David, how influential his profiles could be, his ability to uncover personal history, to paint a nuanced portrait, never for the sake of sensationalism. He had integrity; he had started his career at the bottom rungs of Radio France. She had an affinity for those who worked their way up.

She hastily put away things in the living room, her gestures betraying a person who rarely cleans by instinct. She took a pile of clothes from the couch and carried them to her bedroom. She placed cups and glasses in the sink and wiped dust from the coffee table with a sponge. You'll be at the interview, she said, her words final.

All day, as I drifted from class to class, I dreaded seeing David and the kinds of questions he might ask. I wasn't a seasoned actor like my mother, skilled at divulging my emotions when thrown into the spotlight. I was better at omission.

Juliette and I waited in line at the cafeteria for a half hour, almost our entire break, and for once I wasn't starved. That day there was spaghetti Bolognese, and people rushed to retrieve plates of the steaming pasta. The noodles were always too soft and watery, but the portions gigantic and the cheese endless, so spaghetti Bolognese days were among our favorites, along with cordon bleu and fries. I sat across from Juliette and mounded my fork with sauce, leaving the spaghetti behind. The sauce was too cold for the cheese to ever melt, but we continued to add more, not wanting to pass up bottomless food.

I told Juliette about the journalist who was interviewing us.

What will you say? she asked.

I don't know. Anouk will do most of the talking.

Have you spoken to your father yet?

I shook my head. We hadn't heard from him in a month, and I expected him to call me, not the other way around.

Shouldn't he be the one apologizing for telling the press that we had no relation to him? It had taken him a week to acknowledge the affair.

He's acting like a child, she said. It reminds me of my father. I always have to be the one who breaks the silence. Sometimes I wait for days on end, thinking I'll have the courage to stay away, not contact him. But then I call him. I'm not ready to cut him out of my life.

Because you think he'll change one day.

Juliette nodded. I knew she had a complicated relationship with her father. He was critical of her choices, thinking she should take a more traditional path. Once a month he called her to say she had no future as a filmmaker, that she would be poor and was too dispersed to succeed.

We picked at the food on our platters. I split the bread roll in half and dipped the soft crumb into the Bolognese sauce. I'd lost my appetite over the past few weeks, and I ate with difficulty, nervous when there was too much food placed in front of me. Eventually, I broke the silence.

I don't understand why he's avoiding me. His sons are all grown up, and he doesn't even love his wife. Why hasn't he contacted us?

Juliette considered my question before answering. Who knows what's going through his head right now? You'll probably hear from him when the scandal blows over. Or you could try calling him.

I wouldn't know where to begin. What would I say to him? We don't really argue. It's not like with my mother.

Juliette wiped her mouth with a paper napkin and served us water from the jugs on the table. Her eyelashes were short and light brown, often invisible, but today they caught the light streaming through the windows of the cafeteria.

The thing with my father, Juliette said, is that sometimes he can be extraordinary. We'll have a conversation and I can tell he thinks the world of me, he doesn't really mean to criticize me. He just doesn't see the world from my point of view. Maybe your father is the same way. You should call him. Don't wait too long.

I had thought I had known my father, or parts of him at least. But now when I imagined calling him, I found I was terrified, as if I were about to call a stranger.

You're afraid of showing him how you feel, she added. I understand.

I folded my hands under my chin. I was also afraid of the emotions spilling from me if I heard his voice. What if in my vulnerable state I confessed to what I'd done? Maybe it was wiser to wait until he picked up the phone, so I could be the composed listener.

You're not eating, Juliette said, looking at my plate. She had almost finished hers and we had five minutes until our next class.

I twirled the cold spaghetti on my fork and stared at her as I put it in my mouth, chewing the pasta into a paste until I could slide it down my throat.

Les papas, I said, sighing, as if we knew all of their shortcomings, and as if we didn't love them with every fiber of our being.

At home, I found Anouk pacing the living room. Her eyes were dark and large, enhanced by charcoal eyeliner. She had changed into black trousers and a silk blouse. Her feet were bare, and her crimson toenails gleamed from afar.

David is arriving in five minutes, she told me, glancing at the clock. I almost touched her arm to soothe her. She ran her fingers through her hair, shaking out the ends for more volume. I could tell from its soft and feathery texture that she'd washed it that same morning.

I stepped outside onto the balcony to calm the erratic beating in my chest. My hands were moist and cold. I wanted to seem composed. I looked down at the familiar sidewalk and the clean gutter where I sometimes sat and waited for Anouk whenever I forgot my keys. Across the street the butcher stood in the doorway of his store, hands on hips, apron white as bone. He wiped his forehead and disappeared inside. He knew our order as soon as we stepped through the door. Four slices of ham and one *pâté de campagne*. The evening sky cast a fragile blue light onto our neighborhood.

I came back into the living room and slid the door shut behind me. Anouk was in her bedroom upstairs, putting on more makeup or changing her clothes. I sat on the couch and waited. The light grew dimmer inside and I switched on the lamp next to the couch. A moment later, the buzzer rang and Anouk came bounding down the stairs. I heard her voice in the entrance saying hello over the speakerphone as she pressed the button. Come on, she said, glancing back at me. Don't just sit there.

David looked the same as I remembered, though his hair was cut shorter than before. He was dressed casually, sleeves rolled to his elbows and shirt tucked into his jeans. He carried a leather jacket over one arm. He introduced himself to Anouk and me in a tone that suggested we'd never met. I was grateful for this, and the flutters in my stomach settled somewhat. As he walked into the apartment, I noticed a woman following close behind. She first said hello to Anouk, and then turned to face me. You must be Margot, she said.

Not in a hundred years did I expect David to have a wife, let alone bring her. He'd given me no indication of being married, not once mentioning a partner—he had described the life of a bachelor—and Anouk hadn't thought to mention her either. David explained she was also a writer and often helped him with his assignments.

The skin on her face and neck was golden and bright, like a peeled peach, and she emanated an intensity, as if she were composed of charged particles. I searched for wrinkles or blemishes on her face. Her skin was perfect. She was striking in her boyish Oxford shoes, feet planted a little apart, a long coat that came down to her ankles, almost brushing the floor, and a cotton white shirt underneath.

She leaned in to greet me and I caught a waft of her scent, citrus and wood. Her eyes were black, and yet they had the same golden quality of her skin, as if light shone through them from a hidden source in her head. Her name was Brigitte.

We sat in the living room with a tape recorder placed on the table between us.

David began by saying he'd long admired Anouk's work as an actor. I felt Anouk relax beside me, bathing in the ray of David's admiration. Soon she'd forget I was there. I sunk deeper into the couch while she straightened her spine. She hardly blinked. David mentioned *Antigone,* one of Anouk's first important roles in the eighties. He had read the reviews and there was one scene that stayed with him: When Antigone stands at the edge of the stage, close to the audience, she swings forward, almost tipping into the front row. It took agility to perfect this move, balancing on her toes and heels, using the strength in her abdomen but making it seem effortless. Anouk's training as a dancer allowed her to maintain balance while giving the impression of falling. One critic described it as a pendulum, barely controlled. She wore a strong jasmine perfume and those in the front row could smell her. It created a sense of intimacy, the wall between actors and audience seeming to shatter.

I stared at the coffee table. Anouk nodded at David's description. When I glanced up, my eyes met Brigitte's. She seemed amused by the conversation, and then she propped her elbows on her knees and moved forward as if to speak. David paused, allowing her to ask a question.

We heard he was there, Brigitte said.

I noticed Anouk's shoulders tighten slightly. Who? she asked.

Bertrand Lapierre. Though at the time he was just at the beginning of his political life.

We met after the play. It was the closing night. He loves theater, as you know, and he impressed me with his knowledge of Anouilh.

Do you know if he was seduced by your performance?

We only spoke briefly that first night. We became close years later.

Did he sit in the first row?

Anouk smiled. You would have to ask him.

A lot of people now wonder if he had an influence on your

career, David said, shifting the conversation. He's always been involved in the arts, and more so since he became the minister of culture.

He was supportive of my work and he came to my shows, but he never asked me to change my lifestyle for him. I didn't feel the need to incorporate our story into my art.

You both lead such public lives. How did you juggle this fact, all the while maintaining the secret of your union?

We gave each other the space and independence to grow into our careers. If anything, our arrangement allowed me to continue my work as an actor with more freedom and mobility. It also allowed me to grow closer to Margot.

Anouk turned to me and ran her fingers along my knee. A film covered her eyes. My mother was performing.

Margot and I have developed a unique bond, she continued. It's always been just the two of us at home.

You haven't had other partners? David said.

No.

Do you mind if I circle back to your career? Brigitte asked. I'm wondering how your acting will be changed by this revelation. Your shows are very personal. Will you continue to remain private about your relationship?

I should rephrase what I said earlier, Anouk answered. I incorporated him into my art all the time. Perhaps people aren't as perceptive as they like to think.

Anouk was quiet for a moment. It seemed she was thinking about her next words. Your question, though, seems to imply that there is still a relationship.

My skin prickled. It hadn't crossed my mind that they were

no longer together. We had weathered longer stretches of absence, one or two months during which Father did not visit, but he always returned to us.

So, you confirm that you're no longer together? Brigitte said.

Yes. Anouk held her gaze.

I stood up suddenly from the couch, conscious that my breath had stuck in my throat. I'm going to get a glass of water, I said. Would you like one? My vision blurred as I glanced over at Brigitte and David. They shook their heads, thanking me. I walked away from the living room, aware of the stiffness in my legs, my shoulders tense and drawn up to my neck, a hotness spreading across my nose. I closed the kitchen door behind me and leaned against the wall, my chest heavy. I roughly wiped my eyes and poured myself a glass of water.

With the lights turned off, the kitchen was barely illuminated by the neighbors' windows. I splashed water on my face, dried it with a dish towel that smelled of onions, and stepped out of the kitchen. I found myself face-to-face with Brigitte, who stood in the dark hallway. She was looking for the toilet. This way? she asked, pointing down the hallway.

Yes, I said. On the left.

She paused, as if wanting to speak, and I waited, invited by the soft glow of her skin. I'm sorry if we overstepped, she said.

I smiled gently. It's nothing we haven't heard before.

I remember what it's like at your age, but you know, you're allowed to show pain from time to time.

Brigitte spoke with warmth, but beneath her words I detected a sharpness, as if she either recognized herself in this description or was judging me for it. I ignored her comment. I never knew what to say when adults commented on what I did and didn't know for my age. What more could I do? I'd only lived those years.

You'll write something good, I said. It won't be like the other articles.

I'm not going to do it. David is writing the piece.

I was surprised, having assumed they'd be writing the article together since he'd brought her along. I asked if she would help him with it.

Yes, with the interview.

What else do you do?

In life? She raised her eyebrows. I make coffee in the morning. I do our laundry. Sometimes I write.

I felt myself relax in her presence, enough to venture a joke.

How did David ever find you? I asked her. You're a vestige from the fifties.

I'm something of a relic, aren't I? She burst into quiet laughter.

My eyes had adjusted to the dimness of the hallway. I observed her, the sparkle in her eyes, and I saw how she was younger than I'd first assumed.

I'd like to read your writing one day, I said.

Oh, it'll bore you.

I can't imagine it would. Saying those words gave me a shot of confidence and I stood taller, my toes rising.

She pulled on the collar of her shirt, and I noticed the glint of a plastic thread. The tag was still attached; she'd forgotten to remove it. You have something there, I said, taking care to avoid touching her skin as I broke the thread with my fingers. I gave her the tag. It's better to wash new clothes before wearing them, I said. To remove the chemicals.

She smiled, holding the tag between her fingers. Thank you for your wisdom, Margot. I'll remember next time.

I watched Brigitte walk to the bathroom and close the door. It was quiet on the other side. I stood in the hallway, listening to the muffled voices of Anouk and David, wondering if they had heard us talking. I listened to the trickle of water, the zip of jeans closing, the powerful flush, water running from the faucet. As I turned to leave, I heard the cabinet door pop. Its sound always surprised our guests. The wood was swollen from years of humidity and poor ventilation. I wondered what she wanted in the cabinet. I imagined her eyes traveling over the creams, perfume samples, hand towels folded neatly, the old boxes of tampons. We kept our personal items in the bathroom upstairs. If Brigitte was looking for medications, she'd have to search elsewhere.

10

Before you were born, Anouk told me one day, your father was a different man. He rode his bike to see me on weekends, arriving out of breath, a bag of pastries in his hand. Being in love for him was a revelation. His sons were young, so he always had his hands full when he was at home. I provided an outlet for him. I think our relationship presented itself as carefree and uncomplicated; it fulfilled a part of him he'd kept repressed for years. Your father belongs to the generation that was born after the war, with constant reminders of how little his parents had, how little there still was, and how he needed to begin earning immediately after school. His trajectory was less common: He didn't go to business, law, or medical school; he pursued a literary path. But even in doing so, he fought to be first in his class, received the necessary scholarships, and was financially independent by his early twenties. What was different about his story was his wife. He had married up into a wealthy and educated family. He once told me that he learned all his table manners from her. A woman must sit with the best view in the restaurant, but also with a view of the entrance, in case her lover walks in.

He is five years younger than I am. When I met him, I'd been worried I was growing old, reaching my limit for dancing. I could see it on my face when the light was harsh. Thirty-six felt like the end of the world. I'd begun acting more. There was *Antigone*, of course, but remember, this was before *Mère*. Being with him was a breath of fresh air, a second youth, because he saw me with complete wonder. I was older than his wife, and yet I hadn't borne any children. I danced every day and wore the same clothes I'd bought in my twenties.

I told him it was unlikely I'd have children from all the dancing. I'd gotten my period late and never bothered being careful during sex. The doctors I saw in my adolescence had warned me I might never get pregnant. Some months I barely bled. My hormones were out of whack, and then there was the eating. What a drag it was to eat when there was so much to do in a day. Rehearsals, auditions, dance classes, seeing your father. I ate the pastries he brought me. They were always squashed from his bike ride, the paper transparent with grease.

I was almost three months pregnant when I realized you were inside me. It was a complete shock. My doctor called it a miracle. He said: Well, Madame, at your age, the risks are high, especially for Down syndrome. You are past your prime. I don't see many women your age having children.

The nerve he had! I was thirty-nine. He lectured me about not having children when I was in my twenties. You're lucky it's not menopause, he said.

Your father was shaken by the news. In a matter of weeks, he started to lose his hair. He had rashes along his arms and shins, and he came to visit me less often, as if by avoiding me he could ignore how much bigger I was growing. Most days, when I wore a wide jacket and a thick scarf draped over my stomach, I didn't look pregnant.

I decided to visit my parents. I wasn't in touch with them other than Christmas and their birthdays. I called them to announce my pregnancy and say that I'd be staying with them for a few days. A childhood friend was getting married close to where they lived.

Your grandparents had already retired to that small town in Burgundy two hours from Paris by train. I settled into my seat and placed my hands over my stomach, as I was in the habit of doing, and it was wonderful, the firm roundness of you. You felt extraterrestrial and it scared me at times, how I housed another being in my own body. Sometimes I wanted to turn myself inside out, just so I could see you.

I rested my head against the window and fell asleep. I was woken by the loudspeaker announcing the approaching station. As I stood from my seat, I felt the first kick. It was the strangest thing, to feel uncontrolled movement coming from within me. It sent a jolt up my spine and I almost laughed right there, on the train. I waited for another kick, and then it came, softer than the previous one. I'd felt flutters in the previous weeks, but they were subtle movements compared to this. You were energetic. Strong.

The house hadn't changed since I'd last seen it, with its grand winding staircase at the center and the high ceilings. The windowpanes had been recently cleaned and light flooded all the rooms.

My mother took care of me for three days. She cooked two

meals a day and bought fresh bread every morning. But she managed to avoid talking about my pregnancy, other than asking how far along I was. My father only wanted to know if it was a boy or girl, and when I told him, he was pleased. By the third day I grew resentful. How could my mother ignore this tremendous change in her daughter? Why didn't she ask about the father? What would happen when the baby came?

I confronted her, wanting to know why she was ignoring the pregnancy. She had been busying herself in the kitchen, cleaning the house, pulling weeds from the garden, even though she'd never cared about flowers or plants.

What do you want me to say? she asked. You've always made your own choices. I think I know who the father is. A married man. It's a way for you to ensure your independence, by choosing a man who isn't entirely available, who isn't asking for your commitment. You don't need me anymore.

I wanted to yell at her. Isn't this when one needs their mother most of all? How am I going to do this without you? Who knows if the father of my child will stay with me?

I was shaking, but I couldn't open my mouth. You're an adult now, she said, but even if you were a child, I'd say the same thing.

That night, I went to my friend's wedding. It was at a restored farmhouse in the middle of the countryside, a half-hour drive from where my parents lived. It was a beautiful setting; the ceremony took place in a clearing. You could hear the swoosh and rustle of leaves whenever the wind swept through the trees. There were many children and babies at the wedding. I wore a tight navy dress to show you off, and mothers came to me, asking their usual questions. I glowed from the attention, feeling complete at last, a part of their world. How sad that I needed their validation. I craved it, and all the while I replayed the conversation with my own mother, hurt by her attitude.

During the cocktail hour a little girl disappeared. The mother noticed about a half hour later. Her daughter, who was three, had been playing with a group of children by the edge of the forest. The energy shifted instantly. Everyone started searching for the girl, including the bride and groom. There were ponds and rivers nearby, and we'd been talking about them earlier in the evening, how the venue was surrounded by water holes. An hour later the police showed up. The bride was in a field, holding her dress around her waist, screaming the girl's name. Léa. We looked in the shed and the barn and the house. We followed trails into the forest. A group of boys found bikes and disappeared among the trees, going farther than we could on foot. If you had seen the mother, how she melted into the ground, the horror on her face, and the other mothers as they eyed their own children with a relief so open and tender . . . I hated them in that moment.

A sixteen-year-old boy on a bike found Léa. She'd wandered off on one of the trails and had walked for almost two hours, before stumbling upon two hikers who realized she was lost. It was almost eight P.M. when the boy returned with Léa, drenched in sweat.

The mother didn't move at first. There was a moment of hesitation, as if she was dreaming or hallucinating, afraid this was not her daughter after all. And then the girl cried out *Maman!* The sound of her voice activated something in the mother. She sped in her direction, faster than I've ever seen a person move, and scooped the girl into her arms. The intensity of that moment is hard to describe. It was like seeing two magnets find each other, a field enveloping them, and we knew the mother would never again let the girl out of her sight.

For the first half hour, while the bride tidied up and we waited for dinner, we were subdued. But when we sat down and the wine was served, something unleashed in all of us. It might be the only meal from a wedding that I remember this vividly. Roasted lamb falling off the bone, caramelized carrots and onions, loaves of bread with thick crusts, small bowls of butter. We ate and drank as if this were our last night. We danced for hours. Even me, with my swollen ankles, plodding along to the music. I had never seen that kind of savage fear followed by release. It terrified me, knowing that I, too, would feel this helpless one day.

I came home and slept until late. When I woke up at noon, I wondered if my mother would be a different person if she had lost me in the same way. Had she ever been afraid for my life? On the kitchen table I found fresh bread, salted butter, a new pot of cherry jam, its lid left open. She had loosened the air-tight lock for me.

As I packed my bag to return to Paris, my mother stepped into the doorway of my bedroom. She held a small package in her hands. They were clothes for you and a book she had read while pregnant with me. She had found it useful for childbirth.

I've always wanted to give you freedom, she explained, and one day you'll see how hard it is to step away from your own child. You can't imagine all the times I've stopped myself from grabbing you. But what if I had died? What if I was sick and could no longer take care of you? How would you find your way if you depended on me so completely? Perhaps I was wrong to keep you at a distance and make you believe I was independent. I did what I thought was best, with the tools I've been given.

When I came back to Paris, I told your father we were finished. I'd raise our daughter alone and didn't need his assistance, financial or otherwise. I didn't want his negative attitude. I want to do this alone, I said. For the first time, I felt a true kinship with you. I had lied to him. I wasn't alone. I'd be with you.

Your father astonished me by saying no. He wanted to take responsibility. He would be a father, and he would take care of both of us. His anxiety had receded and his hair had mostly grown back, the rashes were fading. We will raise this child together, he repeated, and indeed, he threw himself into fatherhood with the same determination he deploys at work. He gave us stability by paying for our apartment. But our relationship was going to end one day. It almost did seventeen years ago. I was never stupid enough to believe we would die together.

As I listened to Anouk's words, I saw for the first time that my mother had assumed theirs was a story with an ending. It wouldn't last; one day they would separate.

Even if you knew this day would come, aren't you sad? I asked.

Sadness is a fleeting emotion, Anouk said, just as happiness is. What I want is to continue my work, to perform, to be onstage. Our relationship was fragile from the beginning. It didn't have the strong foundations of a partnership.

Anouk leaned in closer to me and spoke as if imparting a lesson.

My role isn't to explain everything to you. I can't explain your father to you, and you can't understand what it was like. A marriage is a closed world. Anyone who thinks they can explain it to an outsider is a fool.

11

A marriage. The label had slipped from her mouth. She had thought of their union as a covenant, even if it was a vulnerable one. The word haunted me at night, but Anouk didn't notice the effect it had on me. Rather than linger on their relationship, she soon started to spend less time at home, taking on more classes, helping her friends with rehearsals, and disappearing to shows on the weekends.

Four nights a week she worked until late at night, teaching classes. She slept a few hours and was up before my alarm rang. She took on more work to pay our bills, as we were no longer covered by Father, but somehow I had trouble feeling pity for her. I couldn't appreciate her hard work because she seemed to take such pleasure in being out and about with other people, expending her warmth and charisma on strangers. In the loneliness at home, I often took refuge with Juliette.

The days grew shorter and sometimes I awoke in pitch blackness, thinking the city had vanished overnight. It was hard to imagine others alive when our building was so still.

Then I'd hear our neighbors waking, their alarms going off, the music from a radio drifting into the courtyard, light warming a curtain to transparency. They aired out the night. It was comforting to hear proof of their aliveness. I listened for the clink of a fork scraping against a ceramic plate. These familiar sounds accompanied me when I felt distanced from my mother, when I worried Father wouldn't return. Such was the nature of hope—believing that change wasn't swift and dramatic, that certain routines were immutable.

After school at Juliette's, we would make bowtie pasta for dinner. She measured the pasta into two bowls and threw it into a small pot of boiling water. We ate it with melted butter, grated cheese from a bag, and tiny squares of ham she'd cut directly in the packaging.

One Friday night, after we had finished eating, I washed our dishes and placed them to dry on a folded dish towel next to the sink, while Juliette poured us two glasses of wine. We didn't usually drink just the two of us, but tonight we were going to a party in the eighth arrondissement, at the apartment of an acquaintance from school. Everyone in our class was invited.

I drank the wine while Juliette changed into a dress. It was blue, tight along the waist, with loose sleeves. The material stretched across her hips like a surgeon's glove. I was dismayed by my own outfit, jeans and an old blouse made of a synthetic material. I asked her to spray me with perfume. You don't need to wear a dress, she said, the boys stare at you anyway. When Juliette gave me a compliment, it sometimes felt like she was dismissing me and measuring herself against me, maybe so I'd put less effort into my appearance. We were both aware that our friendship wasn't always pure. She was much shorter than I was, with narrower hips and shoulders, and her petite frame made boys want to circle their arms around her. We slipped on our shoes and left her studio.

The exhilaration of being free, even for a few hours, was powerful enough to bury whatever turmoil we both felt beneath the surface. It had been seven weeks since I'd last spoken to Father.

Juliette and I walked down the street arm in arm, our heels tapping on the pavement and echoing against the buildings. Perhaps we weren't popular, and no one described us as beautiful at school, but we had life, our youth, and not a single thought of mortality.

I knew this kind of party. Whenever we were invited, Juliette and I went, even though we weren't friends with the person who was throwing it. We were both relieved to be invited but also ashamed to have given in so easily. We liked to pretend we didn't care about frivolous things such as being seen at parties. At the end of the night, I often found myself on a couch alongside piles of coats, watching classmates eat potato chips and drink vodka. I liked the comfort of bathing in a smog of cigarette smoke and resting upon mounds of jackets and scarves. The coarse texture against my cheeks, the scent of perfume layered with sweat. I loved when hours later my body still throbbed from the music and my fingers and hair smelled of smoke, even though I'd never held a cigarette. The feeling of others brushing against me and having music wash over me in giant waves. I was there and I wasn't, like a silence between two beats. Juliette danced with abandon in the hope of having a boy from the lycée notice her, someone to kiss. Maybe I was too proud to display that kind of invitation around our peers. Whatever she did was magical. By the end of the night, she was always locked in an embrace with someone new.

When we arrived, the party was in its second surge, the floor pulsing. I saw Diane and Camille in tiny black skirts and heeled boots talking in a corner. They eyed us, then turned around.

That night, we danced for hours. I felt that people looked at me differently since the news of the affair, and it made me looser, more confident in my moves. The stereo blasted a deep beat that thrummed our skin, the bass traveling up our feet. I closed my eyes and allowed myself to melt into the surroundings. Spots of light burned the insides of my eyelids. The alcohol spread through my body and unwound knots as it encountered them. I leaned my head back and opened my mouth to laugh. I saw Juliette in a boy's arms. He sucked at her mouth, barely coming up for air.

I danced with a boy I'd never met before, a friend of someone in our class. He went to another school. I liked that he was taller than me, and although he looked young, his face smooth and long hair draping over his forehead, I let him touch my waist. His fingers were warm and gentle. We spoke for a little while, then he leaned down and kissed me. He knew the person throwing the party, he'd been to this apartment many times before. I followed him down a long hallway to a spacious bathroom, far from the living room where the others continued to dance. Wait here, he said.

I looked around at the white tiles lining the floor, a standing tub with high sides and no shower curtain. He returned with pillows and placed them on the floor. He kissed me and lowered me to the pillows. The pillows shifted beneath us revealing the cold tiles and he kept pushing them back into place. How tempting to go all the way. I pulled down my jeans and underwear. He told me he'd had only one girlfriend, and she was a virgin; he hadn't slept with anyone else since then. I'm on the pill, I said, as though it was a given and he was wasting my time with all this talk. Ever since I'd started taking it the previous year, I'd said the words proudly, soon addicted to their immediate, soothing effect on boys. I knew he wouldn't ask who I'd slept with. We were on our sides, facing each other in the dark. Above our heads was a large sink and a mirror, and to the left a window, cracked open. A muted light from the streetlamps shone through the window and onto the floor.

He entered me and moved slowly, holding his breath, fingers pressed into my ribs. I wanted it to be quick. I would make sounds and he would finish. He came inside me, waited a few seconds, then pulled out and stood up. I was always shocked when boys did this. What did they think would happen to the semen trickling down my thighs? That it would magically evaporate? Or did they want me to just stare at their lingering erection? I wiped myself and the floor with toilet paper. He looked embarrassed and turned around to put on his clothes before shutting the door behind him.

Once he was gone, I adjusted the pillows beneath me and stretched out my toes, relaxing against the cool edge of the bathtub. I touched myself until I was swollen and numb, flushing thoughts out of my mind. Anouk dancing on a stage, falling in midflight and breaking her ankle, Father walking through our living room in his slippers, leaving a book on the shelf. I thought about a faceless man who lifted me from the floor with his weight. I waited for the numbness to break and flood me with heat.

Eventually people started leaving the party, thundering down the stairs, until only a few of us remained. I made my way to the couch, now covered in just a few jackets. Juliette's boy had gone home, and mine turned his back to me, pretending we'd never met. Juliette sat down next to me and brought her face close to mine. Her hairline glistened with sweat and her collarbones looked sharper than usual.

I have an idea, she said. Let's get out of here.

We walked for almost an hour. I couldn't remember where we were going or giving her an address, only that I had followed Juliette blindly, the alcohol floating through me, a bitter taste on my tongue. It was three in the morning when we turned onto Father's street. It was cold outside and I was shaking, but I let the tremors roll over me.

This is where they live? Juliette asked, staring at a door. The number gleamed above us in faded bronze. The street was empty.

We should leave. I pulled on her arm.

Do you know which floor they're on?

I stared up at the windows. Most were closed with shutters. Father had mentioned owning an entire floor. Madame Lapierre was a light sleeper, so they kept the windows shut against the morning traffic.

No, I said, but I know the bedroom is on the street.

Juliette started laughing, and then she let out a loud scream. It jolted through me and echoed against the pavement. The street stayed silent, as if it were unsure the sound had happened at all.

What are you doing? I whispered.

We're going to make sure they don't sleep tonight, she explained. Let's give them a taste of their own medicine. Just try it, you'll feel better.

She pushed me against the building and gently moved my head back until my chin grazed the stone wall and my eyes were angled up at the window ledges. She stood next to me, her shoulder against mine. Let's do it together, she said.

We screamed at the same time. We didn't need to count one, two, three. We felt the scream swell inside our lungs and burst through at the same time. Windows opened on the street, but we had chosen a dark spot, and no one could see us from afar.

What's going on? we heard someone say. *Shut up! It's just a bunch of drunk idiots!*

We waited a few minutes until the windows closed again.

I broke from Juliette and ran to the middle of the street. I cupped my mouth and yelled: *PAPA! PAPA! PAPA!*

I hadn't spoken those words in weeks, and they surfaced like a swimmer gasping for air, shredding my throat, making my eyes stream. I think I lost sense of time. I felt Juliette dragging me down the street, and I remember seeing a figure in the window, gazing down at us. The outline not of Father, but of a woman.

I was certain Father would call after the night outside his apartment. The windows had opened, along with the shutters, and everyone in his building had heard me. He'd recognize my voice, the way the mother at the wedding had known her daughter when she'd called out *Maman*.

Whereas before I'd been obsessed with checking the news and studying photos of Madame Lapierre, now I was afraid to go anywhere near them, unsure of what I'd find. I was afraid of articles that portrayed Father as a weak man who had betrayed his wife, articles that speculated whether he'd had other affairs, and especially those that claimed he was still seeing Anouk.

The image of a woman standing in the window stayed with me. I assumed it was Madame Lapierre, but I had no proof, and I pushed the thought out of my mind every time it invaded me. After a while, the woman faded from my memory, becoming a silhouette, until she was no longer there to begin with.

12

A week had gone by since the incident at Father's apartment when I saw Brigitte at the café across the street from school. She had flitted in and out of my consciousness since the interview. I sometimes thought about our encounter in the hallway, the pop of the bathroom cabinet, her long teeth surrounded by painted lips. The surprise of seeing her in our home. I thought about her without imagining our paths would cross again.

I had just finished class and it was already dark outside when I walked into Chez Albert. The table I liked, a small round one in the corner closest to the window, was taken by a woman whose face was partially hidden by a thick sheet of black hair. She was bent over a notebook and her pen moved quickly across the page from left to right. Students sat around her, chatting lazily and sipping coffee. She, on the other hand, was burning, as if racing to meet a deadline. I watched her. As the only adult there, she seemed out of place. No one else noticed her, though, and for a moment I wondered if she was a figment of my imagination. Something about her was familiar.

Then she dropped her pen, swept her hair away from her face, and looked up in my direction.

I recognized her instantly. David's wife. I could have pretended I didn't know who she was and walked away, but I stayed there, feet rooted to the floor. She raised her hand and waved at me.

Margot, she said, recalling my name once I'd walked across the room to her table. She asked if I'd like to sit down and join her for coffee or a glass of wine.

My school is right there, I said, pointing to the building across the street.

Really, she said, widening her eyes.

Her hair was the kind of black you rarely see on someone's head. It hadn't struck me the first time, but now I saw it more clearly in the light of the café. Its surface shimmered blue and purple. She wore the same red lipstick and her lips barely closed over her teeth.

I asked if she and David lived close by. No, she said, they lived in the ninth, but she had studied at a university nearby, and she liked coming to this neighborhood; it reminded her of being a student once upon a time. Before meeting with her adviser, she always came to a café just like this one and reviewed his notes.

Brigitte ordered a glass of white wine and asked if I'd like the same. Coffee, I said. We were silent for a few minutes while we waited for our drinks to arrive. All the tables were taken, and we were surrounded by loud chatter, people tipping back on their chairs, exchanging notes, ordering the specialty, waffles with Nutella. The windows were fogged from the heat.

Outside it was almost winter. Brigitte took a long sip from her glass. Not bad, she said.

I liked the article David wrote, I said.

It had come out a few days ago, and Anouk and I had read it over breakfast. He'd barely mentioned the affair with Father, instead focusing on Anouk's career as a stage actor.

Brigitte smiled. David's editor wanted more of your father, but he pushed back. It's a good article, isn't it?

My mother was pleased. I held my cup of coffee in both hands and noticed they were slightly shaking. Do you and David ever work together? You asked a lot of questions during the interview—that's why I thought you might be writing the piece with him.

Sometimes, yes. I mostly help with the research, and I read what he writes before it's sent to the editor. But you know, I also write my own books. I'm a ghostwriter.

A ghostwriter, I repeated, in admiration. I hadn't met one before. So, you pretend to be someone else? I asked.

Brigitte rolled the sleeves of her shirt, a stiff canvas material, and placed her bare elbows on the table. She had almost finished her glass of wine.

It's less about pretending to be someone else and more about becoming, she said. Through their language. I find the words they use to describe their world.

Do you like being a ghostwriter?

She told me she liked to slip into her author's world, the hours of research, learning how someone else's mind worked. She even liked transcribing interviews. The hardest part was translating their experiences for an audience who didn't know the author personally. To bring coherence to an intimate world, make sense of it for an outsider. She also liked the anonymity. It lowered the stakes. She was less affected by bad reviews. David, however, took things more personally.

He doesn't seem like someone who would, I said.

I've had to stop him from reading comments on his pieces.

How did you become a ghostwriter?

Oh, I sort of fell into it. I was finishing my studies in educational psychology. I didn't know what I wanted to do next, if I wanted to start practicing, working in a clinic, or if I wanted to change careers. I loved my studies, but something about making a career out of it didn't settle with me. Unfortunately, I couldn't be a student forever. I was always writing, working on essays, researching. Writing is the muscle I developed the most, but I wouldn't have considered myself a writer. David was the writer in our relationship. Brigitte took a long sip of wine before continuing.

You know, we'd met the previous year and were still trying to impress each other. One afternoon, David called me to tell me about a woman who was writing an important piece for a special magazine issue. She was a famous chef and she had a story to tell; in fact, she'd promised the magazine an exclusive interview. But the weeks went by and she kept asking for more time. Soon the editor realized the chef wasn't going to write the piece, let alone meet her deadline.

David referred me to the editor, saying I had a talent for bringing stories out of people. He thought of me as a therapist who could see into someone's soul. Perhaps I could help with the article. At first the editor told me my role would be to encourage the chef. Ask guiding questions. I expected we'd talk on the phone. I assumed she had writer's block or imposter's syndrome. She'd probably never written about herself.

I called her a few times. On the phone she was vague and often hung up after a few minutes, saying she had an appointment or was heading into work. I read about her. She was a well-established chef, in her early forties, who had worked at some of the best hotels in Paris. She was married to another chef who was younger, a rising star in the industry. She was not a beautiful woman in the photos. Her hair was always pulled back so tightly it was hard to tell what color it was, and her lips were thin, severe. The press often commented on her relationship with the younger chef. How unusual it was for a handsome, young chef to be with an older, less attractive woman. She was discreet in public and I wasn't able to find interviews with her, whereas her husband seemed to enjoy the attention. He always brought the conversation back to her, saying she was *la femme de sa vie*.

Finally, after two weeks of chasing her down, I was able to schedule a meeting with the chef. She agreed to meet if I was willing to come to her place.

I knew she was from the South of France, close to Marseille, and had discovered gastronomy at a later age than most chefs, in her midtwenties. She hadn't cooked in her youth, nor did she come from a family of cooks, but she had a deep connection to the *terroir*. One summer she had offered to help a family friend who had just opened a restaurant in the Luberon. She fell in love. It was the only direct quotation I'd found of hers, where she described the magic of touching ingredients for the first time. She spoke about the slippery flesh of a potato when cut in half as it released its starches. What it was like to hold a ripe tomato and feel its weight. When she ran her fingers over a strawberry it was like caressing gooseflesh. Imagine if she'd never known, if she had gone her entire life seeing ingredients with indifference. Her parents didn't cook. She had been raised on boxed gazpacho and frozen meals.

The chef lived close to the Arc de Triomphe, on a wide avenue. I took the elevator to the fourth floor. It was one of those narrow elevators made to fit in the hollow space between the winding stairs. I didn't want to arrive out of breath. I had my tape recorder, just in case, paper and pen, and my research files hidden in a folder. I rang the doorbell.

When she opened the door, I first noticed her bare feet, and then her face, how unrecognizable it was from the published photos. How to explain her face? I'd never seen someone look so flat in an image, and then so alive and textured in person. The shine of her gray eyes, the flush of her cheeks, the light freckles on her nose. She wore no makeup. Her hair was curled and golden, with a few graying locks. She was smaller than I'd expected. I had met her husband a few times at events with David, and I'd found him charming, but now, faced with her, I thought he had no more than a fraction of her spirit. I tried to regain my composure.

The apartment was immaculate. Carpets covered the floors, leaving thin strips of dark wood along the walls. I followed her into the living room. I searched for the scent of food—she was a chef, after all—but the apartment smelled neutral. She explained how the article had been her husband's idea, not hers. But why? I asked, since it seemed clear to me, from the sarcastic tone of her voice, that she had no intention of writing it.

I'm leaving the industry, she said, and he wants me to explain why.

But you are at the peak of your career, I said.

She shrugged. Is it better to leave when you've already been forgotten? She ran her fingers through her hair. The curls grew in volume, beautifully framing her face. Will you write the article for me? she asked.

I'm not a writer, I said, taken aback.

You'll do a better job of it.

I'm here to help you, ask you questions, guide you. I stumbled over my words.

She squinted at me. Someone once told me to squint my eyes at a dish, she explained. To look at the shapes, the colors, not the details. I was too bogged down in the minutiae and needed to pull back, see the composition. My dishes lacked unity. The trick is to allow the details to blur and fall away.

Your food has been described as off-balance, I said, encouraged by her. An illusion of harmony. With the first bite, you think the flavors marry perfectly, but as you eat more, there's a buried flavor that comes through and disrupts the harmony. Like your famous celery dessert. Then you provide an antidote. A squeeze of lemon to temper the salt and bitterness.

The chef smiled. You've done your homework. See, you can write this. You describe my food better than I do.

I blushed, embarrassed by the audacity of my words. I shook my head. No, no, I said.

She asked how old I was. Twenty-eight, I answered. In fact, I was twenty-seven, but my birthday was in a week, and it felt false to say anything less.

Do you want children? she asked.

I hesitated. In the past I had always said yes. I don't know yet, I replied. What was I going to say? Yes, but not now? It sounded cliché.

At your age it's normal to think that way, she answered. It doesn't feel urgent. I once felt the same way. You assume there's time to make a choice later, when you're ready. Do you mind if I speak frankly?

No, please. I shifted to face her and show I was listening.

I got pregnant when I was a year older than you. It was unplanned. I remember my hands shaking when I took the pregnancy test. I was barely able to hold the stick in place. I was a few years into my career, and I worked all the time, forgetting to eat for long stretches of time. It was a miracle the baby stuck to my body. I was on my feet all day and I hid my pregnancy as long as I could. Plus, the father wasn't an important man in my life. No one in my family understood when I decided to keep the baby. I had an easy pregnancy and I continued to work almost at the same rhythm until I went into labor.

My daughter was born one early afternoon in November. I remember the trees had lost most of their leaves. Their branches stuck out into the sky like needles, with a few yellow leaves hanging on. It was a scene out of a horror film if you looked too closely. I had a migraine that bludgeoned my forehead and made it hard to look at anything too bright. But not even that could distract me from the sudden change I felt inside. A feeling of peace, you could say.

The chef paused and lifted her feet onto the couch. They were short and wide. She looked at the wall behind me as she spoke.

I named my daughter Romane. I stopped working to take care of her. Otherwise it would have been almost impossible to nurse. I hadn't expected to feel attached, and yet here I was, head over heels. It wasn't like during the pregnancy. When I'd felt her move in my stomach, it was just a movement, not my daughter.

She was just over three months old and I was preparing to go back to work. I found her one day after her nap and she wasn't breathing. She was in her crib, eyes closed as if she were still sleeping. I took her in my arms and got in the car. I didn't even think to call an ambulance, I thought I'd be faster, and I needed to move. My only focus was on saving her. I've always known what to do when there's a crisis, whether a fire flares up in the kitchen or we haven't received an important delivery. I drove through the narrow streets and onto the wider avenues. Soon I arrived at the Arc de Triomphe roundabout. I had driven on the roundabout countless times, but this time, I was paralyzed. I wasn't one to be afraid to impose myself among other cars, I often teased my friends who avoided Place de l'Etoile, but on that day, it seemed enormous and chaotic, like a whirlpool. I became overwhelmed by the cars. I don't know how long it lasted, maybe it was just ten seconds. Somehow, I shook out of it and found a police car parked on Victor Hugo. I ran out of the car, leaving the door open, and screamed at him. I managed to explain what had happened, and the police-man told me to follow him. He turned on his sirens. I drove behind him, very close, and together we drove onto the round-about. He escorted me with his sirens, cutting through the cars, like Moses parting the seas. I knew Romane would live because of what this policeman was doing. How could she not? Later, one of the nurses said I hadn't properly locked her seatbelt, a sign that subconsciously I'd known she was beyond help. But I remember hearing the click of the buckle closing around her.

The chef stopped talking there. I sensed the story had ended.

You know the rest, she said. The restaurants I've worked at, the Michelin stars, my relationship with Jérôme, our marriage. Today I'm almost forty-three. I love my work, but I have to leave. I've found a house in the south, close to my parents. I'm going to be a mother. I don't know how, but I know I will be. It's a certainty. But for it to happen, I have to stop working in a kitchen.

Will you go back to cooking? I asked her, not knowing what else to say.

Cooking gave meaning to my life. It was a gift. But I can feel its effect wearing off. Maybe cooking is something I just needed to do for a while, a chapter in my life. Maybe that door closed a long time ago, but I kept it open for Romane.

I spent the next three days writing the article, barely sleeping. I had to use her words, write in the first person. I could hear her voice in my head as I typed. By the end, I was delirious. I would wake up from dreams of seeing her car speeding onto the roundabout, except this time, the other cars didn't stop and hers was engulfed. She told me I could use what I wanted. I wrote about her daughter, sensing this was what she wanted. She read the piece and told me it was very good. I sent it to the editor without telling David. I waited anxiously for a response, certain the writing was terrible, and I'd gotten it wrong. I thought I'd be told I was an amateur. I was surprised when the editor called to express his satisfaction. The piece came out four months later, when the chef was already far away from Paris.

Brigitte stopped speaking and looked down at her empty glass of wine. The strange thing, she said, is that I felt like I had become the chef. Not that I wanted to be a chef and cook, but I could really feel her pain. And I could also understand this liberating choice of letting it all go, starting afresh, perhaps having a second career no one would've ever dreamed of. We always imagine a talented person should only pursue their one talent, as if they can't have others. For a while I was even obsessed with becoming pregnant. David was a bit frightened. Then the feeling disappeared, as it always does when a project has run its course.

Do you feel this every time? I asked. Consumed by your author?

Not always. It depends on the person. Sometimes it's just a job, a paycheck.

It must have been horrible, losing her daughter at that age.

I can't think of anything more violent. But then again, you're never safe when you become a parent.

You wonder if some parents are better prepared for these kinds of events, I said.

My mother, perhaps, was too prepared. Brigitte played with the stem of her glass.

It was late, almost dinnertime. People had started to leave the café. Anouk was teaching tonight. I wondered if there was food in the fridge. I couldn't remember the last time we'd shopped for groceries. Brigitte took the carafe of water and poured out two glasses. She pushed one in my direction.

I know it was you, she said. You told David about your father.

Her words caught me by surprise, and I froze in my seat. I should've known they'd share everything as husband and wife. A marriage is a closed world, Anouk had told me.

It's all right, Margot, she continued, and placed her hand over mine, surprising me with the familiarity of her gesture. Her fingers were warm and enveloped mine entirely. I understand you must be disappointed in your father.

I pulled my hand back and placed it on my lap. It doesn't matter anymore, I said.

He was a coward.

I had called him a coward in private, repeating the word in my head, but I shuddered upon hearing it from her, and my instinct was to protect him.

He should have left his wife, she said, but it's easier to continue as one has.

He's not a bad person.

That's irrelevant, his goodness or badness.

You sound like my mother.

Brigitte laughed. What an awful thing to say. The last thing I'd want is to sound like your mother.

I felt heat rise to my cheeks. I pressed my fingers to them, trying to cool my skin. We stared at each other. I couldn't tell what she thought of me in that moment.

He'll come back to us, I said, but it'll take some time.

So, you will reclaim him.

Something like that.

I know your father, she said, the kind of man he is, and you are right, what he needs is time. It's his turn to show his loyalty to you and your mother. He owes you an apology, doesn't he?

Brigitte wouldn't let me pay for my coffee. She pinned down the receipt with a few coins. It was a pleasant surprise to run into you, she said. She wrapped a cashmere scarf around her neck and slid her arms into the same long coat she'd worn at the interview. I wondered if I should kiss her on the cheeks. She touched my elbow, her fingers barely resting on my coat, and told me to take care of myself.

What did she mean by the kind of man he is—what *kind* of man was Father? Was he what Anouk claimed him to be, someone who fled conflict and shut his eyes at the sight of an ugly truth? Would he come around with time, as Brigitte said, or drift further away from us? Whenever I remembered standing outside of his building, screaming for him, I felt embarrassed and hoped no one had seen me. Now I was embarrassed because he hadn't called me. The woman in the window was a hazy memory. I couldn't even say what floor she'd been on, but the harder I thought about her, the more I believed it had been Madame Lapierre witnessing the spectacle of me crying out.

I thought about the chef and her daughter often. The disbelief she must have felt once she arrived at the hospital and the doctors told her it was over. As long as she was in the car, it didn't matter that Romane had stopped breathing. They were moving, fighting their way through traffic to reach the hospital where she would be healed, and while they continued to go from one point to another, there was hope.

It was different with Father. There was no moment of recognition. *C'est fini, enfin.* The sense of an ending, what others
call closure, though I've often wondered how the love for a
father can be replaced, if there's even a loop to close.

I remember sleeping at Juliette's on a Saturday. In the
morning, the sun shone on our faces through her sheer curtains. When the alarm rang, I rolled away from her. She didn't
open her eyes. I was used to hearing the alarm, and I no longer
differentiated it from mine. I washed my face in the kitchen
sink. I glanced over at Juliette before leaving. Her hands were
tucked under the pillow, her face peaceful as she slept. I had no
other friends like her. The intimacy of this realization was
painful and enormous. I wanted to fall back asleep next to her.
I closed the door quietly behind me.

Anouk had left two voicemails on my phone. She wanted to
know when I'd be home. It was unlike her to nag, and I was
worried I'd done something wrong. On the métro I thought
about the homework I needed to finish for the next day.
Whether I should buy milk on my way. I thought about my
conversation with Brigitte and if Father would make the first
move to apologize, or if it was better to call him. I had avoided
calling him, but what if it was the only way to see him again?
Don't wait too long, Juliette had said. I felt a burning in my
chest, the ache of wanting to hear his voice again, to see him
walk into our apartment and untie his shoelaces. It always took
him a while to settle in, to remove his jacket and put down his
heavy briefcase. I also knew he almost always answered the
phone when I called him. Since he was averse to conflict, I'd
just have to pretend nothing had happened between us. I could

ask him about his day, what he'd had for dinner the night before, if he had seen Audiard's latest film.

The train jolted to a stop. I stood from my seat, warmed by the possibility of hearing his voice again. Yes, it was as simple as dialing his number. I was an idiot for waiting. The walk to our apartment felt longer than usual and I hurried up the stairs. I was coated in a thin layer of sweat by the time I opened the front door.

I expected Anouk to be out, as she often was, and at first I didn't see her sitting in the dark living room, blinds rolled down and knees folded into her chest. Her hair partly obscured her face. She lifted her head. She looked at me as I walked over to her. What had I done?

She blinked at me a few times and then I noticed the tears wetting her face. I saw a look of bewilderment and something else that terrified me. It broke her cheeks apart. A dozen ideas flew into my mind. Something bad had happened. She is sick. We can no longer afford this apartment. Or was it Father? Had he called to say that he never wanted to see us again? Perhaps he had lost his job, no longer was the minister of culture—and all because of us, because of what I had done. I looked at her and asked softly if she wasn't feeling well. Then, more insistent: What is it?

She sounded nervous when she spoke. There's something I have to tell you, Margot, she began. She took my sleeve and pulled me closer.

Your father died last night.

I stood there without moving or saying a word. She spoke again, repeating the same sentence.

Everything went silent, as if the apartment had fallen away, leaving us in a vacuum. I kneeled on the floor. A numbness spread through my chest. She took my head in her lap.

Oh, my darling, she said, her voice breaking. I'm so sorry.

Our home had never been this quiet, all the sounds absorbed into some other place. I could feel my heart thumping out of my ribs. It was just us, two bodies breathing and sweating. Anouk told me his sister had called in the early morning; Father had had a heart attack and died in his sleep.

And then it started, the sounds returned, a car screeching down the street and water gushing from a nearby apartment, a loud banging below us and a high-pitched scream. I stood on my feet, but the scream was coming from me and nowhere else. Anouk covered my mouth with her hand.

13

How to believe Anouk's words, even when I saw the announcement for his funeral?

Father had been sick around us before. His stress manifested in visible ways: a scalp covered with sores, the skin on his elbows flaked from scratching. I knew he had vulnerabilities like anyone else, but I'd never imagined him dying. I wasn't afraid of his complete disappearance. The newspapers used that word. We mourn his disappearance, as though he had vanished, boarded a plane to a tropical island. Alive, somewhere.

After all, those were just words. Everything inside me fought against accepting his death. Some would say it was because he hadn't been a greater part of our lives, and we hadn't seen him in two months. They said: How can she feel the loss of someone who didn't live with her?

I waited for something inside of me to change, for his death to materialize into an absence, but I couldn't accept it. I waited for him to call and laugh at the articles, say it was an absurd joke. I continued to feel his presence. I kept this hot secret to myself, knowing no one else would believe me, and because it brought me some relief.

Time had a swollen and heightened quality. A strange softness that I would later miss, as if my skin was thinned to petals, and I was constantly evaporating into my surroundings. I felt that nothing good or bad could happen. I'd sit in a room and no longer feel my legs, my arms, my feet, as if I was disappearing, too.

Memories of Father resurfaced. He had once showed me a paper on which he had written down a list of dates, including the year I was born.

He'd said: Your mother has the memory of an elephant, whereas I am forgetful. I only remember the good things. I wrote these dates to remember the bad years.

What else had happened that year?

He once showed me the scars on his body. His deformities, as he called them, in case I ever had to identify his body. He pointed at the chickenpox crater on his eyelid above his left eye, the shiny scar on his shoulder from an old surgery, the birthmark on his leg. I had imagined identifying his headless body.

Anouk had a more immediate reaction. She understood he was gone, and something inside her broke. Unlike me, she felt his absence viscerally. The first two nights I sat in my bedroom staring at the wall, listening to Anouk crying in her room. It angered me to hear her. She didn't even try to hide her pain, whereas I cried into my pillow. Mathilde and Théo stayed with us, sleeping on the two couches in the living room and preparing meals for us during the day. I remember hearing them move around the apartment, filling the space. Mathilde encouraged Anouk to shower. She walked her to the bathroom at night when Anouk vomited.

On Tuesday, Juliette came by with our homework assignments. She hugged me for a long time. It was the first time someone had properly touched me since Anouk took my head in her lap. I'd stiffened in Mathilde's embraces, feeling she was here for my mother, not for me. In the warm fold of Juliette's arms, I started weeping. I buried my face in her shoulder. Her soft hair rose around me. It was hard to breathe. There was so much I wanted to flush out of me. I just wanted it all out. My ribs ached from the effort.

Juliette continued to hold me in silence, her hand rubbing my back. I kept thinking that if I cried a little harder against her then it would all be gone, but when I stopped, the pain in my chest remained. It was worse, pulsing in my throat.

By the fourth night, Mathilde and Théo had gone home, and it was just Anouk and me again. I ran a bath for her and sat on the tub's edge as she soaked. She placed a wet towel over her eyes. There she was. Reddish hairs whirling between her legs. Breasts flattened and falling to the side. Her inverted nipple missing its tip, a little dot suctioned into her chest. She searched for my hand and I moved it closer until she could grasp it. I felt a prickling in my eyes and nose, and as if she knew, she squeezed my fingers. The loud shrill of the doorbell startled us.

I opened the door. It was Madame Bonnard from our building. We didn't like her. She voted for the National Front and spied on our street from behind her curtains, convinced that drug dealers met in the underground parking lot. She handed me a bouquet of roses and tried to look past me.

Is your mother home? she asked. I wanted to give her my condolences.

No, I said, and thanked her before shutting the door.

I trimmed the stems on the kitchen counter and placed the flowers in a vase. I stayed in the dark kitchen for a few minutes, staring at the apartments across from ours. Most of the neighbors were home, their curtains drawn open. The windows emitted such a reassuring glow from afar. I heard a shuffle behind me. Anouk stood in the kitchen door, dressed in her coat and leather boots. The skin on her face was still inflamed, but I noticed mascara thickening her eyelashes. Where was she going?

Those are from Madame Bonnard, I said, pointing at the vase. She sends her condolences. Anouk touched a petal and shook her head.

Put on your jacket, she said. We're going to see your father.

For a moment, I thought she'd lost her mind. He was gone.

We're going to see his body, she specified. At their apartment. He's on display until tomorrow.

Tomorrow was the funeral.

How do you know? I asked.

She swept aside my questions and told me to get ready; we didn't have time to waste.

It had only been two weeks since I'd last been there with Juliette, rue Mirabeau, but I saw it with new eyes. It was not our Paris. It had the pure scent of mountains. Their street was silent aside from the swishing of trimmed trees guarding expensive homes. There was no butcher or baker or other *commerçant* in sight. Anouk paused in front of a building. Here, she said, retrieving a piece of paper from her bag and typing in the code.

The door buzzed, and we pushed it open onto a vast entrance. We read the names on the directory and pressed on LA-PIERRE. We waited for a while. It was almost eleven and I wondered if Madame Lapierre was asleep. The murky memory of what Juliette and I had done coursed through me, screaming at the top of our lungs in the middle of the night, drunk. I was sure they'd heard the alcohol in our voices, the sloppiness and laughter, and had dismissed us as *voyous*. I remembered standing in front of their building, calling out to him. If Madame Lapierre had seen me and known who I was, what had she thought in that moment? That I was an uneducated, stupid girl, asking for their attention. I decided I'd deny anything she said. I practiced the words in my head. You imagined me there. I was at home.

Anouk rang a second time, longer. She was determined to get us inside. A man's voice spoke on the other end.

Yes, who is it?

Anouk Louve and my daughter, Margot.

There was a silence.

Are you there? she asked.

It's the third floor, said the voice, and the door clicked open.

We climbed the stairs without exchanging a word, and for a moment we were suspended in time, the possibility of not meeting Father's other family hanging by a thread.

Their door cracked open and a young man swung it back. He was in his midtwenties, hair parted neatly to one side. He wore a suit and the same leather shoes Father always had, a classic style with laces. I recognized Father's favorite brand, Heschung. The resemblance was uncanny. Similar stance, feet angled out and hands folded at the lower back.

I'm Jacques, he said.

You are his son, aren't you? Anouk asked. She spoke with surprising warmth.

I was silent and continued to stare at his shoes, polished a glossy burgundy. I imagined his toes nestled beneath the leather. Father's eldest son.

I can't let you in, he said, sounding apologetic. He stayed in the doorway, his hand on the knob. I don't want to wake my mother.

But you answered, Anouk said. You allowed us to come to your door. This is our only chance.

Even in the poor light of the hallway one could see the red rim of my mother's eyes and the puffed skin on her cheeks.

I'm sorry.

Maybe you'll allow Margot to say goodbye. She hasn't seen him since August. She pushed me forward toward him.

His eyes flitted over my face as if noticing my presence for the first time. My mouth twitched.

Jacques glanced behind him into the apartment. We waited. I knew Anouk wouldn't budge. It felt like an eternity, though perhaps it was minutes, seconds. The light in the hallway turned off with a click. He sighed and stepped aside. Come on, Margot, you can see him. Please be quiet. Better my mother never know you were here.

Anouk thanked him and pushed me forward again.

But what about you? I whispered in panic.

He would have wanted you here. That's enough. Go on. She pressed her hands into my back, toward the apartment.

I followed Jacques into the hallway. I felt Anouk's presence behind me, standing straight, her eyes lifted and her chin very still. I thought I might be sick.

We entered a living room where the lights were dimmed. Long curtains swept the floor and hid windows to the street. I saw large bouquets of flowers on a glass table, the stems tightly wound together, putting Madame Bonnard's to shame. We were not attending the funeral. We hadn't been invited.

I'll leave you alone for a few minutes, Jacques said. He disappeared into the hallway.

Father was on a smaller table the length of his body, surrounded by chairs for visitors. I stayed a few feet away, afraid to smell his decomposing body. I'd never seen a corpse before and it frightened me. I glanced at him from the corner of my eyes, just barely recognizing the shape of his face. It wasn't him.

I waited for my real father to join me. I waited for him to flush the toilet and appear from a nearby room, to be astonished by my presence, to smile with the bottom edges of his teeth barely showing. Margot, he'd say, *ma chérie,* what are you doing here? Would he be shocked, would he still kiss me on the cheeks, or would he want me to leave immediately? Warm air billowed inside me and I felt lighter all of a sudden, soothed by the thought of him appearing.

As my eyes adjusted to the dim lighting, I noticed framed photos on a dresser close to the table. His wedding day with Madame Lapierre. I barely recognized her, a pretty bride in a white dress, and he looked young, with thick wavy hair. His two sons on a boat, their legs spread apart to keep their balance. A more recent photo of the four of them at the beach. He was at the center, holding his sons around the shoulders, while Madame Lapierre stood in front of him, her head leaning into his shoulder. Their happiness winded me.

I heard footsteps, heels clicking away from me, and then a woman's loud voice.

How dare you, she said.

I recognized Anouk, speaking with equal force. Her voice traveled down the hallway. They must have been standing in the entrance of the apartment. It was possible she had stepped inside.

We have a right to be here, I heard my mother say.

Haven't you done enough?

Please, don't play the victim.

He was so easily distracted by beautiful women like you. Do you think you are any different from the others?

Their voices lowered, though I could hear the violence in their speech. I pressed my hands into a chair and closed my eyes.

When I opened them, a moment later, she stood there, just an arm's length away. I jumped at her presence. She had traveled silently down the hallway.

She looked nothing like the woman I'd seen on the street a few months earlier. Madame Lapierre wore a skirt and a matching jacket, her clothes without the slightest wrinkle, but her face was deeply lined and her skin a ghostly white. Her hair, usually lush and shiny in photos, clung to her head and revealed the uneven shape of her skull.

I waited for her to accuse me.

You're so young, she finally said, her voice catching.

I wrapped my arms around my chest. Jacques appeared behind his mother and took her arm. He spoke gently, telling her to give me some time alone. Come here, *Maman,* he said, leading her to the door. She stepped away from me.

Yes, it's true, she said. You haven't done anything wrong. You are like us. She spoke with regret. They left the room, and I was alone once more.

Her words chilled me, bringing tremors along my hands. I moved toward Father. His lips were thinner than I remembered, as if someone had stolen his teeth. It was his skin that was the strangest, without the lift of movement beneath. It made him look deflated. I bent over his head until my lips touched his hair. It was soft and smelled of his shampoo, a slight medicinal scent. I recognized him there. I breathed in again. It was him.

We miss you, I whispered. Come home to us.

Anouk waited for me on the street. At some point she had gone downstairs on her own. I had let myself out, the door locking behind me with a click. She paced back and forth in front of the building and came to a halt when she saw me. How was it? she asked. Her voice was aggressive, and then it softened. How did he look?

The same, I said. The tightness in my throat made it hard to speak. If you cry now, I told myself, I'll never forgive you.

She drew me into her arms. It surprised me. I felt my body stiffen even more. I wasn't able to surrender, allow myself to be comforted. She held me until I somewhat relaxed. I tried to remember what it was like when Father took me into his arms, the shape and breadth of him, but it wasn't his style to be this affectionate.

Anouk smelled of her rose cream. She seemed invincible. I felt her strength pour into me. The exchange with Madame Lapierre had left her charged.

I knew the feeling wouldn't last. She'd never want to indulge this fantasy for too long.

I was reminded of many years ago when a girl slammed a door on my hand. I was six or seven and Anouk had picked me up from school to take me to the hospital. My hand was swollen and purple by the time she arrived. The mother of the girl was there, too. She apologized to Anouk, but her attitude was dismissive, and she immediately shifted her focus to her daughter. She consoled her, saying it was an accident, the door had shut on its own. I remembered it otherwise. The girl had been deliberate in her movements, staring into my eyes as she threw the door shut. She called me a liar when I told her I had a father who was an important man. You have no father, she said, and your mother is a slut. I quickly whispered all of this to Anouk.

Anouk walked over to the mother and stood over her, taller by a head, and threw her hands in the air, dangerously close to the woman's face. I remember the daughter crying in response to seeing her mother attacked by another parent. I couldn't recognize many of the words Anouk used, but her tone was vicious. I was ashamed and wanted my mother to take care of me rather than berate a stranger. I regretted telling her the truth. I hated when she blasted her emotions in public, how loud she could be. But that was Anouk, not caring how others perceived her.

Remember who we are, Anouk whispered into my ear. She released me and we began walking to the métro.

No one but the two of us could understand what it meant to be the hidden ones. His secret. Others pitied us, and Anouk once called us second-class citizens. She said it with humor, because the truth was too taboo to say aloud. We were the chosen ones, the better ones. Better than Madame Lapierre and her sons. The ones he loved. And because we felt loved and special, we endured. He was married with two children, and yet he had sought pleasure and family elsewhere. There had been a hole in his life that needed filling. For years we had made him whole. That's who we were, and I drew comfort from this.

14

I felt a change in Anouk after that night. She continued to grow more distant from me. I couldn't help but internalize this shift and think I had caused it by seeing Father alone. I thought she resented me for being with him, whereas she hadn't been allowed into the apartment. She spoke openly with Mathilde about all the sacrifices she'd made over the years when I was out of eyesight although she knew I could hear every word. Mostly she said she regretted raising me in such privilege. That I was spoiled. I didn't understand the value of money. (*Margot's father paid for this apartment; he brought her gifts to make up for his absences.*) She claimed I didn't know how hard she worked, and how it sucked up her creative energy to be teaching almost every day. (*I need to recharge. I need time to think, to dream up a new show, and I can't do that if I spend my days teaching classes to pay our rent.*)

You forget, Mathilde said, she's just lost her father.

A darkness filled me. I began to wonder if I had caused Father's heart attack. If we had continued our hidden life, perhaps he would be safe. What if the exhaustion and stress of the affair had tipped him over the edge? What if my shouting *Papa* at night had deeply affected him, further damaged his relationship with Madame Lapierre? Anouk had told me he didn't like change or confrontations. I remembered that he'd spent a lifetime crafting the polished persona of a faithful husband and upstanding Catholic, and I'd set this image on fire, revealing him as a fraud. I thought about the time he fell asleep in the car, and how tired and vulnerable he looked. He didn't share Anouk's bottomless energy.

Some days I found myself almost speaking the truth to her. The desire to admit what I'd done was so powerful I could feel the words surge in my throat. Sweat broke along my temples, under my arms, and my heart rate accelerated. It amazed me she couldn't hear its beating. But I always held back at the last minute. I was too afraid of how she'd respond. She might never speak to me again, and I didn't want to lose her.

My grades dipped for a few weeks, and I got my first four out of twenty in physics-chemistry. Madame Roullé spared me the humiliation of returning our exams in order of the grades and simply wrote: *There is work to be done.* Despite her kindness, the grade felt like a failure. I was embarrassed and turned the exam over, promising to submerge myself in work. Juliette had done well. Her grade glared at me, written in red, with a *Très bien!* marked beneath. I resented her for having it so easy.

During the past weeks, Juliette had begun to write a script for a film. She wanted to start now; the best filmmakers had when they were very young. She'd have to complete at least two years of studies, probably a *prépa,* before she could apply to the prestigious La Fémis film school. I asked what her script was about. She answered mysteriously, saying she would show me once it was finished.

Is it romance or a comedy? I teased.

Who do you think I am? She pretended to look shocked.

An amateur.

I was wondering, do you think I can persuade your mother to act in my short film?

We sat on a bench outside of the lycée. Juliette wore a puffy blue coat and old, scuffed shoes, the white laces now gray. She looked at me eagerly.

It's really not the right time, and we're not getting along.

Of course, she said, her voice softer, I understand.

I felt guilty for saying no to Juliette, but I couldn't imagine asking Anouk for this kind of favor when she already complained about being overworked. Could I vouch for Juliette's film? How did I know if it was any good? The cold air seeped into my mouth through my cheeks. It was already dark outside. We always finished class after the sun had set.

In that case, you'll have to do, Juliette said. You can be my actor.

I don't know how to act.

It's a film, don't worry, I'll just edit the scenes to make you look fabulous.

I smiled at her. I couldn't take her seriously. We'll see.

She thanked me and hooked her arm in mine, resting her head against my shoulder.

In the mornings, I woke up with a distinct feeling of my heart being broken. I knew something inside me was bruised, but it was in the past and now there was just a floating sadness. I couldn't remember what had happened. Those few seconds of forgetting were a blessing. Then it came back to me. He was dead. My stomach flopped violently.

I filled my head with other thoughts. Juliette at her window, lighting a cigarette. The simplicity of her movements as she dusted ash. Mathilde slicing and washing leeks from the market. Théo turning on the radio in the living room.

I walked onto the street without seeing cars and buses. I enjoyed this feeling of disconnection. I wouldn't admit it to anyone around me, but I liked how easy it was to lose weight, since my stomach was permanently clenched, and how the sound of cars honking always jerked me awake. I felt broken after a night of weeping, my cheeks and lips irritated, the skin under my eyes damaged from the salt. I waited in vain for Anouk to see and make a comment.

Instead she buried herself in projects, her Hermès perfume wafting through the apartment, her voice coming from under the bedroom door when she spoke with Mathilde on the phone. Later, I understood that she had wanted to protect me. In her own way, she took her role as a mother seriously.

But then, when she thought I wasn't looking, I noticed a sudden vacancy in her eyes, her hands shaking as she cut an apple. I saw the swell in her cheeks when I came home from school. It still made me furious, for she wasn't able to spare me even if she tried.

When we ate dinner together it was mostly in silence. We focused on getting food into our bodies, rotating the same dishes every week. Fuel for tomorrow, she said. Prepared meals of rice and salmon, the plastic pouches heated in simmering water, or sliced tomatoes and mozzarella, half a melon with prosciutto, frozen *pommes dauphine* roasted in the oven. When the fridge was empty, I ate cereal.

One night, Anouk rattled on and on, telling me about a play she was acting in as a favor for a friend. It had become an obsession of hers. A low-budget production. She was underpaid, but her friend, the director, was a talented man. She had been excited to be a part of this project. And yet, she spoke about it with bitterness. I noticed something was wrong. What's bothering you? I asked.

Her friend was sleeping with the lead actress. He was twenty-three years her senior, but more troublesome was the difference in achievements. She was a nobody. This was her first role. Seducing the director so early on in her career was a stupid mistake.

Why does it matter to you? I asked.

Because I've known him for a long time. He's a powerful man. He can make or break her career. But he also has no qualms and is capable of impregnating her. That would be the end of her. And she's just his type. Long legs and a mouth like an octopus.

Does she love him?

Why would she? Anouk retorted. He's fat and has rotten teeth.

In that case, he seduced her, not the other way around.

I've seen the way she looks at him, how she places her hand on his knee under the table during rehearsals.

Maybe she's happy with him.

Anouk ran her tongue over her teeth, checking for stray food.

You can be so cruel to people who remind you of yourself, I said.

She sighed impatiently and took my plate without asking if I was done. She scraped its contents onto hers to throw away. I couldn't always tell when I had taken it too far. We both had a high threshold for each other's jabs of aggression. We wouldn't dare act like this with anyone else, not even Théo and Mathilde, because even we could see that it was hurtful and ugly.

I want her to make informed choices about her future, Anouk said.

No, you want to save her. What are you going to do? Tell her to leave him?

I hope they're using protection, that's all.

I replayed her words. She implied motherhood was an obstacle to professional success. Wasn't Anouk grateful to be a mother, to have me? I wanted a mother who laughed with her daughter in obvious camaraderie. When I spoke to Mathilde, she told me to be patient. Your mother is doing what she does best, she explained. Isn't she there for you, day after day?

I knew there was truth in Mathilde's words. Perhaps Anouk, too, didn't want to eat the food on her plate and walked out onto the street without looking left or right. She'd never cared for food and now she shoveled it into her mouth, chewing, maybe so I would imitate her. Sometimes she caught my hand when we walked down the street.

I thought about this when I picked up her belongings, returning a book to its shelf or clearing a plate. I imagined her leaving these objects behind for me to see. Only then, when I folded a scarf or cleaned the sink, did I feel a hot wave rise inside me.

* * *

We slipped into November. I felt exhausted by the cold and gray, the pavement wet from constant rain. Our apartment was just as damp as the streets outside. Anouk hated wasting money on trivial comforts like heat.

On Saturdays I would sit at Chez Albert, at the round table by the window, and drink coffee. I stared at our school across the street, the heavy doors locked on weekends, the silver plaque with its name written in block letters. Sometimes I studied and read for class, but most of the time I pretended to write in a notebook as my mind turned blank. I drank more coffee to counter the drowsiness and for the electric charge that pulsed through my hands. It made the simple act of being feel dynamic.

It was the first or second weekend of November when I turned onto the street of the lycée and saw a man who looked like Father. The beige building rose in the distance with its long windows. The man walked past me. He was middle-aged and of average height, a scarf tied around his neck, his feet angled out, his gait just like Father's, and for a moment I lost my vision.

I remembered the pale skin of his ankles, only visible when he tied his shoelaces. The cotton fabric of his weekend trousers pressed into straight folds, the bottoms frayed over time. The papery warmth of his hands. He had once massaged my shoulders when I was studying for the Bac de Français, telling me I would do well. I should have picked up the phone and called him. Perhaps he had waited for me to call. I closed my eyes and tried to picture his face, but all I could see was his throat, the soft skin rising and falling around his Adam's apple. I pressed my hands into my eyelids.

I doubled over, a pain searing through my stomach. A woman on the street asked if I needed help. I made it to Chez Albert, running the last stretch, and flew into the restroom. My body often felt like that, wrung inside out.

I was feeling his presence less and less.

I washed my hands and opened the door. The table in the corner where I always sat was taken by two boys I didn't recognize. I scanned the café, looking for a seat, but it was unusually packed for a weekend. I saw my classmates gathered around the small tables, bent over our books. None of them were friends enough that I could go up and join their circle. It was better to go home, I told myself, as I weaved through the tables toward the door, although it was the last place I wanted to be. Even with the lights turned on, the apartment felt gloomy. I thought about calling Juliette to invite myself over, but when I'd spoken to her a few hours earlier, she'd mentioned that her mother was in town. I squeezed past the counter. A woman seated on a stool at the end moved suddenly. Her elbow must have touched the person next to her because I heard her apologize. She faced away from me, her long black hair falling down her back. How strangely familiar she was. Who did she remind me of? I paused right behind her, close enough to touch her hair, and, as if sensing me there, Brigitte turned around.

II

1

They lived on the second floor of an old building in the ninth arrondissement. A carpeted staircase led to the entrance and muffled our footsteps. The floor of their apartment was warped from age and humidity, giving each room a lopsided feel. Brigitte had chosen the location; she liked being steps away from the rue des Martyrs and its vendors. According to legend, Saint Denis had carried his head all the way up the street after being beheaded, thus becoming a saint. The streets were narrower and cramped in this part of Paris, a sinuous elevation that led to the heavens of Sacré-Coeur by way of Pigalle's red-light district.

David was raised in the South of France, not far from Nîmes, and preferred small towns and suburbs to the city. He'd suggested the possibility of moving to a town outside of Paris, but Brigitte had set her foot down. It was a stuffy town with old mansions, barely maintained from the outside, crumbling from within and eaten away by mold. There was often a single toilet in the basement. Ghost houses, their spirits stoked by the last

dimes of family money. She much preferred an apartment in
the city, where there was life and activity. Just thinking about
those broken-down mansions made her want to die. What an
awful place to raise children. Winter was dreary to begin with,
but there? From the beginning I liked her confident way of
speaking. She could get away with bold statements.

The entrance to their apartment was dark. There were no
windows in the staircase and the wooden door was painted
black. But the apartment itself was bright, every surface worn
by centuries of touch, large windows flooding the rooms with
a soft light, specks of dust floating through the air. Brigitte
liked to work in the living room, where she sat on the leather
couch, legs folded and a book resting on her knees. The kitchen
was in the back of the apartment with a view onto the courtyard. David's office was down a hallway, close to the bathroom. It was a small room with indigo carpet and a couch that
transformed into a narrow bed.

Close to the front door of the apartment hung two paintings
of Japanese goddesses dancing in the waves. Their bodies were
round, their nipples orange. I liked these goddesses, feet brushing the water's surface, peaceful faces and delicate triangles of
black hair between their large thighs.

It felt like a miracle when I saw Brigitte at Chez Albert on
that Saturday afternoon. I stepped out of the restroom, my
stomach a swollen, knotted sack under my jeans. I almost
walked past without seeing her. It was only when she turned
slightly as she opened her bag that I recognized her bright red
lips, the sharp angle of her chin. She'd hung her coat on a hook
under the counter, but it was too long and half of it swept the
floor. I felt like a stalker, standing so close to her. Margot, she

said, how nice to see you. I smiled at her, though I felt it was strained. You look pale, she said. Are you all right? The weather. I gestured to the window.

She was on her way out, she told me, to meet David for dinner. She offered me her seat. I sat on the stool as she slipped her arms into her coat, tucking her hair under the collar.

Margot. She said my name gently. I'm so sorry about your father.

She touched my wrist. I wasn't able to speak. My neck felt inflamed, the painful knot in my throat swelling into my mouth. I knew that if I kept my face still, it was less likely to collapse. I managed to nod, and she seemed to understand what I was conveying.

Why don't you come over one day? she asked.

I'd like that, I said, wondering why she'd ever want to spend time with me.

What days are you free?

Any day, in the evenings. I didn't have much scheduled other than school.

Good. Then I'll see you on Monday?

Yes. I smiled.

The following Monday, Brigitte greeted me with a clafoutis. It was five thirty and I had come directly from the lycée. Anouk had begun nightly rehearsals for her next play, so there was no need to mention my whereabouts. Brigitte opened the door and kissed me on both cheeks. The scent of butter and stewed fruit wafted through the apartment, and I complimented her, inquiring after the origin of this intoxicating smell. She smiled, seeming pleased with herself, and led me to the kitchen.

The clafoutis sat on the table, the plate hot from the oven. Caramelized slices of pear hid beneath the custard, and the top was sprinkled with shards of toasted almonds. She scooped a portion into a bowl and placed it in front of me. Steam clouded the underside of my spoon. She started speaking almost immediately, as if we had known each other for years.

The other day she had thought of me. She was cleaning her living room and came across a book she'd read many years ago, *Bonjour Tristesse*. Did I know it?

Yes, Françoise Sagan. It was a classic, but I hadn't read it.

The book was a sensation when it came out, Brigitte explained. Sagan was only eighteen. Of course, it wasn't a perfect book, not quite a masterpiece, but it had a daring intensity. Sagan described exactly what it was like to be that age. She couldn't have written it at a later age. Her story was authentic, there was nothing artificial about it.

Brigitte paused to take a breath. She served herself a bowl of clafoutis.

It was one of the first books I read when I got to Paris. I was just a year older than you.

Sagan made an impression on you, I said.

She nodded. The narrator, Cécile, has just finished her last year of high school. She's seventeen and has failed the Bac. She's been living with her father for two years. The novel takes place during the summer, as they vacation on the Mediterranean.

Cécile's life was so different from my own, Brigitte continued. It was a life of privilege, drinking, hours spent in the sun, but at the time of reading the novel, I felt I could relate to her story. Maybe it was the way she wrote about cruelty, youth, and the passage of time. Like her, I thought I understood grown-ups and their games—I looked at them from above—and yet I was often disappointed. Once their games had played out, I inevitably found myself discarded, not having anticipated how my actions could have unpredictable consequences.

I asked if she'd lend me her copy to read.

Of course.

Brigitte finished her clafoutis and asked if I wanted another serving. I offered her my bowl. She seemed to study me as I began to eat.

I had a thought. She spoke slowly, as if she were working through a complicated idea. I hope I'm not being too forward, but I want to share it with you. Maybe you'll find it ridiculous.

Her eyes were a shade lighter and they seemed to absorb the light around us. I noticed how the skin on her neck was looser than on her face, especially when she twisted her head around. The only part of her that didn't look taut. I set down my spoon to show her I was listening. What is it? I asked.

Here we go, she said, laughing nervously. Have you ever thought about writing? Writing about your father, your family, everything that has happened since?

Like keeping a journal? I wasn't sure where she was going.

Not really. I don't mean in a therapeutic way, though there's nothing wrong with writing for yourself. More like Françoise Sagan. A book about you and your father.

A book? I said, taken aback. And then I laughed and waved my hand in the air to dismiss her idea. Brigitte had seen a Françoise Sagan in me, but she had gotten it all wrong. I wasn't a writer.

Listen to me, she said. I can tell you want to talk about him.

You feel wronged. Deep down you know something isn't right, you're unsettled, otherwise you wouldn't have taken the drastic measure of talking about him to David. You asked for change. Opening your world for others to see. You wanted this, but when you gave him a chance to publicly *be* your father, he resisted. People still don't know who he was to you. They just think of him as someone who fathered you, maybe even abandoned you. They don't know the truth, of how he took care of you and your mother. He loved you both a tremendous amount. Didn't he?

I sat in silence as her words sank into a tender space, making small explosions. It hadn't occurred to me until now—how much I yearned to speak about him, after a lifetime of holding him into my chest and having to justify his affection to Juliette and even Théo and Mathilde. Not just reveal his identity, but describe him and his relationship to us, prove that he also cared about me. I'd seen them look at me with pity. They thought I'd been deprived of a father, that my life had been lesser in some way, but I'd had a father, just not the same as theirs.

Wouldn't you want him to be remembered as more than the man who had an affair? Brigitte asked. As more than the man who rejected his own daughter? And maybe you even regret having passed along the story without asking your parents.

I stared at her and blinked a few times. I think she saw the pain contorting my mouth because she instantly apologized.

Forgive me, she said, I didn't mean it that way.

Yes, you did, I replied. He's the son-in-law of the famous Alain Robert, his political career had potential, and how is he remembered today? As the man who lived a double life for twenty years. It's the last thing people read in the obituaries and it has overshadowed his other accomplishments. I may as well have thrown him under a bus. You thought of me because I was like the narrator in *Bonjour Tristesse*. I thought I knew better.

It was hard to say the words and I wiped my eyes, holding my lips in a flat line.

It's true, I continued, steeling myself. Sometimes I sit on my bedroom floor, close my eyes, and imagine our lives if I'd never met David or if I'd kept my mouth shut. I should've known it could kill him. I think about my father coming over, and I can almost see him in our apartment. But every day the memory of him becomes weaker, and soon there will be nothing left. It's the longest I've been away from him. Anouk has already donated his clothes, and whatever food he kept in the fridge is rotten or was thrown away. When I stop to think about what I've done, I have only one idea in mind: to erase it all.

Margot, he died of a disease. You couldn't have known about his heart. You may not understand this, but his work was demanding, his hours very long, he didn't choose an easy job. Have you read the articles? What Madame Lapierre said? How he worked around the clock, sleeping as little as three hours a night, a true workaholic?

I swallowed my tears, feeling worse.

What can I do? I'm not a writer. Anouk will make a play out of it. She's probably already writing about it. She'll find a way to memorialize him.

I'm not telling you to publish a book, but to record it while it's still fresh. How you feel, all the memories with him, the emotions of *this* very moment. Your mother isn't capable of your transparency. She will tell her own story, but as a theatrical embodiment.

Maybe in a few years I'll write about it.

You should be writing it now.

Why does it matter? I felt drained. I looked up at Brigitte and repeated my question.

Because you experience the world differently at your age. Your family, this upheaval with your father, is everything to you. You haven't been in love yet, have you? Your world is still contained, small and intense, and every change to the status quo feels like a rug is being pulled from under your feet. It knocks the air from you. I can see it on your face. When you're older, you'll experience these things with more distance and forgiveness. They won't be earth-shattering in the same way. They won't be a matter of life or death. Right now you want it all to go away. I've been there, shutting my eyes and blocking my ears. This feeling will lessen over time, as will the immediacy of your emotions. See, Françoise Sagan couldn't have written *Bonjour Tristesse* in her twenties. It would have been a different story, with a whole other energy.

Brigitte paused to take a breath. She spoke slowly now, as though conscious of the torrent of words rolling over her tongue.

If I'd had a story like yours, she said, I would have written it down before I got old.

But I'm not you. My voice sounded small. I couldn't match her passion.

Of course. She nodded, a soft smile on her lips.

Because you're a writer. It's your job to tell stories.

What you have is precious. I won't force you. It's your

story. Sometimes I have an idea and it torments me. David tells me I can be obsessive. I know I often make people uncomfortable.

She stood and took our empty bowls to the sink. I considered what she'd said. I had tainted Father's name. He'd barely had time to recover from the affair. He once told me, all we have in our life is our good name, our reputation. I replayed our conversation. Brigitte's words started to make more sense; they revealed an urgency. But I couldn't do it alone. As I watched her turn on the faucet and sponge the dishes one after the other, a thought formed in my mind.

What if you were my ghostwriter?

Brigitte glanced at me, her expression unreadable. I can see I was pushing you, she said. Let's forget about it. I didn't mean to upset you.

It was dark in the kitchen, her lipstick the only streak of color. I loved how it transformed her face when she smiled. I decided, when I was older, I would wear lipstick and no other adornment.

But what if we wrote it together? I continued. You're the writer after all, and you'll know how to find the words. That's the part I can't do. I can come over after school, a few times a week. It'll be like what you did with the chef. I can't pay you, but I can tell you everything I remember about him. I can transcribe interviews, write summaries of books, go to the library for you.

She dried her hands and returned to the table. In front of her was a paper napkin that she unfolded and smoothed along the creases. We heard the front door open and close with a bang. Brigitte smiled at me.

David is home, she said. He always announces his presence.

We heard him walk through the apartment, the thud of a briefcase or bag on the floor, water running in the bathroom, and soon enough his footsteps in the hallway coming toward the kitchen. He stood in the doorway, still wearing his leather jacket. He seemed surprised to see me. As he came over to greet me, I caught a whiff of the jacket's faint animal smell. Brigitte watched him from across the table, waiting for him to come around and kiss her.

He placed his hand on her shoulder, just at the base of her neck, near the opening of her shirt. He hung his jacket on her chair.

Isn't she beautiful, my wife, he said. Brigitte's face colored a warm shade of pink. Yes, I agreed.

The last two times I'd seen Brigitte, she was alone, but now in the kitchen they coalesced as a unit. I was troubled by the tenderness of his statement and I realized I'd been hoping they weren't happily married. I was immediately ashamed by the cruel nature of my thoughts.

I think I've interrupted something, David said. I'll leave you both to it. He walked out of the kitchen.

Brigitte drank from her glass of water. A line shone above her lips.

It's not a terrible idea, she said, me helping you write a book. She seemed to be choosing her words with care, as if unsure of what direction to take. It's not a bad idea, is it? she repeated. Who was she asking? I wondered.

I'd rather we not tell my mother, I said.

Why?

She won't understand.

Brigitte nodded. Because she'll want it to be about her, won't she?

Already then, Brigitte had a capacity to pluck sentences from my mind, though she was able to echo my ideas in a more sophisticated and assured manner. How not to trust a woman who articulated my thoughts as if they were her own, without judgment, who for once sided with me?

As I left their apartment, I looked at the Japanese goddesses in the entrance and admired their nonchalance. They were brave in their nudity, unaware someone might judge them for their roundness. I thought about how much wider their skin must stretch out than ours when unraveled, their hugeness a source of comfort and horror.

2

December was the month when everything began to tip and unravel, like the old wooden floors of an apartment slowly sinking or the seam of a sleeve coming undone from a loose thread.

It started with a story Anouk told me. She had heard it on the radio one morning while getting dressed. A mother was traveling on a train with her children. They were fleeing a war and the train sped through the countryside for days without stopping. There was no food, her children were starving, and they hadn't eaten a proper meal since leaving. The train finally stopped in the middle of the countryside. Far in the distance, the mother saw the outline of a village. She recognized it from a church, rising higher than the other buildings. She left her children on the train and walked through the fields in the direction of the village. They wouldn't survive another day without food; this seemed like her only option. While she was gone, the engine rumbled to life and the train began to move. The children stared through the window, waiting for their mother to appear. They begged the conductor to wait, but he ignored their pleas. The next day, they arrived at their destination. A big industrial city. The children lived, but they never saw their mother again.

Anouk was convinced the mother had died in the village. She concluded that the village was abandoned and the mother hadn't found any food. By the time she got back to the field, the train was gone. Or the war had caught up with her and she had died from a stray bullet. If the mother had lived, she would have found her children eventually. She would have known where to look, even if it took her entire life.

Like Anouk, I also became obsessed with the story. We took comfort in their tragedy and endlessly discussed the possibilities. What had the mother found in the village? What had the children felt as the train began to move, traveling farther away from her? Had they thought of jumping from the train? I was also persuaded of the mother's love. She had sacrificed her life for them.

By then I knew my way to Brigitte and David's apartment by heart. Transfer to line twelve at Sèvres–Babylone. I arrived at their apartment when night had fallen and people clustered on the sidewalk under the orange electric heaters of cafés, smoking and drinking small glasses of wine.

It had only been a few weeks since our first meeting, but we had progressed quickly, with an intensity that reminded me of when I became friends with Juliette, a mutual hunger and admiration. I thought about my outfits on days that I visited Brigitte and I often looped around the block to pick up a small cake or pastry at the boulangerie. I felt I shouldn't arrive empty-handed when she was the one doing me a favor.

At first it was hard to talk about Father. My thoughts flowed freely, but they were unstructured. I'd lost my sense of chronology. I'd start a memory midway and fifteen minutes later I'd peddle back to the beginning, realizing my story made little sense to an outsider. Brigitte was patient, though, and she knew when to ask questions and when to sit back and listen, her golden dark eyes staring at me. I knew she took notes because at the end of a session, her notepad was covered in her dense handwriting, but during our conversations I never noticed her hand moving or the pages flipping.

To accommodate this new schedule with Brigitte, I invented vague excuses to spend less time with Juliette, or I told her I was tired. She gave me space, perhaps thinking I needed to be alone to grieve. I felt pangs of remorse throughout the school day, especially given her gentleness in those weeks, tiptoeing around me, but how could I explain that all of a sudden, my father felt more alive than ever? That in some ways, the hours spent with Brigitte brought him back to life and validated his love for me?

We were now at a point in our collaboration that made it impossible to tell Anouk without upsetting her. I was too engaged in the project; plus I didn't want to share it with anyone else, though subconsciously, I must have known that what I'd decided was not without its risks.

When Anouk called me, which happened rarely, I told her I was at Juliette's, studying. I planned most of my visits to Brigitte's around Anouk's evening rehearsals. She was weeks away from performing again, her first role since the summer, and even if I'd been home more often, we wouldn't have spent that time together. I woke up an hour earlier on school days to catch up on homework, and because I was only getting five to six hours of sleep, I was sometimes drowsy in class, digging my fingernails into my palms to stay awake.

One evening, I told Brigitte about the mother on the train with her children. I wanted to know what she thought, why the mother hadn't found her children, if she should have stayed with them on the train.

We sat in the living room. Brigitte held a pad of paper to take notes during our conversation. She turned off the tape recorder.

If they were my children, she said, I wouldn't leave them. What are the odds that I'd come back in time? That I wouldn't be killed along the way?

But don't you think she was acting out of love? She saw the possibility of saving them.

Perhaps. But a mother still has the power to soothe her children with her presence, hold them, tell stories. She has techniques to distract them from their hunger.

So you think she was wrong not to stay?

Maybe it was easier for her to jump off the train. Maybe she thought: If I don't make it back in time, I won't have to see them die. If she returned with food, they'd be fine. Perhaps she felt free, running through the fields. We don't know her. What if she wasn't a good mother? We assume she was a good person. What if the war did things to her that we can't even fathom? Or what if she stayed in the village too long, searching for food that didn't exist?

You see what she did as a form of abandonment.

She could have taken her children with her. Brigitte's eyes darkened. She told me it was the kind of thing her own mother would have done. Faced with disaster, she would have taken any opportunity to flee. Thank goodness Brigitte and her sister hadn't been raised during a war. They'd never have survived.

I sensed Brigitte came from another world, not this one in the ninth arrondissement. She described a dark apartment with two bedrooms. A small room she shared with a sister she no longer spoke to. A father who was lazy and absent. She mentioned these sparse details in a sarcastic tone, making it clear she had distanced herself from them. I tried to push her onward with questions, but she changed the subject.

We are like snakes, she said. Throughout our lives we shed our previous selves like old skins. We're always changing, never the same individual. Nothing, not even a terrible thing, can fully consume us.

I wondered if she said this to reassure herself, for she had still identified with her childhood when I told her a story about a mother who made a difficult choice.

Do you want children? I asked.

You don't ask that kind of question to a woman my age. Her smile was elusive. It's rude.

I was mortified. I told her it was none of my business, but I thought she'd be a good mother.

How would you know that? I don't have the most maternal disposition.

But you have a strong sense of self.

I suppose I could only do better than my own mother.

That's what Anouk had said about raising me. It was all about improving who her mother had been, being aware of her shortcomings, not repeating those toxic patterns.

Brigitte was silent for a moment. She had a pensive look and she jotted something down in the notepad. I felt tired from our conversation. Had I spoken adequately? Did I sound intelligent? I'd tried to remember everything Anouk told me about being a mother, but now I was afraid I'd offended Brigitte. It was the first time in our meetings that I worried we might not always be in agreement, which was puzzling as she'd praised my instincts, encouraged my opinions, and almost always agreed with them. She turned the tape recorder back on and continued to ask me about Father.

I told her about his love for cinema. I explained how at fifteen he'd started the cinema club at his high school in a city thirty kilometers from where he was raised. It was a boarding school where the boys slept in one large room and paid tuition based on their needs. He sought obscure films with subtitles and wrote reviews of the newest releases. His favorite movie was Truffaut's *The 400 Blows*. We had watched it together in May, Anouk sitting behind us with her foot massager as she read a new script. When I described these memories to Brigitte, I often came back to those precise moments. It had been a cool day, a few weeks before the end of the school year. I'd worn a dress and the wind had nipped at my bare legs when I stepped out to buy bread. The air of the apartment was thick with dust. We hadn't vacuumed in a while and Father had commented on the dust, saying he should hire a cleaning service for us.

His childhood was very different from mine, I told Brigitte. He wanted his children to have everything he didn't have, and more. His parents could barely afford to buy meat. After they had served their children, they tossed rice or pasta in the pan they'd used to cook the meat, taking whatever fat was left behind. But my father never called his childhood *difficult*. His parents gave him what they could, and he was grateful for never being hungry or cold. In a way, I think he knew what he had was temporary, and one should always be prepared to return to a simpler life.

What do you mean? Brigitte asked.

Well, he often told me that he was proud of his career up until then. He said, I couldn't have dreamed of coming this far. Like he was implying that he'd gone further than he had ever expected. I got the sense that he appreciated the fleeting nature of status and glory.

You mean someone who is raised in wealth isn't able to imagine losing it. Whereas he understood the other side.

Yes. I think he believed he was better equipped to fail.

Let me ask you a difficult question. Brigitte leaned forward. Do you really think he was capable of abandoning his comfortable and glamorous life? The apartment in the sixteenth with his wife, her family, his greater political aspirations?

I was silent. I stared at her, waiting for more.

Or should I reframe my question? If he was willing to return to a simpler life, as you say, why did he choose two lives? Why not leave his wife and sons, if he loved Anouk and you just as much, if not more? Why turn his back on you?

Because he felt a duty toward both families.

What if it's because he loved the perfect bourgeois life he'd created with his wife?

A small flame flickered in my stomach, an electric blue like from a Bunsen burner. It was true that I'd always wanted to protect him from an undefined danger. I had sensed a fragility in him. But then I remembered how Father had identified with

Antoine Doinel. That's why he loved Truffaut—he wanted to be the boy who roams Paris at night, takes refuge in the printing room, steals milk from a doorstep, the boy who knows how to survive on the street.

Maybe he wanted to be that person, I told Brigitte. He wanted to be the kind of person who can abandon everything, because he saw nobility in it.

Or because he looked down on people who've been handed the tools to succeed, she said, picking up my train of thought. He didn't want to become one of them. Those who've had it too easy. He was afraid of losing his identity, where he came from.

We sat in silence for a few minutes, listening to the cars drive slowly down the wet street. I heard the splash of water hitting the sidewalks. I wasn't looking forward to the long walk from the métro to our apartment.

To answer your earlier question, Brigitte said, interrupting the silence, I do want children. David and I have been trying for some time, but it doesn't seem to be working. Our doctor can't figure out what is wrong with me or David. Meanwhile, my friends are onto their second or third, or have grown children.

Brigitte's voice was hard, even though she tried to speak lightly. She looked away, and in profile she appeared much younger, her long hair turning her silhouette youthful in the evening light.

It took my mother a long time to get pregnant, I said. She didn't even think it was possible.

But she was younger than me.

I don't know.

I'm thirty-nine.

She was your age.

Brigitte nodded slowly. I know it's not that old today—women have children well into their forties—but should it take years? There must be something wrong with us. We started too late.

I thought about how to provide comfort. What was I supposed to say? I remembered a detail Anouk had shared recently.

My mother's doctor thought she was going through menopause when she told him she was pregnant. He didn't believe her. I think an older mother is better and wiser.

Brigitte laughed and shook out her hair. I marveled at her flat stomach. Even when she tucked shirts into her jeans, they remained loose around her waist. She closed her notepad and put away the tape recorder. I think we've done enough work for the day, she said. Let's go eat.

3

Perhaps it started with the films we watched with increasing frequency. After our conversations about Father and Anouk, where Brigitte would push me until I struggled to answer, sometimes my throat closing in, we liked to take breaks by eating or watching films. I soon learned Brigitte preferred horror films, but she didn't want to watch them alone.

She liked the heightened sensation triggered by the films, the adrenaline, especially. Imagining the sharp tip of a knife lifting the shower curtain. A hand seizing her ankle when she slept. A face drenched in blood, coming for her.

The shared experience of watching a horror film together and being terrified precipitated a physical familiarity. We sat on the couch and grabbed at each other's arms during the most frightening scenes.

Her favorite was *Trouble Every Day*, the only horror film Claire Denis ever made, in which an American man goes to Paris with his wife for their honeymoon. But the trip has a darker purpose. He's seeking a doctor who will cure him of a disease. Whenever the man is aroused, he hungers for human flesh. His desire turns into cannibalism. The man finds a woman who has the same disease. She preys on strangers, eating truck drivers on the side of the highway. Her husband, the doctor who hasn't found a cure, keeps her locked up in their house. In one of the most horrifying scenes, she devours a man's face, taking bites from his mouth moments after kissing him.

I wasn't troubled by these scenes like Brigitte, who turned her face away and covered her ears, asking me to tell her when it was over. *Trouble Every Day* made me see our skin in a new way, such a thin membrane separating our vital organs from someone's sharp teeth.

Brigitte thought humans were remarkable in their ability to contain this mass of liquid with an almost transparent casing. She pointed at the veins on the underside of my arms as proof. I can practically see those irrigation canals, she said.

I'd stop after the first bite, I told her, because I didn't like the metallic flavor of blood. I couldn't even eat steak tartare.

Brigitte wasn't so sure. What if she liked the taste? Hadn't we all started somewhere, trying ingredients at a young age and deciding whether we enjoyed them? Was there a reason why babies weren't fed raw meat? Better not to know one's compulsions. She ate her steaks rare, almost blue at the center.

But a human was more complicated, she agreed. It wasn't just flesh. There was fat, tendons, bones, all the hair, too.

She made me laugh with her exaggerations, though something in her voice rang true—this fear of losing control, as if she yearned for an opportunity to spin out of her tightly wound world and be excused for a horrific act.

It seemed in line with her ambition, one that intimidated me. I knew how to work hard at school, but this was something else. It boiled at her feet and shot up. She worked longer hours than I did, transcribing interviews into the night, sending me emails long after I'd gone to sleep.

I was haunted by the few details she revealed about her mother. You will be a fat girl if you eat too much, her mother told Brigitte as she gave her cotton balls soaked in warm water to swallow to quell her pangs of hunger. She weighed her daughter every morning before breakfast. Brigitte had been taught at a young age that beauty and slenderness were necessary qualities for a woman to succeed. The gnawing feeling of your organs eating themselves from starvation was a good sensation.

As much as I complained about Anouk, I'd never known that kind of maternal cruelty. I was more fortunate. But I recognized myself in Brigitte, the way she rejected where she came from.

One afternoon she asked if I'd ever thought about Madame Lapierre. How do you think it was for her to learn about your father's relationship with another woman?

I was embarrassed to admit that I hadn't thought about it. When I saw Madame Lapierre last summer, I began, I didn't recognize her, because I had no idea what she looked like. Later, when Anouk told me who she was, it was a shock. This woman was completely different from my own mother. My father had chosen two opposites. I was so caught up in her physical appearance for a long time that I wasn't concerned with her emotional state, what she knew and how it would affect her. I told my father about seeing her. I asked him if she knew about us. He said no, but I didn't entirely believe him. It didn't make sense that she was in the dark when we'd known about them our entire lives. That's probably why I assumed she was less innocent than she appeared.

I heard that she had no idea about you and your mother, Brigitte said.

From who?

Did you read the interview with her in *Madame Figaro*?

I shook my head. I'd stopped reading the news after his funeral.

She said she never suspected another woman.

Do you believe her?

I remember her saying that she felt deeply humiliated when the articles were published. She received no warning, and it was one thing to learn that her husband had spent the last twenty years with another woman, but a child? It was devastating. Brigitte spoke with her gaze fixed on the coffee table. She glanced up, as though expecting a response.

You're saying this as if we're at fault.

No, I'm just saying that you have to consider who else suffered.

Brigitte swept her hair around her neck. It draped over her shoulder like a long, faceless animal. I felt the tears fall down my cheeks before I could stop them. Usually I was able to hold them back in public, contain them in my swollen throat, but this time they escaped. Brigitte stayed seated across from me as I covered my face with my hands.

After a moment, she spoke in a softer voice. I know you didn't want to hurt them. She handed me a tissue, and I wiped my eyes. It's hard to know who to blame, isn't it? Whether it's your father, someone you deeply love, or your mother, for choosing him and staying with him.

You have it all wrong, I said. He chose to stay with my mother, not the other way around.

Your mother would have left him?

I was silent, no longer sure. Maybe Brigitte was right.

Why don't you stay for dinner?

We often ate snacks in the kitchen. Tea or coffee if it was earlier in the day. Slices of cheese with toasted bread. Almonds and dried apricots. Sometimes I picked up a pastry on my way over. Brigitte cut it into small pieces and served it with home-made pear or plum jam. But I always left before dinner, not wanting to intrude. Back home, I often ate alone, soup in a carton or a can of sardines or mackerel. I forced myself to eat the entire can, chewing on the small bones and sopping up the oil with bread. It made me nauseous, but I didn't want to throw it away, knowing it would stink up the kitchen.

That evening, Brigitte cooked for us in their small kitchen. I sat at the table watching her boil water for spaghetti. She sliced the onion thinly and made a sauce with caramelized onions and bacon pieces. She opened a bottle of white wine and added a splash to the pan. It evaporated almost immediately. As the pasta cooked, she made a salad with radishes and herbs.

How was I going to eat all of this? I worried. Brigitte tossed the spaghetti in the sauce and added a few tablespoons of cream. As she placed bowls on the table, I recognized a con-traction in my stomach. Hunger.

I ate slowly, taking my time to twirl the spaghetti around my fork. For dessert, she served pieces of dark chocolate and opened a bottle of red wine.

We'd drunk half of the bottle when David came home from work. I looked at him in the brightness of the kitchen. Despite my spending hours in the apartment, I hadn't seen him all that much, and we hadn't emailed since our last exchange before the interview. There he was, the thickness of his hair, a warm energy emanating as he poured wine into a glass, and the sharp scent of sweat as he brushed past me.

Let's watch something, Brigitte said, finishing her glass. Can you stay, Margot?

I just have to tell Anouk. I took out my phone and sent her a message saying I was at Juliette's.

What are we watching? David asked.

We migrated to the living room to look at their collection of DVDs. David settled into the couch while Brigitte rummaged through cases and loose disks. I placed my glass on the coffee table and sat down beside him.

You're taking Brigitte's seat, David whispered into my ear. It's where she likes to sit. Am I replacing my wife with a younger woman? His tone was light, and he furrowed his brow, obviously wanting to make a joke, but I was unsettled by his comment and moved to the other end of the couch.

Brigitte turned around, triumphant, holding a disk in her hand. *Contempt* by Godard, she said. Her eyes fluttered over me.

Have you lost weight? she asked. Before I could reply, she said it suited me.

I placed my hands over my stomach.

I can't believe I never noticed this before, she added, but you look like a young Brigitte Bardot.

No, I don't, I stammered, flattered. I'm not even blond.

She used to be a brunette. And then she dyed her hair and kept it that way.

What did she look like?

Brigitte searched for a photo on her phone. She found a black-and-white picture of Bardot posing on the beach at Cannes. She was sixteen at the most, with a slender waist and long, dancer's legs.

I know that photo, David said, peering over my shoulder. You do have the same mouth.

Is it the teeth? I asked. Do I look like a donkey? Like Balthazar?

Au Hasard Balthazar! David exclaimed. Brigitte loves that movie, don't you?

You love that movie, she corrected him. She turned to me. No, it's the lips. They are like your mother's.

I told you, David said, just quietly enough that I didn't think Brigitte heard him. He took the remote and pressed a button. The screen flickered to life.

Brigitte inserted the disk and came over to the couch. Stand up for a moment, she said, addressing me. I stood in front of her. She circled my waist with her hands and pressed into my stomach. Her fingers were hard through the thin material of my dress, and they sank deeper than I'd expected. I thought of her mother, demanding that Brigitte remain empty for the sake of beauty. She pulled her hands away.

Such a beautiful waist, she said. I used to wear dresses like that when I was your age.

You still can.

I'd look like an old witch. I have a friend who has beautiful hair without a strand of gray and this incredible, athletic build. She's almost sixty now, but people always mistake her for being much younger, especially from afar or from behind. Once a boy, no older than you, whistled at her on the street. When she turned around and showed her face, he apologized and ran away. I'd never want to be like her. What an embarrassment.

The windows of the living room were open, and an evening breeze swept through, carrying the smell of food cooking from a nearby kitchen. It was warm and humid for this late in the year. We watched the movie in silence. The colors on the television screen were Mediterranean, bright and warm, especially Casa Malaparte, a spectacular orange villa with a slanted roof made of stairs. Father had shown me photos a long time ago. I remembered the house belonged to an Italian writer, Curzio Malaparte.

Brigitte sat between David and me. His arm was wrapped around her shoulders. When I glanced to the left, I saw his fingers caressing her neck. They seemed porous to each other, so comfortable existing in each other's space. This is what a marriage must feel like from the inside.

Later that night, when we had finished all the wine, I twirled and kicked my legs in the air. They did look long and graceful. We laughed about the opening scene, where Bardot was naked on a bed, her body golden and shimmering like a mermaid.

Brigitte cheered me on. She was a little drunk.

Et mes cuisses? Tu les aimes? Mes genoux, tu les aimes? I asked, imitating her voice.

Yes, I like your thighs and knees, Brigitte answered, playing along in a deep masculine voice.

I sensed we had achieved a new kind of closeness.

The trains had stopped running and David offered to call me a taxi, but Brigitte insisted I spend the night. It had started raining again, and at this hour it would take a long time to find a taxi. You can sleep on the couch in David's office, she said.

She took a pillow and two blankets from a closet. We tucked a sheet into the sides of the couch. She gave me an old nightgown, the material almost transparent from wear, and wished me good night. Make yourself at home, she said. Use whatever you like in the bathroom, and if you need anything, just knock on our door.

I changed into the nightgown, which smelled of soap. The cotton was soft along my bare skin. I sat on the makeshift bed for a while, thinking about our evening together. I listened to David and Brigitte as they washed dishes in the kitchen and walked around the apartment, preparing for bed. I thought about her black eyes aimed at the television, her hands squeezing the skin around my waist, her nails filed into perfect halfmoons. I felt guilty, thinking about Juliette alone in her studio. She had asked if I had plans for the weekend and I had lied, saying I needed to spend time with Anouk. Oh, that's fine, she'd answered. I need to work on my film.

Once the apartment was quiet, I stepped out of the office and walked down the hallway to the bathroom. A sliver of light shone beneath their bedroom door. It beckoned me. I paused and listened to their muffled voices, too soft to distinguish words. Perhaps if I stopped breathing for a second, I would hear them. I knew I should continue on my way, but instead I crouched down by the door and lowered my head, one cheek against the floor, until I could see into their room.

At first I saw their feet walk across the bedroom. The floorboards creaked beneath David's feet, heavier than hers. I adjusted my angle to better see their calves and knees. When they climbed into bed, I lost sight of their bodies. I waited for the lights to extinguish, but they remained on.

I heard sheets being pushed aside, the rustle of cotton as they slid into bed, the gentle sucking of mouths kissing. I imagined their tongues licking, bodies pressed against each other, his hand dipping under the covers to find hers. How often did they have sex? The bed scraped against the wall. I listened to their moans, louder, and I could almost smell the wine on their breath, hear their wetness. I was paralyzed by the thought that they'd see the shape of my body through the door. The bed stopped moving and their feet dropped to the floor. My stomach swung violently, as if I'd been thrown down a tunnel. I braced myself to be discovered.

But they stayed by the bed, paying me no heed. I could see their legs now, even the hairs on David's ankles and the red polish glinting on Brigitte's toenails. Her feet turned to face the bed. David stood behind her, muscles visible on his calves as he rose onto his toes. He bent his knees and she tipped over onto the bed. I couldn't see above their thighs. Their breathing grew sharper and hoarse as he continued to push into her, his skin smacking hers, and I finally smelled it, the sweat of their bodies combined. She spoke to him, just loud enough for me to hear. Is this what you want? she said. Her voice was feminine and delicate. And then she said something else so quietly I wasn't able to catch it. David's legs buckled against hers.

I closed my eyes, trying to picture myself as Brigitte, and was flooded with a feeling of euphoria. I'd been so afraid they would discover me before they finished. Now it almost didn't matter if they found me. I sat with my hands pressed tightly between my thighs, not daring to move for a long time. My own breath was shallow and drops of sweat slid down my ears and neck. I waited for them to turn off the lights, then I returned to the office and fell into a deep sleep.

The following morning, I was slow to remember where I was. My feet touched the hard end of the couch and a bluish light seeped through the cracks between the shutters. I folded the sheets and brushed the couch, erasing the shape of my body. Through the window I saw an old man in the courtyard, sweeping leaves into a plastic bag.

4

What can you tell me about your father that no one else knows?

My mother will always say that he wasn't made for a career in politics. Like it's a big secret! Yes, it's remarkable to see how far he came: minister of culture! Even *professor* was an accomplishment. Anouk will tell you that he lacked a skill necessary for the political life. He was too rigid, his sense of right and wrong too black and white, his definition of justice too absolute. Which may seem ironic to you, considering how easy it was for him to rationalize his personal life. But in the professional sphere, he had an intransigence that sooner or later would have cost him his career.

Think of it this way: A group of thirty people are boarding a small boat. The captain of the boat knows that one of the passengers is a thief and murderer who will not hesitate to kill the other passengers and steal from them. The captain can either allow the thief to board the boat, or he can throw him into the ocean. A clever captain doesn't hesitate to eliminate the thief, even if this compromises his broader sense of right and wrong.

Father wasn't cunning in that way. He was intelligent and worked hard, but when it came to human relations, he didn't fundamentally understand what motivates others. He couldn't empathize enough in order to disarm them, and he didn't know how to massage a situation, how to choose between two evils. In those situations, he was paralyzed. Perhaps he could have learned more from the way he so cleverly managed his two families.

She doesn't think he could've run for president, despite his popularity among the center-right?

No, though perhaps because she always hoped to steer him to the left.

What do you think was at the origin of this weakness?

His family. The town he was raised in, a feeling of being small that never really faded, even as he gained wealth and status. Anouk once saw him at an event with another man, an ultra-bourgeois who was raised in the sixteenth, where Father lived with his wife. She later recounted how Father shrank in his presence. The other man didn't notice—he wouldn't have cared enough to notice—but Anouk saw the flush in Father's face, his body language immediately shifting, both submissive and outraged. Something the man said triggered this reaction.

Made him plump up like a rooster. Most of the time he suppressed these feelings of smallness, but in certain exchanges, like this one, his insecurities flared up.

How did you perceive him in the private space of your home?

His weakness was to attribute meaning and status to beautiful objects. He was not a frugal man. The opposite even, someone who saw his generosity as proof of how far he'd come. He wanted to show others he was comfortable and could also make their lives comfortable. I've got this! he'd say, delighted, swooping in to take the check. I think what he hated most was walking into a supermarket and having to purchase the brand of the store. He thought it was invariably inferior. He was the perfect consumer, whether it was buying Maille mustard, Ariel laundry detergent, or Spontex sponges. He didn't even need to watch the ads. He had already absorbed the idea that buying *real* brands is a marker of quality, and therefore reveals what you can and cannot afford.

It was the same with other things. He didn't care about owning an expensive watch, but he wanted the best shoes, the best hairdresser, the one who only cut the hair of politicians, actors, famous people. Ever since he could afford a car in Paris, he preferred to drive. He's never owned a flashy car, always something solid and durable, often a Saab, but he loved the luxury of being able to choose not to take the métro.

As we drove around in his car, going from one store to another, he told me stories about his grandmother, who cleaned bars late at night well into her sixties. The vomit and urine she washed from the floors of restrooms; the heavy bags of trash she put out in the outdoor bins. He admired her more than anyone else in the world. She never complained about her work, and when he stayed with her, she spoiled him. She made him hot chocolate every morning and bought him his favorite magazines.

I remember Father once taking me to Brasserie Lipp. We barely went out together, but his wife and sons were away, and it was in the earlier years, when he was less worried about seeing people he knew. This was the kind of restaurant he loved, traditional and timeless, where a customer is always respected. He ordered leeks with vinaigrette, sole meunière, endives, gratin dauphinois. Perhaps at Brasserie Lipp he felt comfortable because it was anonymous—you were respected for simply dining there—and yet entering that space symbolized an ascension of some kind. He knew the menu by heart.

And what about your mother?

When I want to think of her fondly, I try to imagine what she was like in her twenties, before she met Father. Were we alike? Would we have been friends?

She spent her childhood in Le Vésinet, a wealthy town west of Paris, the opposite of where Father was raised. Her parents had a studio nearby in Saint-Germain-en-Laye and as soon as she was old enough to leave, she moved into the studio. She couldn't afford her own place in Paris yet. I like to picture her living in this small studio, one room the size of our living room today, folding out her sofa bed every evening. The studio was close to the park. She took me there last year. It's a beautiful park designed by the man who conceived the gardens of Versailles, with a long terrace that opens onto the Paris skyline. I remember her excitement as she brought me through the iron gate and past the high schoolers who sat on the patches of grass in circles, their backpacks thrown into the middle, so no one would steal them. We stood at the railing. She pointed to the Eiffel Tower and La Défense. She told me this was where she came to clear her head after an audition. This is where she spent hours when she found out she was pregnant. She wondered if she'd keep me, how her life would change, what would become of her relationship with this married man, how they might build a life for their child.

She looked at the Paris skyline not with hunger or apprehension, but with the excitement of someone who already owns it, who can't wait to live there and fit right in.

But what you may not know about my father is that he never really took a day off, not for his wife and sons and not for us. He believed in the value of work. Even during holidays, he was attached to his phone, reviewed papers after everyone had gone to bed. Because he felt this enormous responsibility to take care of us all. He was afraid. What if we asked him for something and he couldn't give it to us? That would've been the greatest embarrassment. Being empty-handed? I think he would've gone into debt or sold his most expensive shoes before saying no. He also loved to work, to be in the middle of a crisis and make things well again. He liked to be the calm one in the eye of a storm.

At the end of the day, is your mother that different from Madame Lapierre? Don't they come from similarly privileged families?

As you know, Anouk's father was a doctor. He had his own practice in Le Vésinet and the same patients for decades. Her mother worked until her early sixties. Anouk was the rebellious one, that's why they sent her off to boarding school for a few years. She didn't do well at the Catholic private school. She clashed with the teachers, refused to attend the catechism class. She wasn't a brilliant student because she never studied that hard. She wasn't interested in getting the best grades, she just wanted to pass the Bac. Yes, my grandparents are privileged. They live in a three-story house in Burgundy and travel to European cities, staying at five-star hotels, a few times a year. But they're not refined intellectuals like Madame Lapierre's family. They're not celebrities. Not like Alain Robert, Madame Lapierre's father. I bet they've already drafted his obituary to be published the minute he dies. And Anouk didn't fit into the mold the way Madame Lapierre did. Anouk wanted to define herself against her upbringing. She wanted to be an artist, a creative. She never wanted to get married, let alone in a church, nor did she ever want to baptize her children, if she had any. She wanted to do it all differently from my father and his wife.

Does she know how her parents played a role in her success as an actor? The stability of her upbringing, the studio in Saint-Germain-en-Laye, the weekly checks they sent her for years—it all gave her the confidence to succeed in her vocation. In their own way, her parents supported their daughter.

Oh, she knows, and she hates it.

5

Anouk and I barely crossed paths during the week. She continued to teach her evening classes and preferred to rehearse at the studio. She came home late, sometimes taking the last train home, and was asleep when I left at seven-thirty A.M. Three evenings a week I went to Brigitte and David's, and the other two I saw Juliette. On the weekends I floated around the apartment alone, sometimes cleaning, most of the time sitting on the couch and staring at the balcony as the plants lost their leaves until all they had left were spindly, darkened branches.

One morning I was awoken by the sound of Anouk's alarm. I waited for her to turn it off, but the longer I waited, the louder it shrieked, until I stumbled from my room thinking something had happened to her in the night. It was a wicked thought and it blazed through my head. I turned off the alarm and searched for her long shape in the bed.

I thought you had died, I said, pushing her shoulder. Why didn't you wake up sooner? Are you deaf?

Let me sleep. She said my name with visible annoyance and

closed her eyes. She turned away. I wavered, then put myself back to bed. She'd want me to soothe myself. Sleep wouldn't come. I pushed my hands onto my stomach where there was only a floating mass of tubes. I moved my hands lower, remembering Brigitte and David.

The date of Anouk's play approached and soon it was the opening night. Théo and Mathilde had gotten us seats in the second row. Anouk never wanted us in the front row in case we distracted her. I'd offered to go during the previews, but she didn't seem to care either way.

To see Anouk for the span of two hours as a woman who had never birthed me, could be shattering. She slid across the stage and her eyes glossed over us without recognition. I wanted her to look in my direction just once and acknowledge my presence. I focused on the other actors. The woman who was sleeping with the director was a revelation. Anouk had been right; she was talented, and the audience was immediately drawn into her orbit.

The heat in the theater was stifling, and we were sweating beneath our winter clothes. Mathilde wiped her upper lip more than once, and Théo fanned us with a program. Anouk's skin, however, didn't even glisten. She stood on a different plane from ours. Juliette, who sat next to me, beamed at her. I tried to see my mother from her point of view. I closed my eyes and listened to her voice.

After the play, we went to dinner at a nearby brasserie, a place famous for its steak frites and oysters. We picked on bread as we waited for our food to arrive. Anouk began to tell us about a conference she'd gone to the previous week. It was for women in the arts. There was a presentation in the morning, followed by a conversation with a filmmaker, a retired actor, and a professor who taught at La Fémis. The morning was long and tedious, and the conversation dragged on until two in the afternoon. Everyone was famished when they finally stopped for lunch.

The women were shuttled to another room, where they were welcomed by a magnificent platter. Rows and rows of sandwiches, filled with cheese, ham, hard-boiled eggs, and tomatoes. Anouk was caught up in a conversation with the professor. She saw the women descend on the table, taking at least two sandwiches per paper plate, even though the sandwiches were each half a baguette. Why would they ever need more than one? It was extraordinary to see them lunging for the food, afraid they wouldn't have enough.

Anouk stared at them in wonder and continued to speak with the professor. Eventually the women around the table dispersed. There was nothing left. Those who had gone to the restroom or stepped outside for a moment were left without lunch. The others stood in corners, chatting and pausing just long enough to take another bite, holding the second sandwich close to their chest.

Weren't you starving? Juliette asked.

Anouk shook her head. I lost my appetite within minutes. If you'd heard them all chewing, the same would have happened to you. I could feel my stomach shrink as their chewing grew louder. But I waited to see if everyone would finish their food. Most couldn't even manage one sandwich—they were so big! I left as soon as I noticed people putting down their half-finished plates.

Our food arrived on the table. Anouk cut a piece of steak and placed it in her mouth. She moaned with pleasure. It's very good, she said. Juliette and I stared at our frites.

Did the professor notice? I asked. Did he see you had nothing to eat?

Oh no, he didn't bat an eye. But those women weren't wrong. If you're hungry, you have to move quickly. Maybe I'd have done the same. We weren't friends before walking into that conference room. What did we owe each other?

A few days later, Juliette took me aside after class and told me she had been inspired by Anouk's story. I've been thinking nonstop about those women and their hunger, she said. I keep picturing them huddled around the table, taking the equivalent of an entire baguette onto their plates, and ignoring the ones who didn't serve themselves in time.

We walked down the hallway and through the heavy front doors. Outside the wind was cold, as if speckled with bits of ice.

It was probably less dramatic in reality, I said. You know Anouk has a tendency to exaggerate events. Maybe she even got a sandwich herself. We'd have to ask someone else who was there.

I know how she is, Juliette said. Either way, the scene made its mark on me. I've told you that I've wanted to make a horror film for a while, but I didn't have a good idea until the story of your mother's lunch.

We crossed the street and opened the door of Chez Albert. Our table in the corner was free. We took off our coats and

ordered two coffees and our favorite item on the menu, a panini with mayonnaise, ham, and cheese, and stuffed with fries.
We tried to eat it no more than once a week.

Tell me about your horror film.

Juliette rubbed her hands together. A woman who is devoured by other women.

I laughed and drank my coffee in two gulps, while it was
still burning hot, the way Father always did.

Tell me more, I said.

The panini arrived. I ripped it in half and divided the portions between our plates. Juliette pulled her chair in closer and
began to describe the film. She had written it out as a story, and
she recounted it with all the same details, so I could better visualize the scenes and characters.

The film took place in an isolated town, somewhere in the
countryside where the winters are brutally cold. As long as the
townspeople could remember, the mayor had always been a
woman. There was a tradition of selecting a new mayor every
ten years. She wasn't chosen by vote, but through an old ritual.
Once a decade, all the women aged eighteen to forty gathered
in the town hall. A group of older women presided over the
ritual. They kept the men out of the premises and recorded
every detail for later retellings.

On the morning of a new selection, there was a hum of excitement among the candidates as they waited. They were impatient; most hadn't found sleep the night before, and they
were nervous as they stood against the town hall walls, wring-
ing their hands and whispering to each other. Many had flushed
faces, skin scrubbed to hide the dark bags under their eyes.

Their hair was pulled back into tight buns, stray strands flattened with gel.

The current mayor was an astute woman. She'd been thirty-nine when she was selected, almost the maximum age, and in her ten years of leadership she had learned the different facets of human nature. She surveyed the younger women with a benevolent smile—even the forty-year-old ones seemed so young to her. She, too, sensed their excitement. It was contagious and made her own skin prickle. She was light-headed, as she hadn't eaten in fifteen hours. She had emptied herself one last time in the morning. It was better not to make a mess of one's body. The room had tall windows and as the sun rose higher in the sky, it filled the room with a hot white light. It was time to begin.

The mayor stood from her chair and came to the center of the room. An older woman described the ritual. As the mayor listened, she felt the rise of an emotion, the first hint of terror. She had expected to feel afraid but hadn't anticipated the way time both slowed down and quickened, like her erratic heartbeat, and this sudden feeling of being exposed. She was clothed, but her skin felt bare, reminding her of the first time she'd undressed for someone she loved.

The young women were to line up and take turns biting the mayor. The one who took the bite that killed her became the new mayor. They could only use their teeth and lips. Some of the women had gone through the ritual twice. They had studied late into the night, first practicing on unpeeled oranges, then small animals—pigs and calves were best. The more devoted ones had trained on cows. They knew it was important to be patient and start with small bites. When their turn came around again, they had a better chance of delivering the fatal bite. It also depended on how the other women proceeded. The selection usually took a long time, as each woman was allowed to bite only once during her turn.

One woman chose a section too wrapped in flesh and her bite did little more than draw pinpricks of blood. Another's hair came undone and fell loose around her face, making it hard to see each time she bent her neck. The youngest—she had just turned eighteen that very morning—took her first bite out of the mayor's thigh and was immediately sick.

And what of the mayor?

She started on her feet. Then she kneeled, as if in a prayer. She tried to keep her limbs exposed and accessible. She had been in their position before, and she didn't want to shame the women into having to nudge her legs and arms with their mouths. It was all too vulgar. At the end she fell on her side and formed a crescent shape on the floor.

The older women praised her; they were sad to see her depart. There was such grace in the way she arched her neck and stared at the candidates with kindness when they stepped forward. Twenty years ago there had been a fiasco. A mayor who screamed and battled until they had to tie her down with chains. What an embarrassment. This one was silent and majestic even as blood poured down her chest. The novices wondered if she had been drugged. But no, she was lucid. She knew what to do, as if this was not her first time.

It was almost noon when she died. Sometimes it was hard to tell who exactly had finished her. The mayor simply bled out from all the wounds.

They carried her punctured body outside, the clothing

heavy and wet. Through the streets, children would detect an iron tang for days. The new mayor wiped her mouth and brow. She would be twenty-four in a month. The sound of the old mayor's last breath rattling through her weakened lungs would haunt her for a long time. She ran her tongue over her teeth before smiling at the crowd.

I was reminded of *Trouble Every Day*, but I didn't want to mention it to Juliette. We had seen almost every movie together in the past years and she'd want to know why I hadn't told her about this one sooner and who I had watched it with; it would lead to a million questions about who Brigitte was. I thought about how counter to our nature it was to bite down on human flesh, to harm someone with no other weapon than the sharpest part of ourselves.

I want you to play both mayors, Juliette said, interrupting me in mid-reverie.

I was startled by her request. I hadn't believed her when she'd mentioned it in passing. Whenever someone asked me if I'd be an actor like my mother, I always said no. Juliette knew it was the last thing on my mind, that I'd never be drawn to the stage or screen.

I thought you could do me a favor, she continued, sensing my hesitation. I don't know who else to ask.

But how am I going to play two characters at the same time? I softened my tone.

I'll show only body parts for the older mayor. We can make do with your arm and close-ups of your skin. It's for my portfolio, to increase my chances of getting into a program. Juliette offered me the last bite of the panini. Specks of oregano clung to the melted cheese, and a few fries had spilled onto the plate. I laughed and squeezed her arm.

All right, then.

The old Margot would have pushed back, but it occurred to me that this kind of project could bring us closer during a time when I worried my avoidances were growing awkward. One day Juliette might question me about where I was going, why I seemed distracted, and I might stutter, turn red in the face. Plus, what was I to do if the book Brigitte and I were working on was published? How would I explain it? I swatted away these concerns before they took on substance. It seemed far away, an indulgence. In the meantime, her film was a welcome distraction. I finished the panini and gave Juliette the last fries. They were no longer warm but had retained their softness.

We left Chez Albert arm in arm. Margot, do you think it'll be good? Juliette asked. Do you think people will like it? She sounded anxious. It was rare that she asked for my approval, and when it happened it was usually about a boy. All I could think about was how much Brigitte would like this kind of story.

I think it's brilliant, I told her, drawing her closer to me. We'd gotten to the bridge and noticed a crowd gathered at the barrier. Juliette pulled me toward them. A group of ten or so people stared down at the Seine, pointing at a shape in the water. I soon realized what I was looking at. A man floated on his stomach. Even in the dark we saw his shoulders popping above the surface like two bald scalps, the black water lapping at his pale skin. He's dead, someone said.

I stepped away from the barrier and felt a crushing weight in my throat. An ambulance siren rang in the distance. Had it been like that with Father, a siren in the middle of the night, tearing through their neighborhood? Blood rushed to my feet and a cold wave surged inside my chest. Had he woken Madame Lapierre, had there been time, had someone tried to resuscitate him, had he spoken to her, and if so, what had his final words been, what did he think in that precise moment?

I looked at the other side, where the river flowed undisturbed. It was often like this. I forgot he was gone, and then for a brief moment the fog cleared, and my mind was the sharpest it had ever been.

It was becoming harder to believe Father might call me one day, still alive but just away for a little while longer. Over time this fantasy was losing its soothing effect, as if I had built a resistance and the drug no longer worked its magic.

6

It was in those early days of our friendship that I learned the most about Brigitte and David. She was happiest in the months of autumn, around the time we first met, and she retained some of that glow as we transitioned into the winter. From the kitchen window, she often watched the old man I'd seen rake leaves in the courtyard. She was soothed by his patient movements, the shuffle of his feet. It reminded her of autumns spent with her parents, looking down at the trees in the playground. They lived in a twenty-story building with walls so thin between the apartments that she could hear the neighbors cough at night. That world, thank God, was now buried. It was a reminder of how far she'd come. And she also liked when the weather turned colder. It made her skin contract to a tighter self. In the summer she felt loose, as if her insides were on the verge of melting.

Brigitte had qualities that reminded me of Father. She could be a snob and refused to drink tap water. She criticized David for buying Evian, because she preferred the flavor of Acqua

Panna. She made tea and coffee with mineral water. She had a tendency for commenting on my clothing—when I wore a dress that revealed too much skin, for instance. She wasn't prudish, but she had specific ideas about style.

In many ways, David was the opposite of Brigitte. He loved the summer and thrived in the heat. He even enjoyed the smell of rubbish stewing on street corners. Brigitte had fallen in love with the sour scent of his sweat mixed with his deodorant. Still now, when she caught a waft, it aroused her. On anyone else it repulsed her. She showered twice a day.

My favorite moments, I discovered, were watching her cook. She didn't do things as if for the first time, unlike me, who was a novice in most realms.

One afternoon she showed me how to make soft-boiled eggs. She filled a saucepan with water and placed it on the stove. In the winter she kept eggs by the windowsill. She plucked two from the carton and slipped them into the roiling water one by one, her fingers almost touching the water. She turned the heat down to a gentle simmer and stirred them for thirty seconds. We waited six minutes.

It was an act she did mindlessly. She had made eggs hundreds of times, whereas I only knew how to scramble or fry them. As we waited for the eggs to finish cooking, she drizzled slices of bread with olive oil. We ate the eggs with sea salt and a splash of red wine vinegar.

She had learned from the chef, so many years ago. During their meeting, the chef had described making these barely cooked eggs with bread fried in oil, and Brigitte had re-created the recipe from the tape recording.

As we ate, Brigitte told me that during her childhood she

sought to imitate others. Like me, she was dissatisfied with her body, her mind, everything her parents had given her. She understood my insecurities. But unlike me, she fought hard to adopt the gestures of her classmates who seemed happy and confident. She wanted to be more like them.

I told her that if those girls saw her today, they'd be dying of envy.

It took years of discipline to arrive here, she said. I detected a giddiness in her voice. You can't imagine how much work it takes, still today.

To illustrate her point, Brigitte told me about a girl in middle school named Eloise. She admired Eloise for her curly blond hair and pink skin. The teachers adored her. She sat next to Eloise every day and tried to be more like her, twirling her hair around her fingers so it would curl, except hers was charcoal black and straight. She sensed this girl had a superpower, and she needed to learn it.

What she loved most about Eloise was her handwriting. Circular letters, evenly formed, fitting perfectly between the tiny blue lines of their notebooks. After school, Brigitte copied her handwriting until she was able to imitate the round letters. She wrote until her thumb held the imprint of her fountain pen. She was proud of this accomplishment.

And then, one day, the teacher left a note on the margin of Brigitte's assignment, saying she shouldn't copy another person's handwriting. Brigitte was deeply hurt. She knew she had transgressed. It was humiliating, like getting caught cheating. She came home and cried for hours. She almost didn't go to school the following day. She spent days unlearning the handwriting she'd so carefully studied, but she could never truly change it, and even today her writing bears traces of Eloise's. She used to be disgusted by the circular letters, but with time she'd come to see this writing as her own. It was an important lesson. Brigitte was an inherently weak person, unable to take ownership of her own writing. She learned that those who imitate others and get caught in the act are punished.

Brigitte's story chilled me. I imagined a young girl coming home to her dark apartment. A mother who pushed her daughter onto a scale every morning. I imagined her throwing out pages of handwriting. Imitation had to be invisible and effortless. Or it had to be done within an acceptable context, such as ghostwriting.

The phone rang, its shrill cutting through the apartment. Brigitte jumped from her chair. I have to take this call, she said, disappearing into the hallway. I waited in the kitchen, first clearing our plates and washing them in the sink, then flicking through an old issue of *Marie Claire*.

I heard David open the front door. He was home early. I waited for his footsteps to become louder, closer to where I was. He walked into the kitchen and sat at the table with me. She's on the phone, I said.

David nodded, saying he'd seen her on his way in.

Do you have more work to do? I asked, glancing at the briefcase by his feet.

Just an hour or two.

You must have a deadline. I don't want to keep you from working.

No, not at all.

You don't have to keep me company. Brigitte will be back soon. I lowered my eyes to the magazine.

I have deadlines almost every day, he said. I'm used to it, and sometimes I can take a break. He placed his elbows on the table and smiled. Am I bothering *you*? he asked. I blushed and closed the magazine.

Has Brigitte told you what we're working on?

She hasn't said much. She's guarded when it comes to her projects. You're writing a book together, isn't that right?

I doubt it'll be a book. Probably nothing much.

I was surprised Brigitte hadn't told him more about the time we spent together.

Does she really not talk about what she's writing? I asked, curious. I assumed you shared everything.

David laughed. Is that how you see us? An old married couple who tells each other everything?

You're not old.

I'm older than you.

Anyway, what do I know about relationships? I sighed and looked up at the ceiling. Small black bugs clustered under the lightbulbs. You know, I thought my parents were a normal couple. I thought the three of us could live happily. But everyone probably knew what would happen. You surely knew.

What do you think I knew?

That he would stay with them. What does it take for a man to leave his wife, for a woman to leave her husband? What would I know about it?

I'd thought about these questions for a while and had wanted to ask Brigitte or David about them. They had sounded intelligent in my mind, but spoken aloud, they were stiff and melodramatic, and I wished I'd held my tongue. David took a moment to answer, and when he did his voice was gentle. You seemed certain of what you wanted. I still remember your first email. You were different from other seventeen-year-olds I've met, more mature and in control.

They train us well at school.

I did try to warn you. I told you there could be repercussions.

Was that true? Those early weeks of September had the imprecise quality of a dream. I flinched at the memory of our written exchanges.

David fiddled with a bottle opener on the table. I looked through the window at the gray sky above the neighboring apartments. It was going to rain.

What about you? he asked. Do you have a boyfriend at school?

Not at the moment.

He smiled. You're right not to waste your time on high school boys.

Should I stay alone, then? I heard the snap in my voice, and I tried to temper its tone.

I'm not telling you what to do.

I'm sorry. I didn't mean to be defensive. I pulled my chair up to the table. I don't seem to interest anyone at school.

I can't imagine that's true.

Maybe one day I'll be wise like the two of you. I immediately reddened at my comment.

No, you'll do better than us.

I laughed and licked my lips. They felt dry, and I wished I'd thought of wearing lipstick before leaving home. I knew the pale, drab color they took on in the winter. We couldn't hear Brigitte from the kitchen, but I could picture her in the living room, holding the phone between her shoulder and ear, writing notes against the coffee table.

Look at your lips, David said.

What about them? I brushed my hand over my mouth. I was sure he'd tell me they were like my mother's.

They're a little swollen.

It must be the cold, I said. The wind irritates them.

David shook his head. No, your lips are always like that, swollen and rounder than you'd expect.

As I walked through the ninth arrondissement toward the Seine, flushed by David's comment, Anouk's voice rattled in my head. I touched the warm padding of my lips. Those huge lips I'd inherited from Anouk, the only feature on my face that made us look alike.

In the past, when she was angry at Father or her life, she'd often lash out at me and accuse me of being spoiled. She wanted to remind me how hard I needed to work in order to be good. I absorbed her words completely. Your father has spoiled you, I remembered Anouk saying throughout my childhood. You don't know how to look beyond your navel. He's rotted you like milk. You rotten, rotten girl.

If I wasn't so rotten, I might have known it was better to shut up about our family. I might have listened to David's warnings.

She was right, I was spoiled. Something dark grew inside me, spreading like mold. I thought I wanted transparency, but in truth, I enjoyed keeping secrets. It wasn't difficult. I enjoyed the ease with which I hid things. I was duplicitous, like my parents, and I loved the feeling of controlling what others knew and didn't know about me. This is what I should tell Brigitte to write about, but to do so would require courage. I pictured Brigitte and David's faces in the bedroom, heads tipping back, David's breath blowing aside strands of Brigitte's hair, her scalp glowing like a lightbulb beneath a mass of black hair. I had loved being on the other side of the door, hidden and close to them.

I thought about Mathilde, who was a cautious woman, who told me women should not salt and pepper their food in public beyond the age of fifty to avoid showing their flabby arms. She rinsed her salad with vinegar to kill any insects. Anouk had chosen her for those secure qualities. She trusted her. Mathilde wore her emotions on her face. She wasn't like us. In a way, she reminded me of Juliette, an open book.

I walked for a long time. The air was thick and wet, almost tropical, and the rain remained suspended in the clouds. When the sky finally broke, yellow light streaked the sidewalk and gigantic drops splattered onto the ground.

The walk home would take almost an hour. By the time I reached Beaubourg, the rain had stopped, and people gathered around the Fontaine Stravinsky. Tourists sat alongside boys and girls my age who used the landmark as a meeting spot. I continued south, past the shoe stores and Châtelet, speeding by the crowds on Île de la Cité and barely glancing at the cathedral. I'd never been inside Notre-Dame. Anouk, who every few years had a sudden yearning for the spiritual, would stop in to light a candle. Once on the other side of the river, I felt an ache in my feet and I slowed down. I was almost there. These were streets I could walk in my sleep: The movie theaters to my right, the entrance of the Jardin du Luxembourg up ahead,

Monoprix followed by the post office, and the sand-colored Panthéon with its bulbous gray dome. Father was proud of us living close to the Panthéon because it housed the remains of his favorite writers.

I turned onto our street and saw a woman and a little girl standing in front of the entrance of our building. I didn't recognize them. The woman was too old to be the girl's mother. I assumed she was the grandmother. She stood over the little girl and shook her finger angrily, chastising her. I paused, not wanting to interrupt them. All of a sudden, the woman slapped the girl. I flinched as though I'd been hit. The girl stayed silent and didn't move. A moment later, they both ran down the street and disappeared around the corner.

Was it like that with Anouk when we argued in public, when we ran to the métro, one marching in front of the other and casting dark glances at each other, jostling the other as we pushed through the turnstile? Did others pause to look at us and, if so, what did they think?

7

I'd never looked forward to Christmas, and in some ways this year felt even more oppressive. Christmas was the time of the year when Father was least available and when we most felt his absence.

Brigitte and David left for Switzerland the following week to spend the holidays with David's family. His parents had moved to Geneva to be closer to their daughter, who lived there with her husband and three children. They'd be gone almost a fortnight.

I read *Bonjour Tristesse* in one sitting a few days before Christmas. I began in the afternoon and I took a break only for dinner. I read in bed late into the night. It was past midnight when I finished, the slim book propped on my chest against the duvet. I hadn't been prepared for the relationship between the narrator, Cécile, and her widowed father—it wasn't an aspect Brigitte had emphasized. But now it shone brightly as the emotional crux of the novel. They were less father and daughter and more friends in their manner of being; they drank together and encouraged each other in their romantic pursuits. In the last chapter, which I read a second time before turning off the lights, Cécile says of her father: *You have only me, and I have only you. We are alone and unhappy.*

I was terribly jealous of their closeness, what Cécile called a companionship, and yet the book also provided comfort in its depiction of sorrow. My sorrow could be like Cécile's, melancholic and beautiful, a silvery trail running behind me on the street and through the lycée's hallways. I fell asleep with the hope of a transformation when morning came, and in some ways, the mood in the apartment warmed, and I found myself seeking out my mother.

We spent a few quiet days leading up to Christmas Eve listening to Diana King and Sade, Father's favorites. Anouk swayed to the music as she arranged gifts under our plastic tree. It was decorated with red and white lights but no ornaments, as we'd never gotten around to buying any. *You think I'd leave your side, baby?* she sang in her androgynous voice, trying to imitate Sade. Her accent was thick, but when she tried, she could sound British.

The previous year we had gone to Strasbourg to spend Christmas Eve with my uncle, Anouk's brother, and his wife, but this year they'd decided to visit a childhood friend in the Alps, close to Chamonix. And so instead, we invited Théo and Mathilde for dinner. We bought a roast chicken with potatoes from the butcher across the street, and they came with bottles of wine, walnut bread, and a beautiful assortment of cheeses: a large block of aged Comté, a ripe Epoisses, an ash-dusted chèvre, and a pungent blue. Anouk unwrapped a block of salted butter. The top was imprinted with a cow and the salt crystals glittered on its surface. I set the cheeses out for later, so the Epoisse's creamy center had time to trickle out onto the board, its flavor blooming at room temperature. Théo assembled a festive salad with dried fruit, hazelnuts, radishes, beets, and large leaves of lettuce that we tore in half before adding to the bowl. We toasted chestnuts on the gas stove as an appetizer. For dessert, Mathilde prepared bowls of her own cherries soaked in eau-de-vie.

We drank two bottles of wine and finished the evening with a sweet Sauternes. The sugar made our stomachs churn, but it also gave us a pleasant high. After Théo and Mathilde had gone home, Anouk and I opened our presents. Anouk gave me a pair of earrings that had once belonged to her. They were shaped like flowers with petals made of rubies. She had also written a short card: *To Margot, from your mother who loves you.* I gave her a cashmere sweater I'd chosen with Father in the summer, on sale at Printemps. It was dark blue and low-cut, to show off her angular collarbones. She wore it for two days straight, and for a short spell we formed a happy family.

The week after Christmas I woke at the crack of dawn and studied until the sun went down. The days were short and dark. I wrote an essay on the difference between manual and intellectual work for Monsieur H.'s class. On the twenty-eighth, Juliette returned from Brittany, where she had spent Christmas with her family. We studied in the afternoons, making note cards for biology, math, and physics-chemistry. We tried to memorize every word, testing each other until we could recite proofs in our sleep.

For New Year's Eve we drank half a bottle of tequila and ate ravioli in Juliette's studio. We cooked the ravioli for too long and the lining ruptured, the ricotta filling dissolving in the water. We covered the empty pouches with cheese.

Juliette asked when I'd be available to help with her film. In the weeks I had spent with Brigitte, she had made admirable progress on the project: The script was finished, and she wanted to begin filming soon. Brigitte and David were coming back in a few days and I hesitated to commit to an entire weekend in case Brigitte needed me. So again, I invented excuses. I said I needed to check with Anouk first, and Théo and Mathilde who complained about not seeing us enough.

Since when does your mother need you? Juliette asked, sounding hurt.

She's been working on a new show for the summer. This one is important because it'll be a solo performance. Autobiographical. She wants to recite lines with me.

I could help her, she offered.

That's very generous of you, but she doesn't like to share her work. She barely shares it with me.

Another lie, since Anouk never rehearsed with me before a show. She could practice lines on her own.

My film can wait a few weeks, Juliette said. I should work on it some more, anyway.

I tried to sound casual as I apologized.

You're not upset with me, are you? she asked.

Not at all. I was just tired, I explained, from all the studying.

It was easier for me to keep these worlds separate and contained, easier for Juliette not to know about a friendship I had with an older woman, the book we were writing, all the stories about Father. She might not like me as much if I were a mass of contradictory selves, if she knew I'd been keeping this other secret from her. I noticed with some relief that she no longer asked if I knew who had leaked the story. I was always nervous someone might mention it. The question reverberated in my head late at night.

A few days later, I had a violent dream about Father. He was shot in the stomach and when I covered his wound, more blood poured through my fingers. I padded him with a towel. He didn't cry out in pain, but I knew he was dying. I saw it in his eyes, the irises losing their shine. I counted the seconds, thinking there was a chance he might live forever. He was wounded but still alive. Now that I had him in my arms, what should I say to reassure him? *Papa,* I said, holding him harder. A faint sob croaked from my mouth. In the dream I could see his eyes, their pale hazel color, but the rest of his face was undefined, it had lost its features—there was no jaw, forehead, no large nostrils to recognize him.

I woke Anouk in the middle of the night to tell her about my nightmare. I'd broken out in a cold sweat and I shivered, barefoot, in the doorway of her room. She lifted herself onto her elbows. It was just a dream, she said. Go back to sleep.

I'm afraid I'm forgetting him, I said.

It's possible you'll forget some things about him.

I keep thinking about those weeks before he died. I should've called him, made more of an effort.

You were upset with him, Margot. It's normal you didn't call him.

But he was ill. Who knows what he was going through—I abandoned him.

Anouk took a deep breath, as if I was testing her patience.

You have to remember that he didn't call you, either. Sometimes you have a tendency to idolize him.

There was a note of anger in her voice and it bothered me. I had expected more empathy.

You forget that he left us, she continued, her voice growing harsher. He died with *them*.

And you probably told him to stay away. I didn't even know that you were no longer together. You could've asked him to come home.

Home! She laughed dismissively. He left us.

What did you do to fight for him?

I grabbed the bedsheet and drew it away from her. Sunspots covered her chest. During the day she hid them with foundation.

You think I pushed him away? she asked calmly, sitting up in bed. You should be all grown up now and you should know better, but you idealize him, you have this grand idea of him, larger than life, a magnificent man. She swept the air with her arms. You think he was flawless.

No, I don't. I felt defensive and I was frustrated by her tone.

Good. In that case you should know he wasn't a faithful man, and I'm not just talking about his wife.

Her words jolted me. What do you mean? I asked.

He went with other women. You would've found out at some point. Better you know it from me.

I sat on the bed and returned the sheet to her, smoothing it over her legs. Were you jealous?

All the time.

But you still stayed with him.

She was silent, as if considering her options.

I was in love. And I didn't know what he was like at first. When I found out, it was too late. She pulled the sheet to her chin. Now I'm going back to sleep. She closed her eyes.

Father had been unfaithful to my mother. How had I not known, and what else didn't I know? Who were these other women? It seemed pointless to ask Anouk more questions. I sat in the darkness of the bedroom, my body a rod of white heat, with the dawning realization that I hadn't known who he was outside of being my father. I would have to tell Brigitte. I don't know who else he's been with and whether he loved Anouk, I'd say. That night, I lay scotched to the bed while Anouk slept, the pale light from the window rippling over her forehead.

8

When David and Brigitte returned to Paris, I waited for her phone call to schedule our next work session. A week went by before she contacted me. She sounded distracted, and I felt like I was imposing by asking when I'd see her next. I've been so busy, she said, and David has a mountain of work, but how about on Thursday?

I wondered if she'd grown less interested in the book. Had the time away from Paris and me changed her priorities? Did she continue to see me only to indulge me, because she pitied a girl who had lost her father? After our call, I couldn't shake the feeling that something was wrong, that her heart was no longer in the project. I had no concrete reason to worry, and yet I grew intensely insecure.

They came back glowing. It was the nourishing mountain air, she said, unlike the smog of Paris that clogged you right up. Her lungs had shriveled at the first contact with the city's toxic fumes when the train pulled into the station. She boasted about their festivities. We were in bed for an entire day after

New Year's, she exclaimed. She had taken eight aspirins to nurse a headache.

I imagined them in Geneva, seated on cushioned chairs around a mahogany table, eating pea soup out of ceramic bowls. A piece of roasted meat with skin that crackled under the blade of a knife. Though in truth, I had no idea what David's family was like, whether they even lived in a house or a small apartment. At night, I was certain Brigitte and David made love. In my imagination, they always stood against the bed. I remembered their sounds as if it were yesterday. His calves straining from the effort. The silence after. With that image alone, my stomach rolled to another depth.

When she opened the door that Thursday evening, Brigitte eyed me from top to bottom and declared I'd put on some weight. I looked healthier, filled out. How was it possible if she'd told me weeks before that I'd lost weight? Could it happen so quickly—had I puffed up from all the wine? It was true I'd eaten more over Christmas, our fridge stocked for the first time in months.

I brushed her comment aside and focused on finishing the book. I wanted to be done so I could dedicate all my time to studying for the Bac. I needed a final grade of at least sixteen out of twenty for a *mention très bien* and to make Father proud. Come spring I'd have exams most Saturday mornings from eight A.M. to noon.

I tried to remember the purpose we'd felt before, the hours of interviews, Brigitte prodding me along with her short questions, the flow of words pouring from me. I sensed she was anxious to finish as well, though a small part of me also worried she'd use it as an excuse to cut me out of her life.

I've told you everything I know, I said. Do you need more?

We're in good shape, she assured me. I have enough material for three books.

Soon she'd have to buckle down and write. Shape the interviews into a compelling narrative. We would need an editor. She had a friend at Gallimard, and she'd begin there.

When I told Brigitte about Father being with other women, a strange expression traversed her face. I thought I saw a gleam in her eyes, but maybe it was disgust.

Do you think he had other children? she asked. You're saying he had other affairs. What if there are more children like you?

I was disturbed by her question; my mind raced to form an intelligent answer.

I told her I hadn't thought about it.

You've never wondered?

If there are others, they're not like me. He probably abandoned them, or never knew about them.

You sound sure.

Do you know something I don't?

No, I only know what you've told me.

Anouk's the one who mentioned his infidelities, and she's not a reliable source. Who knows if it's true? Plus, she's never mentioned anyone specific, just that he was unfaithful in the broader sense.

Brigitte paused, her pen pressing into her notepad. The tips of her fingers were yellow from holding the pen. She tilted her head and smiled.

I only bring it up because I know it's the kind of thing that would keep me up at night, but I'm also prone to imagining the worst possible scenario.

If I knew anything, I'd tell you.

Of course.

I uncrossed my legs. They did seem wider at the thighs, flesh spreading under my black jeans. Brigitte rearranged papers on the coffee table and made two stacks. She pushed one in my direction. Can you take these to David? she asked. I can't stand that he leaves his papers in the living room, when he knows it's my workspace.

I picked up the papers, relieved to step away from her.

Thank you, Margot, she said.

The door to David's office was ajar, revealing towers of books on the floor. His laptop rested on the couch where I'd now slept a few nights. I knocked on the door. Come in, I heard him say.

Brigitte wanted me to give you these, I said, handing him the papers. He thanked me and placed them on the desk.

I know she doesn't like it when I leave my things in her space, he said.

David's legs were too long for his small desk, and they looked uncomfortably folded beneath. He wore a light blue shirt that brought out the color of his eyes. I marveled at how different he was from Brigitte. His energy was boyish, childish at times, caught in the body of a tall, grown man. The few times we'd walked on the street together, I'd noticed women stopping to stare.

As I turned to leave, he called my name. Wait, he said, there's something I've been meaning to tell you.

What is it? I stood near the door, one hand resting on the wooden paneling.

Remember the second time you stayed at our apartment?

I nodded. I'd gone out to dinner with Brigitte at the bistro down the street. The service had been slow, but we'd ordered dessert all the same and by the time we came home it was almost midnight.

Brigitte hadn't warned me you'd be sleeping over, David continued. I came home late from a work event. The apartment was completely silent, the lights turned off, and I assumed Brigitte had gone to sleep. I went to leave my briefcase in the office. When I opened the door, I noticed a shape on the couch. Someone was sleeping there. It had to be Brigitte. It made no sense because we weren't in a fight, but who else could it be? We weren't expecting any guests.

As David spoke, I wondered if he had slept on the couch before when they fought, if their arguments were vicious enough to separate them for a night.

I moved closer to the couch, David said. I spoke Brigitte's name. I think you heard me, because you turned around and then I saw your face. You opened your eyes and said: *No, it's Margot.*

I laughed at this. I had no recollection of seeing him.

The strangest thing is that you didn't say a word about it the next day. Like you'd forgotten. I wanted to apologize for walking in on you, but I didn't want to sound like I'd done it deliberately. It seemed complicated to explain.

How funny. I can't remember you waking me.

I keep thinking about that night. Your eyes were wide open when you said your name. You were lucid.

I'm surprised I didn't scream.

Me too. You weren't scared to find a stranger in the room.

But you're not a stranger.

David smiled and rubbed his forehead with his thumb. Imagine all the weird things people say in the middle of the night, he said.

Perhaps I had been pleased to see him and have his voice rouse me. What else had he said?

Did you leave right after? I asked.

You went back to sleep.

I walked over to his bookcase and ran my fingers over the rows of books. They were arranged by topic: history, politics, gastronomy, cinema. David came by my side and started pulling books from the top shelf. Feel free to borrow any book you like, he said. As he raised his arm to catch another book, he grazed my shoulder. It was a light touch against the material of my shirt. A warm liquid washed over me. I was light-headed. I didn't dare move, hopeful for another swell, and frantic it wouldn't occur again. I closed my eyes and felt a second wave ripple through me. I stepped away from him.

I found Brigitte in the living room, where I'd left her. She was leafing through an art book. She raised her head as I sat on the couch opposite from her.

I was thinking about the first time we met, she said. At your apartment. You seemed unhappy next to your mother. You were scowling, while she radiated confidence. You barely said a word during the interview. And then we met in the hallway.

I remember, you were looking for the bathroom. I was intimidated by you. The long black coat, those leather lace-up shoes, your red lipstick, all your questions.

Brigitte laughed at my description of her, but then her expression turned serious.

You clearly didn't know that your parents were no longer together. I was insensitive, and I hurt you with my nosiness.

I wouldn't have known if you hadn't asked those questions. Anouk didn't speak about their relationship, not to the public and certainly not to me. She probably told only Mathilde.

How come?

She wants to be my mother, not a friend.

Brigitte nodded. She thinks being transparent with you would compromise her authority as a mother.

She's always had these fixed ideas about how she should act with me.

Well, there's something you said that night which I haven't forgotten. You told me you wanted to read my writing.

I wanted you to write the piece.

Brigitte closed the book and placed it on the table. You were flattering me. I was moved by your words. I'm not used to people telling me they want to read my work.

In that moment, I knew Brigitte wanted this book as much as I did.

What else did you think? I asked, trembling with focus. What was your first impression of me?

She took her time answering. Her hands were clasped at her knees. She wore woolen socks, rolled over the bottom of her jeans. She began by telling me about a trip to Jordan.

Two years after they met, she and David had traveled to Jordan. It was the middle of the summer, and their guide was a large man who walked slowly, as if his feet were made of cushions. He didn't sweat, whereas Brigitte's cotton shirt was always plastered to her like a second skin. They drove through the desert, through all the shrubs and rocky terrain. They bobbed in the Dead Sea, and their skin stung from the salt. They walked through the cool shade of Petra. Men offered them hot, sweet tea in small cups. They bought Bedouin silver and let mosquitoes feed on their bodies at night. There was one hotel in particular where she couldn't fall asleep. The bed was a bundle of wire springs that dug into her back. Cockroaches crawled along the walls at night. The restaurant, where they had breakfast and dinner, remained empty during their entire stay. She couldn't remember what they ate. What she remembers, intensely, like a strong white flash, was looking out at the road when they drove. Outside it was hot, like stepping into an oven. For hours she stared at the road and it stared back at her with its wobbly texture, rising and falling, an optical illusion from the heat. She'd never seen something lose its solid properties.

You thought of Jordan when you met me? I asked, in disbelief. I made you think of a road in the desert?

You did, she said. Let me explain. After our meeting, I thought about that road, the way it moved from afar and how it was still when we stepped out of the car and walked on it. It was hard and rippling at the same time. A real mirage. Up until then I'd never questioned my surroundings. I felt superior to my parents, my sister, my classmates. I thought I knew better than anyone else. But just looking at that road made me nauseous and excited. A bit of both. When I met you, I felt something similar to this. You were formed and unformed. You were like me when I was your age.

What do you mean?

I felt like I knew you. It was the boldness of your actions. You were irresponsible. And you had impressed my husband! I assumed you were exuberant, outgoing. Someone who went to parties and got drunk, took drugs, slept around. That kind of *wise beyond her years*. But then I met you and you were so quiet and reserved, blending right into the backdrop, until you spoke to me in the hallway and I saw I'd gotten you wrong. On the surface you were calm and composed, but deep down I recognized that girl, the reckless one, simmering. If you'd seen the way you looked at me.

How did I look at you?

The way men look at me. No, it wasn't quite that. Brigitte shook her head. Like you wanted something from me, something else I could actually give you.

9

I came home to the sound of voices coming from our apartment. Inside, I was surprised to find Juliette and Anouk in the living room, seated on the couch, talking intently.

Margot! I was looking for you, Juliette said. I thought you'd be home.

She's been impossible to find these days, Anouk said.

I was annoyed by Anouk's remark. I could have said the same about her: Lately she'd shut herself in her bedroom and was as remote to me as I was to her. Which made it even more strange to see her curled up with Juliette on the couch.

I went for a walk, I told them, brushing aside Juliette's inquisitive expression. I returned to the entrance to hide the blush in my cheeks. I removed my shoes and hung my coat on the wall.

Back in the living room, Anouk told me to take a seat. I sat across from them on a chair. Juliette had shifted away from my mother. I noticed the way she angled her body toward the armrest, as though to create further separation between them.

Juliette was just telling me about her film, Anouk said. Do you know about it?

Yes, I do, I said.

It bothered me to imagine them chatting away in our apartment for God knows how long. I felt like I'd found them conversing about me and not the film. No matter that I had been with Brigitte, a woman neither one of them knew about.

Go on, Anouk said, encouraging Juliette to speak.

I don't want to take up more of your time. Juliette placed her hands on the couch, as if to stand. I noticed how she avoided my gaze. I'd sidestepped her for weeks now, deflecting her questions, saying I studied better alone in the privacy of my bedroom, saying that Anouk needed me around. What started as an excuse had become second nature.

You should tell her about it, I said. It's a great idea. I tried to control the flush of my skin. The muscles under my cheeks contracted. I looked at Juliette, her eyes open with desire, wanting to please Anouk.

I was inspired by your story, Juliette said, turning to Anouk. The one you told about the women at the buffet who took all the sandwiches.

Ah, yes, at the conference.

The way you described those women snatching up the sandwiches really troubled me, and I kept returning to that image of them huddled around the table, taking more than they could stomach or hold on a plate, while you stood to the side. I knew there was something worth investigating, but I couldn't place my finger on it. Here you are at a conference for women, an event meant to nurture your ties, and it's all gone out the window during lunch. Why? I wrote a script to reflect this dissonance. I imagined a story where women are forced to prey on other women.

Juliette paused and glanced at me, seeking affirmation. Had she practiced these words before coming over? I encouraged her onward with a nod.

The story takes place in a remote village in the countryside, she continued. The mayor of the village is always a woman, and she is selected through a biting ritual. Every ten years, women from the village between the ages of eighteen and forty gather in the town hall. One by one the women take turns biting the old mayor until she dies. The one who delivers the fatal bite becomes the new mayor.

Anouk smiled. I like this, a woman being bitten to death by another woman, who then takes her place.

Margot will play both mayors, Juliette said.

Is that so? Anouk turned to me. And how will you do that? You've never acted before.

The scene will be composed of close-ups, Juliette explained. I'll focus on her skin, and then her face, separately.

You should show as little gore as you can. Have blood only when it is necessary. Leave the rest to the viewer's imagination.

Juliette wrote in her notebook as Anouk spoke. I observed my mother, the comfortable position of her legs crossed one over the other, her hand moving in tandem to her words. She must be a compelling teacher, I thought.

Do you know anything about a play I was in called *Mère?* Anouk asked.

You were the star, Juliette said. I've read the reviews.

The brilliance of that play was in the ending and what happened off the stage. In the climactic scene, I'm kneeling in front of a bathtub with my back to the audience. They've been made to believe that my children are in the tub, although it's only filled with water. I speak to them gently. Moments later, when I kill them, the audience sees my arms thrashing in the water. Meanwhile, off the stage, the young actors who play my children start to scream. Their cries are amplified with speakers throughout the theater. See, what you need is a trigger, something to activate the viewer's imagination, like the children's cries. Better to suggest the violence.

Juliette considered Anouk's words in silence. What if I show the old mayor's hands and feet as she's getting bitten? she asked shyly. I could show them curling, arching, tensing with pain.

Her toes scraping against the floor, Anouk said.

It's just like *Trouble Every Day*, I said, the words flying out of my mouth without a second thought.

What's that? Juliette asked.

A horror film by Claire Denis, Anouk said. It's about lust and cannibalism. Her voice was rich with pleasure. How did you know about that movie? she asked me. I didn't know we had a copy.

Someone lent it to me.

Your father loved Claire Denis, but he could never stomach horror films. I don't think he saw that one. Anouk swiftly turned her attention back to Juliette, and I felt she was deliberately avoiding looking at me. My ears lit up with heat.

So much of the violence in that film, I added, is witnessing the actor's face contort in pain, but not immediately seeing where that pain is being inflicted.

I shivered, remembering the final scene where the man seduces a woman he's been following throughout the film. They kiss against her locker in the changing room of the hotel where she works. He draws her to the floor and undresses her, kissing her stomach. Her face flushes with pleasure, but as the man bites into her, that same desire is replaced with pain, and her moans become cries of terror.

Juliette said she would look for the film, or perhaps I could lend it to her. I wondered if I could borrow it from Brigitte, or take it and replace it without her noticing. I thought about this as I listened to Juliette thanking Anouk for her advice, saying she now felt better equipped to make this film. She knew what to do.

No, you don't know, Anouk answered. You *shouldn't* know. The knowing will unfold once you're behind the camera and then during the editing.

The best stories are created when you surrender to uncertainty, I said, quoting a line Anouk often repeated. She laughed in approval and patted my shoulder. Sometimes I knew how to please her.

I asked Juliette if she wanted to stay for dinner, but she said she needed to go home and finish the philosophy essay. I accompanied her to the door. She glanced at me as she tied her shoes.

You're not upset that I came over unannounced, are you? I called you twice, but your phone was off.

I placed my hand on her arm and caressed the fabric of her shirt, old and soft. I'd worn it once. An unfamiliar tenderness throbbed in my chest, as if we were losing each other. You can always come over, I said.

Where were you this afternoon?

Just nearby. The Jardin du Luxembourg. I spoke vaguely, waiting for the lie to crack through the surface of my face.

She kissed me goodbye and slipped on her coat.

I lingered in the doorway, watching her step onto the stairs. I waved with more energy than usual. Get home safely! I cried out.

Most mornings I woke at five thirty to finish studying for tests. I resented Anouk for staying in bed for another hour or two. How easy her adult life seemed from the outside.

I decided I'd skip the entrance exams for Sciences Po, not that Father was here to judge me or care. Instead I'd sign up to study anthropology, psychology, or literature at one of the universities. It was easier this way, to choose an innocuous subject, and a small part of me was inspired by Brigitte's career as a writer. She had a doctorate in psychology. Until then I believed we were bound to the subject we'd chosen in high school. Anouk had studied at a prestigious conservatoire before joining the Comédie-Française, and Father at l'Ecole normale supérieure, while his sons had studied at the London School of Economics. Who did I have to impress? Anouk, who never asked about my grades? And what kind of job would I hold one day? These concerns were fleeting, as our lives felt consumed by preparations for the Bac, just five months away.

We were troubled by one disturbance. Monsieur H. took a leave of absence for two weeks. It was unheard of at our school; teachers rarely missed a class, especially in *terminale*, our last year. They replaced him with an older teacher who taught a different section and whose curriculum made no sense to us.

He graded one of our essays and gave us all below twelve. Philosophy was one of the least important subjects for us science students; it had the lowest coefficient for the Bac, but we liked Monsieur H. His class provided respite from the mathematical proofs and chemistry experiments. He was the one teacher to ask whether we slept enough, at least seven hours a night, and defended us at the end of the trimester during the *conseil de classe,* when the teachers discussed our grades with the class representative.

Someone claimed to have seen him in the fifteenth, disheveled, carrying two shopping bags. Another person said his wife had left him for a famous photographer who worked in Australia. We hadn't known he was married. Or perhaps he wasn't married. These were all rumors that remained unsubstantiated until his return.

Monsieur H. came back in mid-February without a word of excuse. Until his sudden departure, we hadn't thought about the lives of our teachers outside of the classroom. For us, they existed only as teachers within the confines of the school. It was a small glimpse into their mysterious interior worlds, and then it was over, and we once more drowned in schoolwork, lost in our own worlds.

I had dreams about David. They were mostly innocuous—us having a conversation in the kitchen, him disguised as a teacher at school. Another time I dreamed of him on the street, walking with a woman who wasn't Brigitte. And then one night I had a dream about the two of us. We were in his office. I sat across from him on a chair. He took a fountain pen from his desk. The cap was on and he showed me its rounded shape.

Underneath the cap was the pointed tip. He walked over to me and touched the top of my jeans. I felt his fingers pull the seam away from my stomach, the material stretching like distended elastic. He held the fountain pen in his right hand and slipped it into my underwear. He started to dip the pen in and out, rubbing the smooth cap against my skin. He moved slowly at first. Pleasure began to build in my crotch, and something else, a stickiness between my thighs, shame dripping to my feet. He dipped the pen lower until his fingers reached me. Heat rippled through my legs and I tipped my head back against the chair. I noticed a warm breath on my neck. Brigitte's voice whispered into my ear: *Do you like that?* Her lips pressed against my neck. I felt the cold hardness of teeth as her mouth opened.

I opened my eyes, hands cradling my hot stomach. How terrific, I thought, that a dream could arouse me so, as if breath could turn into flesh.

10

Brigitte and I met at her favorite café on a Sunday morning to celebrate the end of our work together. There would be no more interviews; she'd gathered everything she needed from me. Moving forward she would work alone, channeling my voice from the hours of conversations I'd transcribed from the tape recorder onto her computer.

The temperature had plunged. A cold dampness seeped through my shoes within minutes of stepping outside. The end of our street was cloaked in a dense mist and the tops of our buildings disappeared into the white sky. I ran into the café. I saw Brigitte sitting at the counter, her long hair draped over her shoulders. It was slippery and shiny like in a shampoo ad.

The energy between us felt charged and tense. I sat on a stool next to hers. Steam rose from us and onto the windows. Brigitte ordered two brioches and a tea for herself. I asked for coffee. I'd taken the last empty seat at the counter, and we had to draw in our elbows to fit.

Cheers to us, Brigitte said, when our hot drinks arrived. She sounded neither happy nor sad.

I thanked her for helping me with the book. If it wasn't for you, I'd never have opened up about my father.

All I did was ask you questions. I still have to write it, you know. There's a lot of work on my end. Plus, I have two new articles with deadlines next month. She sounded annoyed, making me wonder again if the book was an unwanted burden and she had grown bored of it. I couldn't pay her, and here she had already given me hours of her time.

I thanked her again, saying I hoped it wasn't too much trouble, that she should take her time because unlike for the articles, we didn't have a deadline.

I'm used to juggling many projects.

Her smile was small, and I had to squint to see it.

Are you feeling all right? I asked. You sound a bit off.

She sipped on her tea and apologized for her bad mood. She'd gone to the doctor yesterday and was irritated by his attitude. The doctor had asked about David, who was also his patient, and when Brigitte complained, saying he stayed at work too late, was rarely home with her, the doctor told her she should try to be more agreeable. Maybe your husband is avoiding you, he'd said.

You should find another doctor, I told Brigitte.

He thinks I'm to blame for not getting pregnant. It always amazes me when a man tells you how to act, offers his advice, as if he knows what we're going through, what *I'm* going through. It requires empathy to tell another person how to be. You have to put yourself in their position and imagine what you'd do if you were the same human being, with the same motivations and history. It's almost impossible for a man to do this, especially with a woman who is trying to get pregnant.

Our brioche arrived. Brigitte picked at it, rolling the pieces between her fingers. The slices were thick with a pale crumb. On the side was a small bowl of raspberry jam.

What did you tell the doctor? I asked.

She laughed. Her laughter rattled in her throat like an animal with sharp teeth.

I told him having sex with the goal of conceiving isn't the most romantic thing. Here I am, trying to seduce my husband when he's home, which is almost never, and this doctor tells me to be a better wife? Do you know what David's mother told me? Over Christmas, she took me aside and said that maybe I wasn't meant to have children, and it would be better for both of us if I let it go.

His mother sounds like a horrible woman.

I've never been good enough for her.

Maybe she's jealous of you.

Her son is a grown man and she still protects him. I know it's normal for her to take his side, but it bothers me.

How about David—does he defend you? Does he want children?

Brigitte spread some jam on the brioche and took a bite. She chewed slowly. Her voice was wistful when she spoke. Like most men, he's afraid of getting old, losing his vibrancy. He's always wanted to be a father and to be free at the same time. Two incompatible desires.

I thought about Brigitte's toes curling against the wooden

floor of their bedroom. What did she mean that David wasn't home? Each time I was there, I saw a strip of light beneath his office door.

Anyway, I've never trusted doctors all that much, Brigitte said, finishing her slice of brioche. My mother once took me to a doctor. This old man who chain-smoked between his appointments. He wanted me to remove my clothes in front of her. I knew she'd notice my fat legs, the overflow of my belly, the stretch marks striping my thighs. I weighed barely fifty kilos, but I thought I was fat. I took off my clothes. I felt violated. She was seeing me naked for the first time.

Just as Brigitte finished her sentence, we were interrupted by a man's voice. I glanced over my shoulder. I didn't recognize him. He was of average stature and wore a brown wool coat and a gray hat. Brigitte Duarte, he said, slapping her shoulder.

Brigitte turned to face the man, and her eyes focused in recognition.

Hello, Georges, she said. Her voice was cold. I could tell she wasn't happy to see him.

Is this how you greet your cousin? He leaned in and kissed her three times on the cheeks. I smelled sweat under his coat, sour like wet wool. I knew Brigitte would hate it, would call it a foul stench.

She introduced me, saying I was a friend. Pleasure to meet you, he said. He laughed at Brigitte. You have young friends. It must be what city life does to you.

Her smile was strained. Do you live here now? she asked.

No, just visiting for the day. I like to come in from time to time. Watch a movie on the Champs-Elysées and take the last train out at night. I was walking down the street and saw you through the window. I couldn't believe my luck.

Georges leaned forward and breathed heavily onto us. His teeth had brown lines running through them like bark. I wanted to close his mouth.

What a coincidence, Brigitte said.

You never visit us. He spoke quickly, almost interrupting her. What about your mother? Don't you want to see her? You know she's cleaning houses, even with her arthritis.

Does she ask to see me?

She doesn't need to.

Brigitte was silent.

She's your mother. You could send her some money at least.

She doesn't have a kind bone in her body.

Brigitte opened her bag and pulled out her wallet. There was such violence in her gestures that I thought she might pay Georges to leave us alone. Or slam the wallet on his head. Her fingers shook as she placed a few coins on the counter. Excuse us, we have an appointment, she said, taking her coat from under the counter. We have to go.

I stood at the same time as Brigitte, my coffee almost untouched.

I'll send my regards, Georges said, yelling after us.

Once we were outside, Brigitte did little to hide her rage. She stormed down the street without stopping to put on her coat. I shivered at the sight of her, thin arms hanging under the sleeves of her sweater. This is why I left home, she said. Because of people like him.

I struggled to keep up with her brisk walk. We were almost

at her apartment. I was stunned by their differences. The loose-
ness of his sentences, how he imposed himself with his chest.
She hadn't slipped once during their conversation, addressing
him with the formal *vous,* articulating each word with care, a
teacher speaking to a young student.

I was out of breath when we arrived in front of her building.
You have to protect yourself from your family, Brigitte said. If
they're bullying you, it's best to cut them out of your life.
When we were kids, Georges used to fondle me at family dinners. That way I'd know what to do later, because no guy
wanted an inexperienced girl, he liked to say. He used to watch
me and my sister. When I turned ten, I begged my parents to
let us stay alone without his supervision.

The words fell from her mouth in a hurried whisper. She
paused, biting her lip. We stepped into the cool entrance, the
heavy door shutting behind us. It smelled like concrete.

All that talk about forgiveness, Brigitte said—her voice
softening now, slowing down to a more controlled pace—all
that talk about people changing: It's a waste of time. People
forgive when they haven't really known hardship or don't have
the courage to push back.

What did that make me, I wondered, if I had forgiven Father for saying I wasn't his daughter, Anouk not the love of his
life? Should I have been harder on him? Was it a sign of weakness? Perhaps it was different, forgiving someone who had
died.

I lingered by the door as Brigitte searched for her keys. She
looked up at me. Her eyes were black, the pupils large, barely
rimmed by her whites. I'm sorry we left like that, she said. You
didn't even get to finish your brioche.

Don't worry about it. I smiled warmly.

I wanted to ask you something before Georges barged in on us. The keys clinked at the bottom of her bag. David and I are going to his family's house in the south, just outside of Nîmes. We're spending ten days there. Do you want to come for a few days? I was thinking you could take the train down for a long weekend. It might be nice for you to leave Paris. You can bring your homework and study. You'd have your own room with a desk.

I had two weeks of holidays at the end of February and was planning on staying home. I pretended to consider her words, but I knew I'd say yes. I would tell Anouk I was with Juliette and I could disappear for two nights and Anouk wouldn't bat an eye. That is how I perceived my mother: oblivious and careless.

Brigitte stood by the stairway holding her keys. She looked at me expectantly, waiting for an answer.

Yes, I said. I would love to spend a weekend with you and David.

11

The journey to Nîmes was three hours long, and during that time I stared through the window of the train, unable to read any of the books I'd brought along. The sky transformed from thick, knotted clouds above lush green meadows to a pale blue with spots of light. We sped by small towns perched above hills and fields separated by lines of trees. I placed my cheek against the window to feel its coolness, not minding the layer of grime on the glass.

If Father were alive today, what would he be doing? I was aware of someone sitting beside me, a woman who had boarded the train after me. I could smell her, a combination of floral perfume and laundry detergent. Father didn't like the train—he preferred to drive even if it took twice as long—so it was hard to imagine us ever traveling together like this. His car was a carapace with darkened windows to hide us. Saliva pooled under my tongue and I swallowed. I thought about whether the book with Brigitte would bring me close to Madame La-pierre. There was almost nothing about her in my interviews with Brigitte because I didn't know enough private details about her life. I imagined reading about us would help her understand what my life had been like.

The train slowed down as it pulled into the station. It was just shy of noon. I took my bag from under my feet and stepped out onto the platform. The air was warmer than in Paris, and the sky overflowed with light from a large sun.

David waited for me outside of the train station. I tried to banish the memory of my dream as I walked toward him, but I couldn't shake the vividness of it. I had to remind myself that David hadn't been there; the experience was mine alone.

He stood next to a silver car, wearing a wrinkled shirt and black jeans. The creases around his eyes deepened as he smiled. I'd grown used to the lines on his forehead, no longer saw them as wrinkles, nor did I think of us as separated by an enormous gulf. We stepped into the car.

He told me about his parents, both architects who designed the house together. Halfway through the renovations they ran out of money and never finished, leaving some walls unpainted and doors with missing knobs. Now they lived in Switzerland because of their daughter, David's older sister, and took care of her two children when she was at work. How boring Geneva was, David said. Everything there closes at dusk. By six P.M. you think it's the dead of night.

Brigitte told me you both had a good time over Christmas, I said.

I was glad to come back to Paris, David replied.

Because of your work?

Does she say I'm a workaholic? He laughed and looked at me.

She admires those who work hard.

We spoke in even tones, our conversation smooth and calm as the surface of a lake, while beneath our legs kicked madly. I stared at his hands on the steering wheel and felt heat rise from them. We drove along a flat road with a view of dark green mountains in the distance. There were no other cars on the road, and soon David released one hand from the wheel and placed it on his lap.

We turned onto a gravel driveway and drove slowly toward a house painted in white. The second floor had wide windows with wooden shutters. The roof was covered in terra-cotta tiles. I spied a patch of turquoise in the garden, the corner of a swimming pool.

I followed David through the wooden door and into the entrance. The floor was made of beige tiles. Its clean, polished surface prompted me to remove my shoes. Brigitte was nowhere to be seen. David showed me my room on the second floor. The window was open, and white muslin curtains billowed in and out like a woman's skirt blowing away from her legs. I closed the window. Here's an example of an unfinished room, he said, and indeed, streaks of white paint revealed a concrete wall beneath. The room was sparsely furnished with a small desk, an antique rocking chair, and a curved lamp hanging over a narrow bed. I placed my bag on the bed. David stood in the doorway, tapping his fingers against the jamb. My neck felt hot, and for a moment I had a powerful desire to fly into his arms. Come downstairs when you're ready, he said. Brigitte is in the kitchen preparing lunch.

I washed my hands in the bathroom down the hallway. The reflection of my face repulsed me. Those dark bags under my eyes and those large pale lips fading right into my face. I rubbed my cheeks and bit my lips.

I walked to the other end of the hallway and opened the door onto Brigitte and David's bedroom. The bed was covered in a white duvet, the sheet ironed and crisp, tucked into the sides under the mattress. Their clothes had been put away, perhaps in the large armoire.

I made my way downstairs to the kitchen. Brigitte was at the stove, steam pluming around her face. You've arrived, she exclaimed. Do you like the house?

It's beautiful, I said, looking around.

Her citrus scent settled around me. How did she always manage to smell fresh, even when cooking? She strode across the kitchen and arranged a bowl of sliced bread. Lunch is almost ready, she said. She picked a speck of parsley from her arm. If we wear sweaters, jackets, and socks, we can eat in the garden, she added.

That same colossal sun from midday warmed us despite it being chilly outside. Brigitte had prepared stewed mussels and a green salad with pickled fennel. The shells swum in a garlic and white wine sauce with bits of bacon. I hadn't tasted the sea in a long time. It reminded me of the restaurant in Normandy, the chef who was Father's friend. I'd drunk three glasses of water throughout the meal and even the following morning I'd felt parched from the salt.

Where did you learn to cook? I asked. Everything you make is delicious. I swished a piece of bread in the broth.

Trial and error. I've been doing this for twenty years. You eventually learn. My mother wasn't a good cook, she said. We ate a lot of pasta and Uncle Ben's rice. Jarred tomato sauce.

Macédoine salad from a can with enough mayonnaise to kill you. I took it upon myself to learn. But it was difficult because I had no one to observe. The best way to learn is to watch someone else. Cooking is all about movements, little gestures here and there. It's like a dance. Most of those moves are intuitive to the cook, who doesn't think twice about them. So you have to look closely. Stand right next to them. Absorb the dance.

I have friends who are proud of not knowing how to cook, she continued, serving herself a small mound of salad. She folded the leaves into squares before putting them in her mouth. For them, being in the kitchen is the ultimate symbol of the housewife. But I've never thought of it as a domestic activity. For me, learning to cook was a sign of education, being better than my parents. My mother called me a fat girl, but she didn't give me the tools to eat well, so what was I supposed to do, aside from starving myself?

She leaned back and held her stomach with both hands. It bulged ever so slightly. She closed her eyes. I've eaten too much, she said, and now I feel like a boa.

I wondered excitedly if she was pregnant, but when she sat up, a minute later, I saw she was the same, not an extra gram on her.

David and I carried the dishes indoors and piled them in the sink. I observed Brigitte through the window. A gust of wind rustled the branches above her head, and she snapped her eyes open. The sun had disappeared. David placed his hands on my waist to move me aside, away from the sink. Let me do the dishes, he said. Their warm imprint stayed with me as I went upstairs to my room.

I unpacked my few articles of clothing and placed them on hangers. I heard footsteps on the stairs, and a moment later Brigitte pushed my door open. She sat on the bed and yawned, covering her mouth a moment too late.

I wanted to know when she had first come to this house.

A few months after meeting David. They'd wanted to travel somewhere just the two of them. His parents' summer-house was the best option. Cheaper than booking a flight and a hotel room in another city, and less of a commitment. Back then the house was run-down, almost abandoned. His parents came once a year at the most and barely maintained it the rest of the time.

They arrived late one night in April. The furniture was dusty, and there was no food in the kitchen. They slept in the master bedroom. She was convinced she could smell David's parents in the sheets, which were slightly damp from the humid, cold spring and obviously hadn't been changed in months. The next day she woke early, washed the sheets, and vacuumed every room, while David drove to the nearest su-permarket. By the time he returned, the sheets were hanging to dry in the garden, the cobwebs dusted, and the bathroom spar-kling clean. She'd used half a bag of stale grinds to make a strong pot of coffee, and just the smell of it brewing had re-vived her after a night of fitful sleeping.

I started to fall in love with him that weekend, she said, or at least this is how I remember it. Maybe because we were in an isolated house, and something about our productivity, us fall-ing into the roles of husband and wife, made it all the more romantic. Back then I imagined spending my entire life with him, although every projection remained in the present, was immediate, even if I tricked myself into thinking I knew what I wanted for the rest of my life.

Do you still feel that way? I asked.

Brigitte stared absently through the window. It was partially hidden by the white curtains. Naked tree branches swayed in the wind.

Now I look at David, she said, and I can see him moving on a different track. I can see a separation between us much more clearly, our differences. And sometimes I wonder what it would be like to step away from him.

To leave him? I asked, tentative.

No, not like that. It's more an out-of-body feeling. As if I'm seeing him from a faraway place but I'm standing right next to him.

You look very in love, I said, my voice gaining confidence. Like a young couple who just met yesterday.

Do we? She raised her eyebrows.

Yes.

Brigitte laughed and stood from the bed. Careful, Margot. If you continue to flatter me, I'll never let you go.

I wondered if there was anything wrong with wanting to keep me forever.

We spent the afternoon downstairs, Brigitte writing on her laptop while I studied for a biology test. David had gone out to run errands and didn't return until nightfall. We ate dinner at the small round table in the kitchen. Pasta with a lemon cream sauce and a bottle of white wine.

After dinner, I asked Brigitte for a towel. I wanted to shower before going to bed. She showed me the closet upstairs where they kept their linens. The towels were rough and worn thin. I chose a green one.

There was no heat in the bathroom and I shivered as I finished removing my clothes, the tiles cold under my bare feet. I stepped into the tub and turned on the water. It took a few minutes to warm. Once it was hot, I held the nozzle over my shoulders, waiting for the heat to penetrate my bones, turn my skin scarlet, soften me.

I was shampooing my hair when I heard a loud knock and Brigitte's voice asking if she could bother me for a moment. She walked right in without waiting for an answer. I crouched in the tub. She was looking for a cream, she said. She opened the cabinet below and stuck her hand inside.

I continued to shower. What else could I do? I rinsed my hair and washed my armpits. She ran her fingers over a row of jars until she found what she was looking for. A small jar that she placed on the counter. She wiped the sink with a sponge. I glanced at her reflection in the mirror. Our eyes met. I could see my small brown nipples, the lift of my collarbones, hair wet and flattened around my face. She leaned into the mirror and rubbed her eyelids, as if it were a window she could see through, not a material that reflected everything behind her, including me.

I wrapped myself in the green towel and stepped out of the tub. Here, Brigitte said, sliding a mat beneath my feet. I thanked her.

She looked out of place in the bathroom in her jeans and socks.

It's obvious you're at ease in your skin, she said. I wish I'd been like you.

Water trickled down my legs. I didn't dare move the small towel along my body to dry myself. Brigitte's face was damp from the steam, and she wiped her upper lip. Strands of black hair stuck to her cheeks. Was she telling the truth—did she admire me? When I'm older, I said to her, I want to be like you. She laughed then, in a way that exposed the tendons on her neck. Her gesture was at once strained and joyful, and I had no other remedy but to laugh with her.

12

I waited for sleep to come, but I was wide awake thinking about Brigitte in the bathroom. What I'd give to see her unclothed. Women were quicker to undress in front of other women because we thought our bodies shared more similarities. I wish I'd been like you, she'd said. But did I really carry myself with confidence? How did she not see me wince at my own reflection?

Anouk's influence had penetrated me after all these years. She walked around oblivious to her body, she stepped into pants without looking at her legs, she never seemed to get in the way of herself. I heard Juliette complain of jeans being too tight after a meal, a button popped, and I felt the same fluctuations in myself, some days better than others. My skin flared up; my hair grew oily. Anouk had imperfections, of course, like a slackness around her buttocks, wrinkles around her knuckles, brown spots on her chest, gaps between her teeth, pink gums that showed whenever she smiled. But she paid so little attention to those flaws that they quickly became inconsequential. Father had always made a point of complimenting me. *Tu es tellement belle, ma chérie,* he would say. I'm not beautiful, I'd reply, as his words sparkled through me.

In the darkness, my eyes grew accustomed to the unfamiliar bedroom: the blue contours of a dresser, the chair by the window with its woven seat, frames hanging on the walls. I couldn't remember the images they housed. I pushed back the covers and stepped out of the bed. I pulled on a wool sweater over my nightgown.

Downstairs the lights were off. The clean dishes were piled on the counter, ready to be put away in the morning. Through the window above the sink I saw the moon and a sky speckled with white stars, a sight we rarely saw in Paris, where the sky remained clogged with pollution. I opened the sliding doors onto the garden.

At first I didn't see David by the pool. He sat on a plastic chair. He wore the same jeans as earlier in the day but had changed his button-down for a long-sleeved cotton top. I wondered how long he'd been sitting here; it was too cold to stay outside without a sweater. I walked in his direction. Brigitte? I heard him ask. Brigitte, he had said to me while I slept in his office.

It's me.

He smiled as he saw me approach. What are you doing here?

I couldn't sleep. I sat on a chair next to his.

Are you having a good time? I don't know how much fun it is for you to be in the middle of the countryside with a middle-aged couple. I'd be bored out of my mind.

I love being here.

I didn't think of Brigitte and David as middle-aged. They belonged to a younger generation than my parents and their friends, who blurred together as one group firmly rooted in middle age. Old. A breeze raked the swimming pool, and its surface glimmered. Even at night the water reflected the sky with white shapes.

I like how the house looks abandoned at night, David said, pointing to the shuttered windows. We don't know if anyone's there.

Brigitte is asleep, isn't she?

She sleeps like she's dead.

I couldn't see the outline of his mouth, but I tasted his words on my tongue.

What was she like when you first met her? I asked.

She didn't have a lot of money, David began. She came to Paris with what she'd saved over the summer. She lived off a government scholarship and worked in the evenings and weekends. She handed out flyers at a department store and stocked the aisles of Carrefour on weekdays before it opened. She had to be there at four in the morning.

David squinted at the pool, as if trying to remember something important.

Did she have any friends? I asked.

Not many, but there was one friend, a woman she met at one of those jobs. She was just a few years older. Her name was Anaïs. They liked each other and decided to live together. Brigitte was able to move out of her tiny maid's room near Château Rouge and into a two-bedroom apartment with a full kitchen. At first Brigitte and Anaïs lived in harmony. They worked different hours and were rarely home at the same time, and when they were, they shared a meal and spoke about their day.

A few months in, though, Anaïs started to act out of character. She became irritable, and Brigitte assumed she had troubles at work. But then Anaïs started what Brigitte called a war of small aggressions. She left empty cans and bottles and dirty dishes at Brigitte's bedroom door if they weren't recycled or washed right away. She used her shampoo and soap, ate her food, leaving all but a few leaves of salad in the bag or the rind of a cheese. She no longer greeted Brigitte in the morning. Instead she marched right past her, as if they were fighting. One day Brigitte noticed Anaïs was dressed like her. It started with the same jeans and shoes, then cutting her hair in a similar style.

Had he already met Brigitte then?

They met right around that time. David thought Anaïs was harmless. A lonely woman in her twenties who hadn't formed her own identity. Maybe she envied Brigitte. She had greasy hair, a body without distinction, needle-thin lips. She wore thick-rimmed glasses before switching to contact lenses, which only further emphasized her small eyes and pale eyelashes.

When David slept over, they avoided Anaïs. He encouraged Brigitte to find her own apartment. Brigitte became obsessed with her roommate. She thought Anaïs wanted to steal David from her. He was amused by the situation and often joked about Anaïs. It was cruel. He had no interest in being with Anaïs, not that it wasn't unsettling for him to see her walk through the apartment in the same clothes and perfume as Brigitte.

One evening, a few weeks into their relationship, David

and Brigitte were in bed. Anaïs wasn't in her room. They'd just finished having sex. They were always more relaxed when she wasn't there, and they laughed and spoke freely. All of a sudden, Brigitte heard a noise from under the bed. She jumped up and looked underneath. What she found there shocked her. There she was, Anaïs, flat on her back and staring at the mattress. She didn't move, like a child pretending to be invisible. That very night, Brigitte packed her bags and left.

As David finished speaking, I felt a sadness for Anaïs. We didn't know her motives, her side of the story, why she'd chosen Brigitte. I pictured these two women circling each other in the apartment, one a pale version of the other, defining themselves according to and against the other. He was right. There was something cruel in how Brigitte had treated Anaïs.

We didn't speak for a few minutes. We sat side by side listening to the rustle of the shrubs in the garden. I stared at the sky. A cluster of dark gray clouds obscured the moon. It shone a softer yellow and lit up the edges of the other clouds. I wondered if I should go to bed. I waited for David to ask me a question, but he remained silent, his eyes fixed on the water.

I walked over to the pool. The wind had settled and the air was still, almost warm, though I knew the water was too cold for swimming.

In the summer we swim in the mornings, David said, when the wasps are asleep. They spend most of the day buzzing over the water. They rarely sting, but it's annoying.

I dipped my toes into the water and wiped them against the brick, the water colder than I expected. I wrapped my arms around my chest. David stayed on his plastic chair, a few feet away from the pool, his face obscured. His long legs looked more impressive when he was seated, forming a perfect right angle at the knees. I noticed his feet were also bare.

Aren't you cold? I asked, gesturing at his feet.

He shook his head.

I took a few steps along the pool's edge, away from him.

Come here, he said.

I turned around and walked over to him. Now I saw his face better. I found his slightly crooked nose handsome. His features were dramatic in the dark, shadows accentuating the angles of his jaw and forehead.

I stood next to him in an awkward stance, my hand resting on the chair. For once I towered over David. He sat deeply in the chair, a bit slouched with his hands dangling over the armrests. He straightened his back and looked at me, his eyes moving up and down my nightgown, an old cotton slip that stopped at my knees, and the loose sweater I'd put on at the last minute to stay warm. The parts of me that were covered instantly lit up, glowing hot like a bulb. He couldn't see a thing, not even the rise of my nipples, hard from the cold, or the curve of my hips. He placed an arm around my waist and drew me closer. I rested lightly against his torso. We stayed there for what felt like a long time.

I could almost touch the current between us. It vibrated like a rope being pulled by two opposing forces. His palm warmed me through the cotton material. He moved his fingers along my waist, back and forth, in tiny movements.

A moment later, he pulled me onto his knees and placed his other arm around me. I sat perched on his legs, the tip of my toes on the ground. I didn't turn around to look, but I imagined a small space between my back and his torso. His thighs were broader than mine, filled with dense muscle. I felt myself soften and my heels fell to the ground, my legs spreading against his. I shifted into his lap until I was entirely ensconced in him, his stomach against my spine and his shoulders rounding over mine. I'd never been held by someone his width before. The boys I knew were skinny and often the same height as me. The closest Father and I got to hugging was when he took my hands at the kitchen table, the last time I saw him. I liked feeling enveloped in David's arms. I was surprised by his soft stomach. It seemed to vibrate, as if he was holding something in.

I felt a hard shape grow against my thigh, first a slight bump and then it was all I could feel, pulsing hard and soft, his arousal so palpable it took me by surprise. A part of me still believed he didn't perceive me this way, that whatever desire I felt existed only in my dreams.

We ignored the hardness at first, our stomachs barely inflating. My legs trembled against his. If Brigitte happened to look through the window, she would spot movement before seeing the distinct shapes of our bodies.

David's breath warmed my neck. An unformed image of a woman like Anaïs flitted through my mind. She stretched out under the bed and ignored the crick in her neck, an itch on her leg, heat spreading above her. The same way I had experienced the pleasure of hearing them through a closed door.

I parted my legs. My feet hung on either side of him. I brought my hand down to the coarse material of David's jeans and ran my fingers over him. I couldn't feel anything other than a hard shape along his thigh. I continued to sweep my fingers, back and forth.

Wait, he said.

Out of the corner of my eye I saw him turn his head, look away from me, his jaw clenched. Maybe he regretted taking me into his lap. He shuddered and for a moment I wasn't sure if it was from pleasure.

Margot. He spoke my name in a pained voice, but he was still hard. I expanded my caress, touching what I thought was the most sensitive part. My fingers burned now. I used my thumb to apply pressure, running down his length. I pressed into him.

His breathing became heavier and humid. He brushed my hair around my shoulder, exposing my neck. I waited for him to kiss me, but he didn't. Instead his hands slid along my stomach, down to my legs, under my nightgown. His fingers were rough against my bare skin. He grasped my legs in place, and for the first time I felt a flicker of fear. He was much stronger, and older, and we were alone. Perhaps he sensed a change in me because he released his hold. I noticed I'd stopped caressing him, had been holding my breath. He smoothed down the material of my nightgown.

Slowly, I started touching him again. I circled up to the warm skin above his jeans. It would be so easy to unzip him and take him into my hands, my mouth, or deeper even. I wanted to wrap my fingers around him and yet I also wanted to live in this moment for as long as I could. If I closed my eyes I could imagine, over and over again, holding him in my hands, squeezing tighter, feeling him explode. We could stop. It wasn't too late.

There isn't a moment I can pinpoint as to when I tipped over. In another life I may have hesitated, moved away from

David. But what I did next felt like something I should do. I thought about Brigitte's wishes to step away from him, how she walked into the bathroom and disfigured me with her gaze. I was naked in front of her just like she was with her mother in that doctor's office, so many years ago. I recognized it now. The humiliation. I thought about sex vibrating through David's clothes right into my hands.

I undid the button of his jeans. My nightgown draped over his knees. I rose onto my toes and pushed aside my underwear with one hand. We didn't move for a few seconds. Then I lifted myself just high enough to slide him inside.

I felt it, the sharp thrill of being entered by someone new. The sensation would fade the moment he was carried away, already I felt his hands gripping tighter, pushing me down and then up. The moment he groaned or gasped, I'd feel pleasure drain from me like water being sucked down a hole.

But there was restraint in his gestures. He pushed himself deeper and held me there. He was scared or no longer wanted me.

I had an intense yearning to unlock him. I wanted him to lose control. This thought alone turned me inside out and drenched me. How to give him pleasure. I closed my eyes and saw sparks behind my eyelids, crackling with light, and I heard him whisper, tell me I was wet. I was ashamed of my slickness. But now I also knew he wasn't indifferent. My cheeks and neck seemed to dissolve. I started to move, rolling my hips. His breathing quickened, and I brought my hand down to touch him. His open mouth fell on my neck. I jolted at this contact, rough stubble against my skin, and a sudden wave of revulsion flowed through me.

My eyelids burned red. I snapped them open. A light had turned on in the house. It was gone before I could blink. The house was dark again. David froze and clenched me against his chest. I understood the mad belief that others might not see you if you close your eyes. The hope that your blindness extends to those searching for you. We waited in the dark for the sound of a door opening.

Did you see something? I asked.

There was a light on the second floor, he said, just for a second.

I pushed aside his hands and stood up. David stayed on the chair. I glanced at the opening in his trousers, the buckle of his belt thrown to one side, his zipper glinting in the dark. He was still erect, tip shiny and exposed. Now that I saw him, I felt no more desire. A moment later he raised himself from the chair, wincing as he adjusted and buttoned his jeans.

I waited alone in the garden. David opened the kitchen door and disappeared into the house without turning on any lights. I hoped he had stayed hard for her. I imagined him slipping into bed, and when I entered the house, I listened for them.

13

For the rest of the weekend, we barely left the house. Brigitte slept late both mornings, appearing at ten or eleven, hours after I'd woken up, wearing a cream-colored bathrobe, her face bloated from sleep. I couldn't sleep much. David cleaned the pool and garden during the day, dumping piles of leaves onto the bricks, pulling weeds from around the house, fixing the gutter. He was avoiding me, I could tell, and I tried not to think about our encounter.

Strangely, in the hours that followed, I felt neither regret nor guilt, as if what had happened between us had taken place in a dream. We had slipped into each other the way one falls into a pool after standing at its edge for too long. But it was real, and I was reminded over and over again from the way he ignored me when we were alone in the kitchen. How he recoiled from my voice, afraid of showing fondness toward me, even in private.

We peeled potatoes, Brigitte and I, seated at the kitchen table. We gathered the peels in a plastic bag and soaked the potatoes in cold water. She kept correcting me, roughly taking a potato from my hands to show me how it should be peeled in one fell swoop. Her expression was placid, showing no signs of distress, though she abruptly broke the silence with a question.

Do you think one day you'll tell your mother what you did?

My heart jumped. About what? I asked.

The press, your father, how you provided the missing piece.

I shook my head and placed a potato in the water, careful not to make a splash. No, she can't find out.

Why?

Because she'll never forgive me.

Just the possibility of Anouk learning the truth filled my mouth with grit, made my stomach heave.

It sounds like you need her approval—you care what she thinks of you.

You haven't seen what she's like when she's angry. I shifted my gaze away from her. The potatoes bobbed in the pot of cloudy water. Why are you asking me?

I was curious. I wonder if your father knew it was you.

Why would he know? I stared at her wildly.

He must have looked into it. I doubt he knew it was you, specifically, but I'm sure he blamed someone, knew more about the origin of the leak than anyone else around him.

Brigitte plucked a potato from the pot and cut it into thin slices. She threw them into an oval baking dish.

If your mother was more perceptive, she'd know it was you.

Maybe it hasn't even occurred to her.

Yes, you may be right, because she's wrapped up in her own

world. She still doesn't know about the book we're writing together, does she?

We decided not to tell her, remember?

Upon your insistence, yes, but at some point it will be public knowledge and you'll have to say something.

I blushed and looked away.

You're good at keeping secrets, aren't you?

I glanced back at her and our eyes met. I was surprised by what I saw—pleasure combined with appetite—like when I brought her a bag of *chouquettes* from the bakery. Instantly, her gaze changed. Don't worry, she said. Like you, I also preferred to keep things from my mother. I had my secrets. She acted the opposite way with me, turned me into her confidante, complaining for hours on end. Maybe that's why I withdrew from her.

Although the mood had lightened, I noticed a tightness in Brigitte's face, as if her skin was stretched closer to the bone. She trembled. I sensed she'd come undone, bits of her fighting to escape. She contained herself with the sheer strength of her skin.

One day, Brigitte continued, I told my mother I'd had enough. It was the summer I graduated from high school. A month before I left home. I found her sitting alone in the kitchen, scowling. There were always flies in the kitchen and they drove her mad. She liked to chase them around with a dish towel. Our apartment was on the twelfth floor and most of the windows faced a neighboring building. We kept our curtains drawn as soon as it grew dark. The kitchen was always bright, with a large window that overlooked a children's playground.

I wasn't allowed to go there at night. Men and women in the neighborhood met at the park and had sex on the slide. Brigitte's eyes narrowed, then she gave a short laugh.

I remember, she was complaining about my father, who preferred to stay silent rather than communicate with her. I stared out the window as I listened. The sky was a beautiful blue, not marred by clouds. I listened to her as if she was background noise, nodding along, giving my approval. I knew I'd be leaving soon, and she'd no longer be my responsibility.

At some point, she stopped speaking and stood up from the table. She must have noticed I wasn't paying attention. She walked to the window. I'm so tired of my life, she said. I may as well throw myself out the window. She unlatched the window and lifted it open. A cold wind swept into the kitchen. She swung one leg over the edge. It was comical, seeing her straddle the window.

I told her: If you jump from that window, no one will care. There'll be a funeral, but eventually you'll be forgotten. You'd hate us for forgetting you, but there'd be nothing you could do about it.

She stayed there, one leg dangling outside. My heart was banging in my chest. I avoided looking at her. I hoped she wouldn't be stupid enough to slip and fall. We could hear the drone of cars from the highway.

I know she was a lonely woman, with impossible expectations and fantasies. She probably dreamed of another life, not cleaning houses, taking the bus for two hours every day. She couldn't see beyond her world.

My sister walked in right then and screamed. She ran to our mother and embraced her. It was a personal victory, though, because after that day my mother stopped calling me a fat fish. I withheld the one thing she wanted. My attention.

Brigitte had finished cutting the potatoes. She wiped her hands on a dish towel. You and I are very different from our mothers, she said.

How can you be so sure?

Because we anticipate what other people want. I've observed you. You care what others think about you.

Isn't that a weakness?

Some people, like your mother, should care more about what others think. Her confidence is a disguise for selfishness, a lack of curiosity, even.

I listened to Brigitte. She was right that Anouk might threaten to throw herself out of the window. She'd do it just to prove the impermanence of being alive, to spite me and make me less attached to her. To perform.

But I couldn't imagine ever telling her to go on. I couldn't imagine risking Anouk's life. The thought of her dying tore me apart. It was so easy to imagine the sound of her hitting the ground, a nut cracking open, a loud thump. To say what Brigitte told her own mother required a level of comfort, no matter how small, with the possibility of losing her.

It occurred to me that Brigitte thought I felt the same way about mine. She saw me as a daughter who was trying to break free from her family. And while I was often the first to agree with whatever observation Brigitte had made and all the more flattered when she pointed out similarities between us, her remarks threw me, especially her assurance when she said our mothers were the same. It made me, in that moment, want to defend Anouk.

I know your mother tried to kill herself when she was your age.

Brigitte was referring to the time Anouk took those pills from her mother's bathroom.

Yes, but she didn't involve anyone else. It was private.

And yet she told you about this episode because she wanted you to know. She's always loved drama. It makes sense that you'd keep so much of your life private from her, and that you'd want to punish her and your father. All those years together and they never asked for your opinion, did they? I would've done the same as you. In a sense, your actions broke them apart.

My first instinct was to disagree, but I also felt a deeper frustration at her delivery, the flippant and measured tone she'd used when she accused me of splitting up my parents. It seemed insidious on her part, to say *I would do the same* as a way to soften the blow.

You're wrong, I told Brigitte. I didn't want to punish Anouk, and I wasn't trying to hurt my father.

Saying those words almost strangled me. Brigitte peered at me sideways, a smile forming on her lips.

Sometimes you talk about Anouk like she's a bad person, I continued. You know, it wasn't easy for her.

Brigitte's expression didn't change, and it seemed she wasn't disagreeing with me, but when she spoke, it was like she'd been holding on to this line for a while, waiting for the right moment to ask her question.

Your mother could have chosen a man who wasn't married. Don't you think?

* * *

Our last meal was strangely festive. David sat by his wife, holding her hand, laughing at her words. He continued to ignore me, and I in turn began to feel a slight revulsion for him. His laugh sounded artificial, louder and crass, and when I stared at him in the light of the dining room, every gesture of his seemed affected. He was growing soft at the belly, and his loose shirts wouldn't hide it much longer.

Brigitte blossomed under his affection. She drank more wine than usual and took bites of fish directly from his plate. She smiled at his jokes. We ate most of the gratin dauphinois. The thin slices of potato coated in cream had melted into a soft mass.

Brigitte drove me to the train on Sunday. She dropped me off in front of the station. I'd sensed that while I was in the house with them, the three of us, she couldn't have known about David and me, but the moment I walked away from her car, nothing held that certainty together anymore. Who knew what they'd say to each other once I was gone from their sight?

I felt her gaze follow me hotly. The strap of my bag pulled on my shoulder and dug into my skin. When I turned around to wave, she was there, hands poised on the wheel, staring at me through the windshield. I was too far away to see her expression.

Most of the seats on the train were taken. I found mine next to an old man who unpacked his food onto the foldout table. He tucked a cloth napkin into the collar of his shirt and spread pâté on a piece of bread. Once he had finished eating the bread, he peeled a clementine. He was slow with the flat ridge of his thumb, his nails trimmed to the skin, and I asked if he needed help. He shook his head and offered me a piece of his fruit. The clementine was sweet and warm; its intense flavor rose to my head. I turned to the window and looked at the mountains. I didn't want this old man to see tears gathering in my eyes.

A memory resurfaced more savagely than ever. A few years ago, Father and I had gotten into an argument. I was furious because he hadn't visited us in weeks and when he tried to kiss my cheek, I turned away from him. I shut myself in my room. He sat by the door while I refused to come out. Anouk was gone, I can't remember where, and it was just the two of us at home.

Eventually, I opened the door and saw his pale face, the red rim around his eyes. He had been crying.

I've tried to be a good father to you, he said. With my sons I was working all the time, but with you I wanted to be more present, see you on weekends, help you with your homework.

But you're always gone, I said, my voice breaking.

I know, but I try to visit you whenever I can.

And then he told me he was under more stress than usual. There had been two incidents with his health in the past month.

What did he mean by incidents?

It was nothing to be all that concerned about.

What happened? I asked again.

He'd blacked out twice. Once at home, and the other time while driving on the highway. He described being blinded, the sensation of falling down a long tunnel. He was close to an exit and as he felt his eyesight slip, he drove off the highway into a parking lot. He threw up behind the car door.

There had been blood tests, a Doppler exam. All was in

order. It appeared he was in good health. He needed to sleep more and eat a healthier diet. His father had died from a stroke in his late fifties.

I know I'm not always here for you, he told me, but I'm doing all I can.

I cried a little and he rubbed my shoulders. He told me not to worry, he had the best doctor in all of France, and his heart was being closely monitored.

But later, when I sat in my room alone, I didn't know how to evacuate the frustration I continued to feel. Would he be here when I fell in love, would he attend my wedding if I ever married, how could he be present at the public events of my life? Why can't we be like everyone else? I insisted. Be grateful for what you have, Anouk would respond. And yet, I couldn't help myself from being dissatisfied.

Whenever I closed my eyes, I was overwhelmed by the image of my own body crashing into a wall, and this image was calming. I imagined flying through the plaster, my bones breaking, my skin turning into powder. I imagined disappearing into thin air. In those moments, my anger toward him and Anouk transformed into an inward loathing, and I hated those emotions, what they did to me. I hated myself.

I wanted his heart to flutter with joy when he thought of us. I wanted to be his favorite. I thought about this often, when I was jealous of the other family. I remembered his words. *I've spent more time with you than with my sons.* I took comfort in this truth. What he was implying is that the second time around, you are a better parent. But then I remembered that my father was trained in the art of self-deception.

14

I didn't see Brigitte or David after my stay in Nîmes. I returned to Paris and was instantly consumed by school. Juliette and I threw ourselves into revisions for the Bac. We had four-hour *Bacs Blancs*—mock exams scheduled for every second Saturday—and we often spent Friday evenings studying until midnight. Anouk was gone for long stretches of time at her studio in the north of Paris, writing and rehearsing, sometimes falling asleep on the futon by accident. The opening date for her new one-woman show was set for July. When she was home, she stayed in her bedroom. I knew she was there from the muffled sounds of her voice filtering through the door as she practiced her lines, followed by an eerie silence when she slept.

Whenever thoughts of David surfaced, I shut them down. I knew what I'd done was wrong, and as the weeks went by, I felt worse. I remembered Brigitte at the dinner table, smiling at David while he played with her hand and gazed at her ador-ingly, when a few hours before he'd been with me. And then it occurred to me: the possibility that this wasn't his first time, perhaps he'd been with other women. Many times, even. Yes, they'd never spoken about being faithful to each other. They were adults with mysterious agreements, and I was the foolish one. I squirmed at this realization, shame twisting up my throat. *Idiote.*

And then one morning, at the end of March, my life was thrown upside down again. Brigitte had once said that people my age experienced events as earth-shattering, the air knocked from us, but this time around it wasn't so much the feeling of losing my footing, as one of loss, pieces of me breaking apart and dividing into smaller pieces until I was barely there.

An article came out in *Vanity Fair.* The author was a journalist I'd never heard of, a man named Julien Toussaint. In the first paragraph I was identified as the one who had leaked the affair between my parents. This journalist claimed to have interviewed me, the daughter of the minister. In the article, I admitted to contacting a journalist the previous summer. I'd given him photographs and had provided enough details to corroborate the affair.

Reading those words printed on paper was a tremendous blow. Anouk had left the magazine on the kitchen table for me to see when I woke up. I interpreted her gesture as an accusation. It was a Saturday morning, and she was nowhere to be seen. It didn't sink in immediately and I read with remove, as though Margot Louve was a stranger living in another city, and I was learning about someone else's life, not my own. A gradual paralysis spread through my limbs with each sentence. I read until the last line and pushed the magazine away from me. Perhaps it was a form of self-preservation, a way to swallow a

horrible thing. Later, I recognized its flavor. Sharp and metallic, the same as when I let blood trickle down my throat when
my nose bled.

The cover glared at me: a photo of me and Father at Parc
Montsouris. We both wore long winter coats. We gazed into
the camera and smiled with our teeth. There was nothing extraordinary about the photo, aside from how young I was, ten
at the most. Anouk had taken the photo on a rare outing together. I'd given it to Brigitte for our book.

The author used direct quotations, sentences I recognized
from conversations with Brigitte, but the way he wrote them
sounded foreign, as if he had taken an idea here and there and
patched them together to form monstrous paragraphs. Had I
ever used those exact words to describe Father? I couldn't remember.

My father despised his cousins who saved money only to pur-
chase gigantic and tacky flat-screen TVs. He loved expensive ob-
jects, because buying them reminded him he had the power to claim
anything. He told my mother that he didn't truly love Madame
Lapierre. He loved what she represented: wealth, elegance, a dis-
tinguished family. He owed his success in no small part to her fam-
ily's fortune.

He had other affairs, according to this journalist, though
it'll come as no surprise to friends who knew him well. He
wasn't like those men who boast about their conquests and
keep count of the women they've seduced, perhaps because of
his Catholic upbringing and provincial values. His wife was
pregnant with their second son when he met Anouk Louve, the
woman who would become his mistress for two decades.

I hadn't known about Madame Lapierre being pregnant when they met. Had he and my mother started seeing each other immediately? Did Anouk know? The thought of it made my stomach turn. I stared at my hands, the fine hairs on my fingers, the peeling skin around my nails. The bone of my wrist popped out unnaturally. Footsteps echoed downstairs and I heard Madame Bonnard's loud laugh. She had a rude laugh, suggesting a mouth open for too long.

The only person who had all of this information, the details and my words, was Brigitte. She knew almost everything, from Father's arrogance to his insecurities to his generous qualities. My legs shook as I stood from the kitchen table. I passed by the mirror in the entrance and caught sight of my splotched face. I fled to my bedroom.

My head seemed to float above my neck, the rest of my body losing its substance. I lay on the bed for what felt like hours. The light faded from the window and my room grew dark, the sun hidden behind clouds. It was going to storm. Why had Brigitte spoken to this journalist? Was it part of an elaborate plan to stir interest in the memoir? Or a cruel attempt to harm me? Had David told her about me and what we'd done? No, she would've confronted me sooner. But if she had known about Madame Lapierre's pregnancy, the timing of the affair, then why had she failed to mention it to me? If it wasn't Brigitte, who else could it be? David? *Idiote*, I said, over and over again, marking my skin with my fingernails.

It had never been part of the project, to reveal the source. She had promised to keep it a secret. No one would know about my involvement with the press. Waves of disgust and sadness rose in my chest as I alternated between thoughts of Brigitte and Father. Who goes with another woman when their wife is pregnant? I wondered. Who does such a thing?

I waited, listening for Anouk's footsteps on the stairs. I waited for the pause as she searched for her keys, the clatter of metal against the lock. Now she knew the terrible thing I'd done. I was unable to move, barely feeling the mattress beneath me. If I kept my eyes shut for long enough, maybe I would dissolve.

Finally, some hours later, I heard the door unlock. I dragged myself out of bed.

Anouk stood in the entrance and stared at me in silence. I couldn't decipher her expression. She frightened me with her long reddish hair and pale cheeks. She hooked her coat on the rack and slipped off her boots, her eyes never leaving mine for a moment.

What do you have to say for yourself? she asked. She stood close to me. Her eyes drooped and the lines around her mouth were more pronounced. I saw her growing old one day, my needing to take care of her when she could no longer leap from one neighborhood to another, carry our suitcases down the stairs, one in each hand, impress others with her physical beauty.

What do you mean?

You know what I'm talking about.

I never spoke to that journalist. I've never heard of him. I think the article is made up.

But you spoke to someone, back in the summer.

Anouk dropped her bag on the floor and walked to the living room. I followed her. She sat on the armchair and rubbed her face, avoiding her eyes and the dark green makeup.

They already knew about us.

Who? she asked.

Journalists. They've known for years.

And *you* know these journalists? You allowed them to go ahead and publish those photos? Who else had that image of you and your father?

I couldn't find the breath with which to speak. I had hoped . . . I paused for a moment and took a ragged breath. I had hoped he would leave her. My voice cracked. I hung my head lower.

Anouk stared at me for what felt like minutes, wordless, as I wished for the air around me to thicken and swallow me whole.

I think I've known all along it was you. Her voice had softened. I looked at her hands, flat on the armrests, the aquamarine ring from Father that she wore on her middle finger. It was bound to come out one day, she continued. How can we expect to keep a secret when everything is public nowadays? But you lied to me, Margot.

Her words rushed into my ears like a cold wind. Her face was composed, as though the sentence were rehearsed.

Sometimes I look at you and I think about who you've become.

You think I'm a bad person, don't you?

Why are you always worried about being good or bad? Who taught you that? It's a way of deferring responsibility for your actions.

Forgive me, I choked. I stood over her, my fists in tight balls, blood rushing to my neck. I repeated my apology, my voice rising, not caring one bit if the neighbors heard us and gossiped later.

You're losing control of your emotions. Anouk spoke coolly. Her calmness drove me madder. I paced around the room.

Did you know Madame Lapierre was pregnant when you met him? I asked her.

I didn't know when we met, but I found out just before their son was born. We were not together at the time, but we knew each other well.

When you found out she was pregnant, you pursued him?

It was more like him pursuing me.

Why would he do that?

I don't know. Anouk sighed. It was complicated, and I can't give you all the details.

You were both selfish.

You expend a lot of energy blaming me, she said. One day you'll wake up, and I'll be gone. You'll realize you don't need me anymore.

Why do you say things like that?

She looked away. I detected a faint expression of hurt in her eyes. Her mouth wobbled before drawing tighter.

I'll always need you, I said.

No, I promise you won't.

We stayed in silence for a while, each of us sitting at opposite ends of the living room. The coffee table was covered in a thin layer of gray dust, dried rain marks dimmed the windows, and our plants had shrunk throughout the winter. Anouk leaned back in the chair.

Look at me, Margot. This afternoon I went to see that journalist, the one who wrote the piece in *Vanity Fair*.

You know him?

He happens to be a friend of a friend of Théo's. I tracked him down at his apartment.

What did he say? My voice was weak, barely a whisper.

I interrogated him. I knew there was something wrong about that article. All the quotes about Madame Lapierre and your father. It just didn't sound like you. He finally admitted to receiving the quotes from someone else. A reliable source, but not from you. I told him that could cost him his career. What a scandal if his colleagues found out it was a sham interview.

I held my breath.

I told him to prepare a correction. It'll go online next week. I also said I was the one who leaked the affair, not you.

You? My stomach lurched in surprise.

Yes. I told him that you knew it was me, but you didn't want the public to know, and that you were protecting me.

She walked toward me.

Why would you do that? I asked. Why lie to him?

As she approached me, I saw concern on her face. I don't want your name to be dragged through the tabloids, for you to be the center of gossip. You have an entire life ahead of you.

But what will people think of you?

Don't worry about what others think. It'll sound like I was bitter, the *other woman*, the jilted lover. I promise they'll forget about it soon enough. Maybe it'll even be good press for my career.

She paused and closed her eyes. I saw the exhaustion on her face, the creases between her eyebrows that she always tried to smooth out with her fingers.

I know we weren't the parents you hoped for. I know you

think we were selfish to stay together. I wanted to separate from your father when you were little. Although I loved him, it didn't take long for the reality of our agreement to surface and for me to see that you and I would be on the short end of it.

But didn't you think about his wife? I asked, interrupting her.

I should have. Anouk lowered her eyes and fiddled with her sleeve. In any case, he refused to leave us, saying he was afraid we'd lose touch if we split up. He really did want to be involved in your life. I agreed to stay with him, but for a long time I wondered if you wouldn't have been happier otherwise, and whenever you told me that your life wasn't fair, it broke my heart. What was I supposed to say? You talk about your childhood as if we abandoned you and suppressed your true spirit, as if we had no idea what we were doing. But, Margot, can't you see how much I've given you? It's all here.

She placed her hands on my shoulders and squeezed them. The light in the living room had changed from golden orange to blue, and now we faced each other in semi-darkness.

Do you remember when you were a little girl, you went through a phase of asking me the same question over and over again? You wanted to know if I would throw myself in front of a bus to save you. You asked if all mothers are willing to sacrifice their lives for their children. No matter what I said, you were never satisfied with my answer, because you'd go on and ask again the following week.

What did you say? I asked.

Anouk raised her eyebrows and smiled. See, even today, you're wondering. She released her grasp from my shoulders and switched on the light. It's time for dinner, she said.

I watched her cook. Every gesture was unnatural. She attacked the ingredients, never pausing to consider their softness or fragility. Did she handle me the same way when I was born? It was almost impossible to imagine her with a baby in her arms. She was known to chop an unripe avocado into tiny hard squares and serve that for dinner.

I understood then that I'd never ask my mother if Father had loved her, because I was certain she'd asked herself the same question a million times. She knew the answer. Either way, whatever emotion he'd felt for her wasn't powerful enough for him to leave his wife. Or perhaps it was us who hadn't been enough.

Anouk filled the saucepan with water and placed it on the stove. She turned on the flame but didn't think to cover the pan. It would take longer for the water to boil. Then she opened a jar of tomato sauce and emptied it into another pan. The sauce sizzled. I went over to give it a stir.

The only other thing there was to eat was salad. Lettuce past its expiration date, the bag ripped open and its contents dumped into a bowl. The leaves clumped together in fermented wads. She set the table with two place mats, napkins folded under our knives, a bottle of sparkling water at the center. She drained the pasta and drizzled oil right into the colander, then served us two portions. Here, she said, handing me a steaming plate. As I took the plate from her, I felt my chest split in half, as if she had stuck her hand in there and cradled my heart.

15

When thoughts of Father washed over me, I learned how to hold myself still. I waited for their intensity to recede, my breathing to even out. I repeated to myself what Anouk once told me: He could be a bad husband, a bad lover, but he was a good father. I gained some of the weight I'd lost that year. Anouk thought I looked better, my bones now hidden beneath a layer of flesh.

Juliette and I locked ourselves in her studio or my bedroom to study. Nothing mattered more than doing well on the Bac.

So, it was your mother all along, she said, when the second article was posted online. The journalist's correction.

Yes, she told the press about us.

I'm surprised she didn't tell you first.

I think she wanted to protect me, in case things didn't go well.

You're not upset at her, are you?

Of course not.

* * *

When I wasn't studying, I thought about Brigitte and the memoir obsessively. I hadn't spoken to her since the train station in Nîmes. She appeared to me throughout the day, a vision clouding my mind, making it hard to sleep at night. I imagined Brigitte in her parents' home, when she was my age. A narrow bed and a wooden stool for a bedside table. Her sister, a thin shape under the bedsheets, facing a wall covered in magazine cutouts.

In my mind's eye I saw Brigitte in the kitchen, the only room with natural light, and I imagined her blinded whenever she entered it, her pupils sharpening to pinpricks. She stood by the window, a film of grease coating the glass. She looked down at the playground where she saw blurry shapes on swings, on the slide, arriving from opposite sides of the street and meeting for a few hours. They made love with their clothes on, she had said. What had Brigitte seen in them? Why did she stare at them?

And what did she see in me? Was there even a book, or had she been planning all along to sell my story to another journalist? Why hadn't she published under her own name, and what if another piece appeared with more alleged quotes from me? I couldn't speak to Anouk or Juliette about Brigitte. I sat in a corner of the living room, simmering under a black cloud. I didn't know what to do.

Juliette was almost done editing her film. We had done most of the filming one Sunday close to the Bois de Boulogne and then at a friend's unfurnished apartment a few evenings after school. I'd discovered that Juliette had a gift for being behind the camera. Because it was a silent film, I had no lines to learn, and this removed much of the stress I'd had about the project.

The script itself was spare and gave few physical directions. I hadn't known where to stand in the apartment on that first evening of filming. But once Juliette began, I forgot she was there with her camera. She moved silently and gracefully, and even her voice was transformed, her directions spoken with eloquence. I found myself bending to her words, following their lead before she had completed a thought. At one point, Juliette had placed the camera on a tripod. She walked over to me and adjusted my pose. We had touched in almost every possible way—held hands, slept blotted one against the other, walked with our arms thrown around the other's neck—but the way she crouched at my feet to better manipulate my legs was different. She worked like a professional, adjusting my ankle to the left and bending my knee into a more flattering position.

For those few days I was absorbed by the film. She told me she wanted to be like my mother when she was older. And for once I was proud of Anouk, that she could inspire someone my age. When Juliette had finished editing the film, she came over to show it to us.

Juliette and Anouk sat at the dining room table, talking about the film, but I was distracted and only caught a sentence here and there, something about my skin being like the surface of the moon, my pores enlarged on-screen. They discussed the long tracking shot at the end, when the camera follows the newly elected mayor as she runs through the streets of the town. She wipes the blood from her mouth but misses a spot on her neck. Slowly, the camera zooms in on the spot of blood, until the screen itself is a reddish blur. We'd made fake blood with food coloring, sugar syrup, and cocoa powder, and smudged it on my neck. I'd run through the streets of Auteuil at six in the morning, before the stores opened, while Juliette followed on her bike, the camera mounted on the backrest.

What are you thinking about? Juliette finally asked, noticing that I was staring blankly into space.

Our math homework, I said. I disappeared into my bedroom and closed the door.

I held my phone. With the door shut, I could no longer hear Anouk or Juliette. I sat at my desk, the point farthest away from the door, and called Brigitte.

She answered after two rings. It was like talking to a stranger; an awkwardness permeated our exchange.

How are you? she asked, sounding normal, innocent.

I ignored her question. I'd like to see you. I was disappointed that my voice had none of the harshness I'd wanted to convey.

How about the day after tomorrow? I'm free in the afternoon.

No, it has to be sooner. I want to talk about the article.

She was silent on the other end.

I'm on my way to a friend's party. Would you like to meet there? I'm sure she won't mind if I bring you. She's always inviting strangers.

I shivered at her use of the word *stranger*, then wrote down the address and hung up.

Anouk and Juliette were bent over a computer screen, reviewing the final edit.

I'm going to buy groceries, I said, standing in the doorway. It was the only excuse I could come up with.

They glanced up from the screen and waved. Ciao! Juliette said.

As I ran down the stairs of our building, I was alarmed by a strange sensation building inside of me. It wasn't fear. It was similar to how I'd felt when I met Father in a public setting, a clandestine excitement strong enough to cut my appetite, erase all signs of exhaustion, and, like a drug, take away the sharpness of life. It was almost like the old times, hurtling toward him, arriving out of breath downstairs, pausing to regain my composure before stepping out onto the street. I unlocked the building door, half expecting to see his car waiting for me.

16

The address in the fourteenth was a ten-minute walk from métro Glacière. It was early in the evening. The sky disintegrated into a grainy blue. The house itself was separated from the street by a small courtyard. A gate opened onto a garden. I followed a stone path to the entrance and walked up a few steps to the door. Music and voices filtered through from the other side; smudges moved behind the tinted glass. I pressed on the doorbell.

A woman around the same age as Brigitte opened the door. She wore an elegant blue dress and reminded me of a movie star, though I couldn't place her face. Her hair was short and black, cut to her chin. She wore no lipstick, but her eyes were circled in dark kohl. She introduced herself as Marie and seemed to know who I was when I told her my name. Is Brigitte here? I asked. She nodded and invited me inside. A man appeared behind her. She introduced him as her husband, Arnaud. He was stout and fleshy and carried his domed torso like a second body. We entered a spacious living area.

There she is, Marie said, pointing at Brigitte. She sat on a chair at the far end of the room, a large cat spread over her stomach.

I stood still for a moment. She hadn't seen me yet. The confidence that had propelled me here was quickly replaced by a feeling of inadequacy. I saw myself from afar, a teenage girl in a room full of adults, wearing a cotton dress with fraying straps, out of place. I was underdressed, I lacked the coolness of everyone else—even crossing the room to where Brigitte sat seemed difficult. The way I walked would betray an overall clumsiness. I took the smoothest steps possible.

You came, Brigitte said. She craned her neck as I leaned in to kiss her cheeks. The cat hissed at me. This is Simba, she told me. My hand settled on his tiny head, and soon he was purring.

We're throwing a party for Marie's husband, Brigitte said. It's his sixtieth birthday and he's taking an early retirement. Marie is an old friend from university. She teaches European law at l'ENA.

We were surrounded by hors d'oeuvres of smoked salmon and mini tomato quiches, but I had no appetite. I had been nervous about seeing Brigitte, but I was relieved by the familiarity of her presence. She hadn't changed. We had been close for months, after all, and on some primal level I responded to that closeness with a vague sense of ease. And yet, of course, I was also uneasy. I cringed at the higher pitch of my voice, the forced cheeriness when I greeted her, the way my hand immediately stroked the cat as a way to hide the banging in my temples. I forced myself to bite into a quiche. The crust was hot, though the custard filling was tepid, as if previously frozen. I dusted flakes from around my mouth.

Across the room we saw a woman spill champagne onto a table and walk away in a hurry. A dark stain formed on the tablecloth. She preferred to run away from the scene of the crime rather than be caught with a sponge in her hand. Brigitte smiled at the woman who now stood on the opposite side of the room, nervously sipping from her glass. I knew Brigitte would have found a creative solution, like throwing a napkin on the stain. We glanced at each other and shared a brief moment of recognition before her expression tightened. She stood from the chair. Simba leapt to the floor with a heavy thud.

Come, Brigitte said. Let me give you a tour of the house.

We walked around the guests who pecked at melon wrapped in prosciutto. I realized most of the guests were women, and I was surprised, given this was a party for Arnaud. Perhaps the men were elsewhere or outside, smoking.

We found ourselves in a dim hallway lined with Matisse sketches. Brigitte turned to face me. We were alone, and I saw now that had been her intention. She placed her hands on my shoulders. Above, the Matisse faces, held together by a few sparse lines, looked down on us.

Where is David? I asked.

He has a dinner for work. She answered immediately, as if she had been prepared for my question.

I watched her skin transform, pink patches blooming on her neck, small veins swelling with blood beneath her eyes. Something was wrong. I broke away from her grasp.

Why did you tell the journalist all those awful things? I asked.

Julien is a friend.

I was silent. A part of me had hoped she would deny it, say

she had nothing to do with the article. Now that she'd admitted to being behind it, I felt a flash of anger. It left me winded. My arms wrapped around my chest.

Listen, deep down you wanted your mother to know, she said.

It's the last thing I wanted.

Does it matter, since she took your side? What a lovely little lie she told Julien. An act of kindness. It surprised me.

I detected a tremor in Brigitte's voice, as if she was hiding her feelings. She blinked a few times.

You wanted Anouk to hate me for what I did?

What your mother feels for you is none of my business.

So then why did you talk to the journalist?

I thought it would be a relief for you, more than anything else.

But the quotes from me, those were details I told you in confidence, off the record.

If you're this upset, why didn't you call me right away?

Her question made me pause. I shook my head, but I knew why—I'd been afraid of asking Brigitte whether she had reason to go behind my back. I thought of telling her about David, but at the last moment I held back. As if sensing I was on the verge of speaking, Brigitte tilted toward me.

I'm glad you called. She spoke gently, and I felt a current of warmth shoot up my spine.

I ventured forward, my voice gaining volume. I had repeated the words out loud to myself on my way over.

There's a reason why I wanted to see you, and why it's urgent. I don't want to be a part of the memoir. It was a stupid idea to begin with and it won't fix anything. I don't want to do it anymore. And I don't want you to do it any longer, either.

A door closed on her face, shutting down whatever kindness I'd detected earlier.

I looked down at the floor, my arms still held in a taut clasp across my chest. A long Persian carpet ran along the hallway. Somehow, Brigitte had turned the conversation around, making me feel as though I was at fault.

You gave me your story, Margot. I barely had to ask and you offered it. Like it was this hot thing burning in your hands and you wanted me to take it from you. I don't understand why you're upset about the article. It's just a piece of writing. The memoir will be much more, it'll be an entire history of you and him.

I listened to her, the confidence ringing through her statements. Once, I would have yielded.

But you misrepresented my father. There was nothing positive about him in that article, none of his qualities, his intelligence.

You're accusing me as if I wrote the article, but I didn't. Julien is the author.

It came from you.

She waved her hand, exhaling loudly. It's just an article.

It's my life.

Brigitte smiled faintly, and I saw it then, the mockery curling her lips, that same expression she'd had when she tried to rid herself of her cousin Georges. I could feel myself losing the upper hand, but still I repeated it: I trusted you with my life.

And why would you ever do that?

We'd been speaking quickly under our breath, almost whispering. I stopped at this last question. I was no longer sure why I'd placed myself in her hands. I tried to recall the first meetings, how we had gotten started, but the specifics blurred in my memory. I saw both of us leaping into an undefined space. The sweet custard of clafoutis, the light in their kitchen going from yellow to blue, David's leather jacket draped over a chair. I had asked her first, but I was no longer certain whose idea it had been.

I'll tell you why you trusted me. She smiled, and I saw she took pleasure in making me guess. You trusted me because you liked me.

I was embarrassed, as if liking her had been wrong. I felt stripped, and I was sure this nakedness showed on my face.

But if you liked me, she continued, speaking louder, why would you betray my trust? You think I've wronged you, but what about you? How do you think I feel after what happened between you and David?

She sounded strangled, barely able to control the pitch of her voice. My heart drummed in my ears. She knew. There was barely time for the realization to sink in before I felt Brigitte's hand on my bare arm. She pinched my skin with her nails, and the sharp pain brought the moment into focus. I wiped a bubble of blood from my arm.

What are you talking about? I managed to say.

Don't think I am so naive, Margot.

There was contempt in her words. She walked away from me before I could answer, down the hallway, and I followed her into a bedroom that resembled a hotel room. It was beige, carpeted, with a white bed and a vase of over-bloomed tulips. She sat on the bed.

I was silent. How to explain that I'd never imagined something with David could happen, and that, in a way, it still didn't feel real?

She smoothed the spread around her. I shouldn't be so angry with you. Her voice was softer. I found out last week that I'm pregnant. She touched her stomach.

The material of her silk shirt swayed loosely. There was nothing to see.

Congratulations, I said, kneeling at her feet.

She retreated from me, folding her hands over her stomach. I know how much you've wanted this.

She considered me from above, still holding her flat stomach.

You know, you are more like your mother than you think. You're both whores.

The violence of her words stung more fiercely than a slap in the face. I moved away from her legs until I found myself against the wall. Is this how she thought of my mother all along, a whore? I felt light-headed, and for a moment I couldn't focus my eyes on her.

He came to me in tears, my husband. I asked if you used protection and he said there was no need. You didn't get far, did you?

He couldn't stay hard.

She nodded with approval.

I wondered if David had lied, or if Brigitte was transforming the truth to prove her control over me.

When he confessed to what happened between the two of you, I told myself, this girl is dangerous. She can't be trusted. The next day I saw Julien by chance. He's an old friend and we see each other a few times a year. We met for lunch, but I was distracted. I could barely hold a conversation. He knew something was wrong.

And that's why you told him about me? My voice faltered. You gave him the photograph, the quotes from the interviews with me.

Do you know the irony of it all? When you walked into our lives, something concrete changed in my relationship with David.

What do you mean?

It took me a while to see the effect you had on David. Then I began to notice him looking at you. And the way you displayed yourself to him! Do you know what it's like to obsess over every little change in your body, wondering if this month you are pregnant? Each time my abdomen was swollen I thought, now it's happened at last. We started making love again, regularly. The times you slept over, David woke me in the middle of the night as if he might explode. And it wasn't just him. I wanted him, too, in a way I hadn't since our first year.

Like when Anaïs lived with you, I thought.

In a way, I loved having you around, Brigitte said. It was so moving to see how you believed us. You believed me when I compared you to Brigitte Bardot. Something magical happened, the compliment opened you up, as if you'd never been told you were beautiful.

She paused. I inched away from her and leaned against the

wall. A question began to take shape in my mind, one I'd privately circled around but had been afraid to ask.

That first time we saw each other after the interview, at Chez Albert. Did you wait for me? Did you know to find me there?

Let me ask you a different question. Do you believe in those kinds of coincidences?

What did you want from me?

She sighed and crossed her legs. The material of her black trousers rustled.

Well, I was curious about you and your father. I was just a few years older than you when the story of Mazarine came out. It was fascinating. Many knew about her existence. Her father was the most important man in France, and he was dying. He had a hidden daughter, a love affair with a younger woman. It became an obsession of mine. I read every single article and book published about Mitterrand and Mazarine.

Your story was different, and that intrigued me. Mitterrand chose to no longer hide his daughter. Your father wasn't the president. Some would say Claire Lapierre is more important than your father. If he was married to a different woman, would the public have cared as much? Would they have cared if your mother wasn't Anouk Louve?

And when I met you and your mother, I felt that same itch from the Mitterrand days. I remembered how much I envied Mazarine. Later, she became a novelist. She could write about her life and make others care. I never had that kind of privilege. My life was small compared to hers.

But now that I know you better, I pity girls like you. You go from invisibility to transparency. First, you're hidden, then you become the symbol of an affair. The reminder of a man who was unfaithful and died a few months after getting caught.

Is that what you think of me?

Some might see tenderness if they look deep enough. The sad story of a second family. But many continue to wonder why he didn't recognize you, why he denied the affair, why he died without saying a word about you. Your memoir would have painted a more nuanced, complete portrait.

I was crying now. I covered my face with my hands. The truth of Brigitte's words blazed through me. He had promised to recognize me, and yet he hadn't; he had died without calling me, writing to me, passing on a note. Had he even thought about me in those last moments?

I know what you've told me. But, Margot, I think it was a lot more complicated than you think. You'll see it better one day. Maybe one day you'll be able to see what it means to love someone. I'm talking about sacrifice, about doing things for another person that make you deeply uncomfortable. I don't know if your father was capable of that.

Brigitte stood from the bed. Her sockless ankles rose thinly out of her men's shoes, the same she'd worn the first time we met. I walked over to her.

Brigitte, I said, speaking her name with more force than I intended. She turned her head. Why do you want a child?

Her gaze became unfocused for an instant.

What does it matter to you? You're not particularly maternal. You've said it yourself.

And your mother is?

No, but she doesn't pretend to be. I know she wasn't expecting to ever get pregnant. But you've been trying for years. You want this more than anything, don't you?

Brigitte stared at the blank wall behind me. I couldn't tell what she was thinking. When she opened her mouth, it was to speak simply.

I want to know what it's like. Most if not all of my friends have children. They've experienced pregnancy. They've gone through that transformation, they've spoken about it, told me how I can't understand the trauma of childbirth, the joy of holding my own child. Some of them didn't want to see me in those first months. They wanted only to be with other mothers. Maybe I'm projecting my fears onto them, maybe I'm being hard on them. Either way, I've often felt lonely.

I reflected on her words. You want a baby for the experience, I said. But would you care if you lost it?

They say your life becomes secondary to the child's. You become selfless as a parent.

You're hoping that being a parent will make you less selfish?

Brigitte blushed deeply. It was the first time I'd seen her color this way. She looked through the window. It was dark outside, and we could barely make out the branches on the trees.

I don't know, she said quietly, still staring at the black window. Perhaps I might turn into my mother.

I thought about the women in the living room, eating hors d'oeuvres in their expensive outfits. In that moment, I could have sworn Brigitte was raised in a place like this, a mansion with walls built to accommodate artwork. I wondered what it took to excise herself from her childhood.

She walked over to me and cupped my chin. I thought of her mother, squeezing her thighs to expose pockets of fat. I waited for Brigitte's fingers to scrape me. Slap my cheek. You should go now, she said.

I left the room and ran down the hallway. I sped past the women in the living room, and this time they turned their heads, as if they could smell my sweat, look right through my clothes. I took my jacket from Brigitte's chair, where I'd left it. Simba's gray hairs fluttered into the air. A woman touched my elbow and I jumped, frightened by her presence. She wanted to know if I was thirsty. I thanked her and said I was leaving. Please yourself, she said, and all I could see was the square shape of her teeth, the tightness of her hair pulled into a bun and shining like a crown.

17

When I walked away from Brigitte at the dinner party, I didn't turn around like the last time at the train station in Nîmes. I was fleeing her, the way someone runs from a screaming stranger on the street. I was afraid to look back because I sensed her following me out of the room and onto the street. Only when I was on the métro, surrounded by other passengers, did the prickling in my neck subside.

For years after, I had this image engraved in my mind: Brigitte, a small woman sitting on that bed, her hands covering her stomach, alone in her friend's beautiful mansion. It was a lonely image and it haunted me often, for I was never able to picture her fully pregnant.

Something about her made it impossible to imagine any growth. I tried to see a child growing in her womb, expanding her flesh like that of the Japanese goddesses riding waves in the entrance of their apartment. How hard it would be for her to surrender. She would gain weight, her thighs dappled with fat, stretch marks along her waist. Anouk had been proud of the sixty-five kilos she weighed at full term.

I searched for traces of Brigitte, anything that might tell me where she was, what she was doing. I created alerts for her name and David's. I told myself a memoir without my consent was impossible. How would she find an editor if I wasn't by her side? And yet the knowledge of everything she had learned about our family clung to me. She could write a different kind of book, if she wanted to.

The week of the Bac went by quickly. The exams were easier than Juliette and I had anticipated. We were filled with adrenaline; we didn't eat or drink during those four-hour stretches. There was no time for a bathroom break, and who wanted to waste those precious minutes? Philosophy was first on a Monday morning at eight. I had already decided I'd do the dissertation, knowing Father would have been proud, as it required forming an elegant argument and inserting memorized quotes for evidence. We were given two questions to choose from. I selected the first one: *Do we have the duty to search for the truth?*

For a brief instant I was overwhelmed by the events of the previous year, and I reformulated the question. Do we have a duty to tell the truth? Our class had studied the concept of truth in the spring with Monsieur H., and I got to work writing down the first quotes that surfaced before I forgot them. But it was mindless excavation—I could write these sentences in my sleep—and soon I returned to Father, the two truths he lived. Is this what I'd been doing with Brigitte, searching for markers of his devotion as a father, or did I want to justify the peaceful coexistence of his two lives? There was no time to lose, every minute in the exam was accounted for, so I banished these pre-occupations and began to write.

Most of the difficult subjects, like math, were in the morning. Afterward, Juliette and I had lunch at Chez Albert. We devoured cheese and ham paninis stuffed with fries. If we had another exam in the afternoon, we returned to school. Otherwise we studied for a few hours at her studio and went to sleep early.

On an afternoon in early July, we gathered in the courtyard of our school where they had pinned a printout of our names and final grades. Juliette and I had both received a *mention très bien*. She scored a half point higher than I did.

And then it was over. All those years of labor, pages of writing, none of it mattered anymore. The grade on the Bac guaranteed our acceptance at certain universities and programs, though in a few years its importance would fade, and we'd forget who had gotten a better grade. I knew that once I was home, I'd throw away the piles of papers in my bedroom, and in a month or less, I'd no longer remember the pages of mathematical proofs I'd memorized, or the philosophy quotes I could recite like poetry.

It had rained for most of June, but now the weather was dry, the sun pleasantly warming us in a final act of kindness. We walked out of the school for the last time as we had every other day, and it was as if everything that had taken place there evaporated in the summer heat.

The day was winding down by the time I arrived at Parc de Belleville. It was the second highest point of elevation in Paris after Sacré-Coeur, overlooking the city with a view of the monuments. Belleville had been the last standing barricade of the Commune de Paris, home to Edith Piaf and Georges Perec. Now it was almost dinnertime and families trickled out, parents going home with their children. I sat on the steps of the open-air theater and pressed my fingers into the cool concrete. Father and I had often found ourselves on the peripheries, in neighborhoods such as this one, closer to the city limits, where few would recognize us. We'd approach the park from the side, so it appeared like a hidden garden surrounded by thick walls of dark green vegetation. On weekends the narrow patches of lawn were taken by young couples, groups of friends, and families who gathered for picnics. I liked the wild variety of plants, ferns shooting up among pink flowers and curled cabbage leaves, the clusters of bamboo.

You'll see it better one day, Brigitte had said. Who would I be today if I was raised by married parents, if our little family wasn't weighed down by a secret? I envied Madame Lapierre and her sons, and their clean conscience.

And yet, was it terrible to admit that I'd also loved the travails of our life, the inconsistency of Father's affection, the hardness of Anouk's hands when they pulled on my ears to punish me, the closeness she and I had cultivated over years of living together? Those moments had been mine alone. They had been all I'd ever known. A small part of me still believed Father had loved us better. I hunched over and held my legs tightly.

A boy and girl my age embraced on a bench close to the fountain. Her long hair shielded her face and he did nothing to push it away, rather burrowing his head beneath her hair. How warm it must be under there. With one hand, he held her legs in place over his lap, and with the other he caressed a hidden patch on her lower back.

It bothered me that I couldn't see her face. The white leather of her sandals sparkled in the evening light. She threw her head back to laugh and her hair swung away at last. But I was too far away to see her features other than the outline of her forehead and nose.

How I yearned, in that moment, to be like them.

It was dusk when I arrived at Madame Lapierre's. I thought I'd know the building instantly, having been there twice before, but I passed by it before recognizing the door with the elaborate engravings. I waited across the street until a man stepped out. The door was heavy and it closed slowly, giving me enough time to catch it and slip through.

The entrance was dark and cool, and it took a moment for my eyes to adjust. Up ahead was a glass doorway leading to the apartments, and to the right the *gardienne*'s window.

A woman stuck her head through the window and called me over. What do you want, Mademoiselle? she asked.

The *gardienne*. What was she doing here at almost nine-thirty P.M.? I lingered by the door before deciding to approach her. She sat behind a window, perched on a stool. Her hair was bleached to the roots. Behind her a small television played a music video on mute.

You don't live here, she said. I know everyone in the building.

She stared at me, rubbing her fingers along her chin. Before I could answer, she spoke.

I know who you are. You're Monsieur Lapierre's daughter. I saw your photo in the papers.

I didn't know what to say, such was my surprise that she'd recognized me. She leaned forward and all of a sudden, I was afraid she'd stick out her arm and touch me.

Why are you here? she asked.

The *gardienne* continued to speak in a voice so low it lured me to her window.

I remember the night they came for him. The ambulance siren woke everyone in the building. They carried him out on a stretcher. Madame Lapierre suffered terribly.

The *gardienne* struck me as a woman who overshared and knew the secrets of each inhabitant in the building. I turned away from her and walked to the glass door with the apartment numbers and doorbells. I searched for his name in vain.

Look for Madame Robert, she shouted from behind her window. Her maiden name.

I pressed the button and waited for Madame Lapierre to answer. I waited for our worlds to collide once more.

There she was in the entrance of their apartment, holding the edge of the door with one hand. She looked different from the last time. There was more color in her cheeks, and her hair had recovered some of its gloss. We stood facing each other for a moment, then she invited me inside. As I followed her through the entrance, I remembered what Anouk had told me, that she should have thought about Madame Lapierre more often. I, too, was ashamed of how little she'd preoccupied me until our sighting of her in the summer. Although I understood who she was, she had remained a formless entity. I was shy in her presence, as though I'd mistreated her all these years and should now absolve myself, show her that my mother and I weren't horrible women who stole married men.

I felt we were meeting for the first time, which in a sense we were, since the last time had been in the middle of the night alongside Father, when she'd emerged out of thin air, more ghostly than alive. I looked at her feet and noticed that she was wearing slippers, the heels worn down. Her ankles were narrow and her calves surprisingly thick with muscle. She glanced back at me and I reddened.

We sat at a round table in her kitchen—the kitchen where Father ate most of his meals. She prepared us some tea.

He always told me he loved your food, I said.

He loved food, she corrected me, but I saw a small smile at the corner of her lips. She handed me a steaming cup of herbal tea and sat across from me. So, why are you here, Margot?

I told her I thought she'd known about me and Anouk. I had assumed my father was more open with his wife than he let on, and that they had both decided to keep his other life separate from their public one.

She looked away from me. Her face was delicate, slender neck and high cheekbones. She wasn't quite how I'd expected her to be—less intimidating and sophisticated—and in some ways, she didn't feel like Father's wife, maybe because I hadn't seen them together when he was alive. She was someone who held her emotions at bay; she sat with her arms on the table, her voice even.

I had no idea. Everyone tells you the signs are easy to read, but I didn't know about his affairs. They say a woman knows when her husband is with another woman. They blame you for being ignorant.

I listened to Madame Lapierre, at a loss for words.

The hardest part was after, she continued, when I waited for him to apologize. Especially to our sons. I wanted him to acknowledge the deception, but he wasn't capable of admitting when he was wrong, let alone saying he was sorry.

He didn't apologize to us, either. He stopped speaking to me after the articles came out.

That must have been painful for you.

Madame Lapierre ran her fingers over the table, pausing for a moment before continuing.

The night your father died, I woke with a start to find the room unusually quiet. It must have been close to four in the morning. Often, your father snored, but there wasn't even a whistle of breath. I touched him on the shoulder to see if he was awake. I couldn't turn him over, and that's when I knew something was very wrong.

He had died, I said, my voice a whisper.

She nodded. He went in his sleep. I wanted you to know, Margot, that he didn't suffer.

He stayed with you to the end.

I didn't give him a choice. I was furious with him. I thought a lot about you, especially your birth. He was with my family when you were born. I didn't know it at the time, of course, but looking back, I remember the exact day. He acted as if nothing was out of the ordinary. It made me angry to know he experienced those intense emotions while standing beside me, not saying a word, playing with our sons in my parents' home.

You know my date of birth? My voice was quiet. I held my breath.

Well, after I found out, he wanted to talk about you. Your birthday is next month, isn't it?

Yes.

I was your age when I met him.

She took a sip of tea. I could feel my throat closing and I also drank, hoping the warm liquid would soothe me.

What did he say about me?

He wanted to share everything about you. So, I set aside my ego and listened. He was relieved to be finally speaking. It made me sad, how lonely it must have been to keep a daughter to himself throughout the years. He was proud of you. He named you after his mother, Marguerite.

I didn't know her name was Marguerite.

Yes, they were very close.

I asked him about you, because I wanted to meet you one day.

You wanted to meet me?

More than anything.

And here we are today. Imagine if he saw us. He'd faint from fright.

Madame Lapierre laughed. Her face relaxed for a moment. It's good that you came to see me. Your mother, I don't want to see her, but you. . . . She blinked a few times and redressed herself in the chair.

Wait here, she said. I have something for you. She left the kitchen.

I finished drinking my tea. The kitchen was small and functional with a large stove and a narrow counter. On the table there was a bowl of onions and shallots. The space was clean and organized, but also warm and inviting, and I could imagine them eating here together, enjoying their meals.

Seeing how comfortable she was with sharing her side of the story further shook any sense of normalcy. It hadn't been peaceful, not for either one of us. I wished I had her facility to say things as they were, but Anouk and I were like those fish at the bottom of the ocean who preferred to stay hidden from the more transparent waters.

Madame Lapierre returned with an envelope. This is for you, she said. We discussed it a few weeks before he died. I haven't had the courage to mail it to you. Maybe you already know from your mother.

I took the envelope from her and opened it. Inside was my birth certificate. I was born at 3:47 P.M. in the seventeenth arrondissement. Anouk's full name followed, her date and place of birth, her profession, but the space for the name of the father was left blank.

Below was a second paragraph, saying that I was recognized by Bertrand Lapierre in Paris. The date of the recognition was less than a week before he died.

Madame Lapierre leaned over my shoulder, reading with me.

He must have gone to the *mairie* with Anouk, I whispered, but she had never said a word to me about it.

Look there, she said, pointing at the end of the paragraph. He also gave you his name.

I tried saying it aloud. Margot Lapierre. I blushed and glanced at her, my words an act of intimacy forced into her world.

It goes together nicely, doesn't it?

I nodded.

I'd heard my name a million times, but still I repeated it to myself once more—Margot Louve, Margot Lapierre—and I agreed, it had a beautiful ring.

18

I came home with my birth certificate clenched in my hand. I found Anouk sitting in the kitchen with a cup of coffee. It was recently brewed, wisps of steam rising to her face as she blew on its surface. She asked if I wanted a cup.

I waved the certificate in front of her. I went to see Madame Lapierre. Look what she gave me.

Anouk's expression stiffened and for the first time in months, she seemed frightened. Within seconds, she regained her composure and slid deeper into her seat, drawing the cup toward her. She cradled it with both hands. When she finally broke the silence, she explained that she hadn't known how to tell me. She was planning on giving me the certificate soon. In ten days, we had an appointment to review his will, his assets to be divided among Madame Lapierre, his sons, and me. As she spoke, she started to cry.

I hadn't seen her cry since the weeks following his death. Maybe she was worn down from the rehearsals and evening classes; it was possible she was overworked—we were just two weeks away from her show. But after a few minutes I saw it was nothing other than sadness. She covered her face and continued to sob silently, though her sorrow was so tangible it rippled through me. I stood in front of her, vibrating, unable to open my mouth. I remembered that she'd covered for me with the article on Father and hadn't asked to know more about the origin of the leak. She had protected me, and she had also seen him without me. It was a selfish move, and the pain of her betrayal made me less susceptible to her tears.

I can't believe you were with him before he died and didn't tell me.

As your mother, I'm not supposed to tell you everything.

You didn't give me a chance.

Anouk stood from her chair and began to walk around the small kitchen. She wiped her cheeks and pulled her hair into a bun.

I was afraid you'd resent me, she whispered.

You got to see him in September without me. All that time, I was waiting like an idiot for him to call me.

Yes, I saw him twice. Maybe I should have pushed him harder to call you. Anouk spoke quietly and shook her head, as if addressing herself.

Why didn't you? I felt like I didn't exist to him.

How many times do I have to remind you that you were important to him? She exhaled loudly and stared up at the ceiling. It took me by surprise, the rapidity with which her mood could swing from one extreme to another. How did she expect me to believe her?

But you could've taken me to the *mairie* for the birth certificate.

You know how your father was. His reaction to difficult situations was typical for a man of his generation. He avoided emotional confrontations. He wanted to wait a little longer before seeing you.

I stood in the middle of the kitchen, now angry at her for withholding this happy piece of information. What else had they withheld from me? Perhaps I'd never know the extent of their deception, just as she'd never discover the life I'd lived with Brigitte and David.

I followed her into the living room. She settled on the couch and crossed her legs. I looked down at her. She played with her hands nervously. Her shoulders slumped forward, and for a moment she seemed frail. I wanted her to act like before, never scared of my reactions and not caring one bit if I disliked what she said, moving forward at her own rhythm without glancing left or right.

I'm sorry I couldn't give you more, she said. If I'd known he was sick, I would have brought you to him right away.

I pointed at the certificate. It says here that he gave me his name.

Yes. If you want, it's yours.

I tried to imagine us living together: Father and daughter, sharing the same space, our bedrooms on the second floor separated by a bathroom. He would be showered and dressed by the time my alarm rang. I wouldn't see him often because he'd be at the office or traveling, and so most of the time, I'd drift around the apartment, sometimes cleaning up after him, although he was much tidier than Anouk and whatever mess he made would be contained to his bedroom. With him, the floor would be clean enough to eat from, and the fridge would be stocked with beautiful ingredients from the Grande Épicerie of the Bon Marché. At night, when he was home, we'd watch Agnès Varda films. I would tell him about *Bonjour Tristesse*, which I was certain he'd read. Perhaps we'd be like Cécile and her father in Sagan's novel, chasing away any woman who came too close and threatened our unit, relishing in our new-found intimacy.

But these images were an invention, colored by the few hours Father and I had truly spent alone. I could count those occasions on one hand. I returned to our weekend in Normandy. The gray skies and fine drizzle, our long walk on the deserted beach, the dishes we'd eaten at the restaurant, the brass molding of the bathroom mirror, and each item of clothing I'd worn. The memories grew sharper over time because I took such good care of them. How to fill a hole when he was barely there to begin with? How to miss someone who was more absence than presence?

Anouk worked around the clock. I barely saw her in the evenings, and I was reminded of how it was each year—that time of the year when she disappeared for long stretches, rehearsing, planning, writing, and rewriting. The meeting with the *notaire* came and went, and we put the money from Father's inheritance into my bank account for when I left home. Anouk wanted me to buy a small studio. For now, I would continue living with her. I had officially signed up at Université Paris 3 for a degree in *lettres modernes*.

It was the opening night of her show. The theater in the tenth arrondissement was a small space, but it was majestic in its own way, with seats made of dark orange velvet and a polished wooden stage. The stage was stark other than a chair and a table. A bright spot of light shone onto the props. It had been almost two years since Anouk performed her one-woman show. She drew from her life: friendships, anecdotes with other actors, books and movies, current events, and sometimes me, though I was never a central focus.

Mathilde and Théo sat to my right and Juliette to my left. She was dressed for the opera in a long silk dress and her mother's Agnès B. jacket, the one she wore for special occasions, and she spoke about Anouk with an even greater level of respect. Between us I sensed a new dynamic, as if Juliette was afraid of stealing my mother's attention from me. Did she see me as maimed because I had one parent as opposed to her two parents? Did she think Anouk liked her more than she liked her own daughter, just because Juliette wanted a career in film? Anouk had helped her with the film, true, and Juliette had displayed a look of guilt tinged with concern. I knew that look well and wondered if she was right. I wondered if I should be more protective of my mother.

The curtains came up and Anouk walked onto the stage. She took my breath away. Tall and muscular, deliberate in her movements. Her legs traversed the stage quickly, like those of a horse. Her mouth was painted dark red, her signature shade, and her hair tumbled onto her shoulders in a mass of red curls. The streaks of gray at her temples shimmered under the lights. She wore a stretchy black dress with tights, an outfit easy to remove and slip back on if she needed to. She had prepared a dance component for the end of the performance.

Her voice was sexy. She spoke slowly, enunciating each word. She sat on the edge of the stage, her legs dangling a few feet from the front row. I imagined Father seated there, as he did when he had first laid eyes on her.

I saw the man I loved two weeks before he died, she began.

We met at a friend's home. A mutual friend who lent us his apartment, so we could spend an hour together. I insisted that we meet in person. At the beginning, he didn't want to, worried we'd be followed, or that his wife might find out. I told him I had something important to say.

The meeting was set for ten P.M. on a Wednesday evening. The door to the apartment was unlocked and I walked right in. I left my jacket on a chair and looked around. There was no one in the entryway. I'd been told to make myself at home. He was waiting for me in the living room. We sat on opposite sides of the couch.

And here, Anouk moved her chair to one side of the stage. She faced the other end, speaking to an invisible interlocutor.

He was like a stranger to me. I knew him better than anyone else, any other man. But instead of embracing as we usually did, we sat far from each other. He looked unhappy, as though he hadn't slept in weeks.

I asked him: Do you want to start over again? We can find a way. We can be discreet. Our daughter and I will leave Paris for a little while. It'll be easier if we're away from the spotlight.

It took him a while to answer. He said: In another life I'd have met you first. We'd have met before I was married, and you'd be my wife and maybe we'd have two or three children. But that's not how it happened, and I don't want to continue like this.

I'm not asking you to marry me, I said.

His words were final: I'm staying with my wife.

It was hard to believe him. I had told him—I'll sacrifice my career for you, I'll leave the city I love, I'll move our daughter who is less than a year away from finishing school. But it wasn't what he wanted. What he'd always wanted was to be this man, married to his wife, even after the illusion was shattered. I felt it in my bones that he wouldn't come home to us.

I heard a rumor, he said. I heard our daughter spoke to a journalist and told them about us. I stayed up all night imagining it was her. But then I thought about it some more and the answer was right in front of my eyes. It was you, wasn't it?

Anouk turned to look at the audience. She spread out her hands, palms facing up.

It was you? he repeated.

Of course, my love, I told him. Who else could it be?

He looked relieved and smiled for the first time.

Anouk stood up and walked to the center of the stage. She leaned against the table. The lights dimmed to a warmer yellow.

Let me begin elsewhere. At the start of our relationship, we tried to sneak in as many moments together as we could. We knew there was a strong mutual attraction, but he was married. His marriage made me looser with him than with other men. He was so straight-edged and spoke about his wife so often that I believed he'd never transgress. I was always testing the limits, directing my attention at him and standing close to him. I never thought he would indulge.

Soon I was in love. I always hoped he'd show up at the same event or play. We avoided making plans for just the two of us, but whenever we found ourselves in a room full of strangers, we gravitated toward each other and disappeared into a corner, onto a balcony, the street sometimes, anywhere to be alone. I wasn't waiting for him to declare his feelings or act upon them. It wasn't in the realm of possibility. And then one day, he invited me to dinner after one of those parties. It was a spontaneous invitation, late at night, and we almost didn't find a spot that would serve us food. We came across a small Italian restaurant on rue du Dragon. We ate lasagna and burrata with artichokes. We drank a pitcher of red wine. He asked if I wanted dessert and I said yes only to prolong the meal, thinking our time together was finite and could not get any more intimate than this moment.

We stepped out onto the street. It was raining lightly, and we stood under the awning of a nearby store. He took my hand and pulled me into his chest. He kissed me. I stopped him. What are you doing? I asked. Until then, he'd shown restraint, barely touching my arm when he greeted me. Yes, I craved his presence, sought out every opportunity to see him. I blossomed under his approval, hoped he would already be looking at me when I glanced over. But this? He had a wife and two young sons at home.

He was surprised by my reaction. I thought you wanted this, he said.

I'd forgotten, he was more literal than I was, and what did I want after all, what had I expected? To dwell in the safety of loving a married man? I'd never wanted what my parents had, and I doubted my body could harbor a baby. I didn't care about having a family the way most of my friends did.

But I wanted him to promise me he wouldn't leave his wife and sons because of me.

I felt Juliette's hand move across the armrest and onto mine. She squeezed my fingers. Did you know about this? she whispered. I shook my head.

Anouk walked across the stage, the suede soles of her dance shoes padding on the wooden boards. She paused by the left wings.

That night in our friend's living room, he asked why I'd made our affair public. What did I hope to accomplish by telling the press? Why now?

I thought about what had changed since that night on rue du Dragon. We were older, his career had transformed in unimaginable ways, we had fought over money, we had a child together. The greatest change was our daughter.

I told him: When I asked you to stay with your wife, it was before meeting the other love of my life.

Anouk moved to the center of the stage. The lights shone brighter on her, surrounding her with a rim of gold. We were plunged in darkness. I knew she couldn't see our faces, only those who sat in the front row if she even paused to look.

She spread out her arms and began to twirl on her right leg. She spun faster, her hands outstretched, her face a blur to us. She arched her spine to form a deep curve. I hadn't seen her dance in years. She retained her balance on one foot, dropping her heel and rising on her toes so quickly we barely saw the movement of her foot. I held my breath, waiting for her to spin out of turn and trip on her own feet.

She slowed down, spinning more slowly until her hair fell away from her cheeks. She paused to catch her breath.

I told him to come home. Margot needs you. Come home to her.

Hot patches spread across my face and neck as I heard my name.

Anouk walked forward to the edge of the stage and stared out at the audience. Somehow, she knew where to look, third row to the left. She caught my eye and winked at me, before disappearing between the dark folds of the wings.

The velvet curtains swooshed across the stage and the lights turned on. Seconds later, Anouk returned, her hair trailing behind her. She paused in front of the audience and raised her arms.

I stood with everyone else and clapped for a long time. I watched her bow once, twice, three times, her torso folding over gracefully. We whistled. My heart and stomach swung into place, having found their origin. I touched my cheeks and found that they were wet. I hadn't felt the tears fall from my eyes.

You have an extraordinary mother, Father often said, as though she was better than all the others. A mother is not a friend, Anouk liked to say, proud of this distinction.

What happened to daughters like us? Would we flee our families, wanting to be far away, wishing to carve out a life that was ours alone, far removed from where we came from? Or were we always destined to return?

I wanted to absorb her into myself so I was never alone. I wasn't afraid.

Acknowledgments

My deepest gratitude to those who made writing my first novel less terrifying and lonely, and who guided me along the way with their intelligence and kindness:

Marya Spence, for taking a leap of faith and helping shape the heart of this book. Thank you for pushing me to my limits with each revision and cheering me on with your marvelous warmth.

Clare Mao, for all the small and big things behind the scenes.

Emi Ikkanda, for believing in me before there was a novel. Your brilliance runs through every line of this book, and I am forever grateful for your friendship.

Cindy Spiegel, for your wisdom and taking a chance on me.

Parisa Ebrahimi, you arrived midway through the book and somehow it was as though you had always been reading my mind and sharing my vision. In our first meeting, you described the novel I dreamed of writing, and then you guided me there. How lucky I was to have found an editor who is as deeply invested in the work as the writer herself. You are just that—unafraid, incredibly sharp, a most perceptive listener.

Everyone else at Hogarth Press and Penguin Random House—especially Alexis Washam, Rachel Rokicki, Erin Richards, Emily Hotaling, Jillian Buckley, and Vincent La Scala—for your tireless work in bringing this book into the world. Francine Toon at Sceptre, for giving Margot a life across the Atlantic and for doing so with such kindness.

Joan Lynch, for solidifying my love of literature in terminale.

Max Apple, for giving me permission to daydream. I wouldn't be a writer had I not stumbled into your class my first year as an undergraduate, and then proceeded to take six more writing workshops with you.

The Kelly Writers House, for being a home to aspiring and established writers alike.

The MFA at Columbia University, for the space, time, and resources to write.

My mentors and teachers who imparted their precious wisdom throughout the years and continue to inspire me: Victor LaValle, Sonya Chung, Rivka Galchen, and Stacey D'Erasmo.

Jason Ueda and Sue Mendelsohn, along with everyone else at Columbia University's Writing Center, for providing a safe and nurturing space for writers. For a long time, it was the one space I could call myself a writer without feeling embarrassed.

Elena Megalos, Yurina Yoshikawa, Lynn Steger Strong, and Eliza Schrader, for your unfailing friendship and love, and the hours spent discussing the woes of writing and navigating the mysterious world of publishing over Thai takeout dinners.

Forsyth Harmon, for your endless encouragement and for

inspiring me to be a better writer. I always hope your intelligence will imprint on me.

Kirsten Saracini, for treating my novel as though it is a part of my soul and yours, with utmost care, and for being the best friend a writer could ask for.

Kerry Cullen, Karen Russell, Crystal Hana Kim, Mai Nardone, Sarah Souli, Florence Coupry, Philippe and Valérie Lapierre, Maud Cavayé, and Eloise Eonnet, for your generosity and time.

Elizabeth Cruikshank and Nanette Maxim, for reading with the sharpest eyes. Susanne Ruppert, for cheering me on to the finish line.

Elaine Sciolino, for teaching me confidence and a million other essential lessons from the Sciolino School of Life and Journalism, and for showing me that writing is an ongoing conversation, a *partage*. It is a privilege to be an honorary member of the Sciolino-Plump household.

Alejandro Milberg, for your terrific imagination, and for introducing me to the cruel Goddess Usagi.

Sadao Milberg and Amanda Sauer, for welcoming me into your home countless times.

My mother, Akiko Okuma, for sharing with me your love of storytelling and invention, for teaching me to appreciate food, go with the flow, and be accepting of our strange family.

My father, Patrick Lemoine, for your unconditional love and belief in my writing.

Geoffroy Bablon, for your infinite curiosity and for reading my novel over and over again, as though it is the most important thing in your life. What a gift to have you as my first reader.

The Margot Affair

SANAË LEMOINE

A Book Club Guide

Questions and Topics for Discussion

1. *The Margot Affair* is a novel of intrigue and betrayal that explores many themes, including family, friendship, romance, grief, motherhood, and trauma. Which theme takes center stage for you and why?

2. How would you characterize Margot's relationship with her father? She specifically recounts a weekend they spent together a few years ago. What is the significance of this trip? How does this weekend inform Margot's perception of their relationship?

3. How does Margot's perception of her father change throughout the novel?

4. What role does Margot's friendship with Juliette play within Margot's life? In what ways are their lives similar and in what ways are they different?

5. After meeting David Perrin, a journalist, at the afterparty of a play, Margot begins writing to him. What do you think motivates her desire to write to him?

6. Describe the ways Margot processes the loss of her father, and how grief seeps into the novel. Does it coexist alongside other emotions?

7. How does Margot's understanding of Madame Lapierre change throughout the novel? What moments mark a change in Margot's perception of her father's wife?

8. How does Margot and Brigitte's relationship develop beyond that of a ghostwriter and subject? What does Margot seek in her friendship with Brigitte? What does Brigitte seek in Margot?

9. What are your thoughts about Margot's affair with David? In what ways does this brief yet intimate and intense relationship influence Margot? Why is she drawn to him?

10. The fragile and potent power of secrets is a returning theme throughout the book. Having been in the shadows of her parents' secret her whole life, how has this shaped the way in which Margot understands boundaries and relationships?

11. Put yourself in Margot's shoes: What would you have done with the secret of your family? Why?

12. Female relationships play a crucial role within this book, and especially in Margot's life. What are the various female relationships she has? Compare and contrast these relationships and their impact on her life.

13. What are some ways Margot is influenced by her mother? Does she aspire to be like her mother or is she motivated to differentiate herself from her mother?

14. Towards the end of the book Margot receives her birth certificate in which her father gives her his last name, Lapierre. In what ways does this change Margot's identity? What do you think she will choose to take: her father's name (Lapierre), her mother's (Louve), or both?

15. Margot and her mother have a tense and, at times, violent relationship. Would you consider this a factor in why Margot decides to share the story of her family with the world without telling her mother?

16. The revelation of her parents' affair not only results in Margot's life shifting from private to public, it also frees Margot from a burden she no longer has to carry. Do you think Margot feels liberated by the end of the novel? Why or why not?

17. Anouk is a successful stage actress yet within her personal life she has remained invisible as the "other" woman. How do you feel about Anouk's performance at the end of the novel?

Did you expect it? Does it change the way you view the rest of the story?

18. What are the different spaces we encounter in the novel, both private and public? How is Margot shaped by those different spaces?

19. The characters of this novel are often telling each other stories, such as Brigitte's story about the chef and her daughter, Anouk's story about being pregnant with Margot and the disappearing girl at the wedding, David's story about Brigitte's roommate, Anaïs, and so on. What role does storytelling play in the novel? How do these stories advance relationships, and what does Margot learn from each story she's told?

20. With Brigitte's obsession with *Trouble Every Day* and Juliette's own attempt at filmmaking, what do you think the author is trying to explore? What did you make of Juliette's film about the mayor?

PHOTO: © GIEVES ANDERSON

SANAË LEMOINE was born in Paris to a Japanese mother and a French father. She was raised in France and Australia, and now lives in New York. She attended the University of Pennsylvania and received her MFA in fiction from Columbia University. *The Margot Affair* is her first novel.

About the Type

This book was set in Fournier, a typeface named for Pierre-Simon Fournier (1712–68), the youngest son of a French printing family. He started out engraving woodblocks and large capitals, then moved on to fonts of type. In 1736 he began his own foundry and made several important contributions in the field of type design; he is said to have cut 147 alphabets of his own creation. Fournier is probably best remembered as the designer of St. Augustine Ordinaire, a face that served as the model for the Monotype Corporation's Fournier, which was released in 1925.